# DEATH OF THE VINTNER

A TALE OF MEDIEVAL MURDER, MYSTERY AND SKULDUGGERY. BOOK TWO OF THE DRAYCHESTER CHRONICLES.

M J WESTERBONE

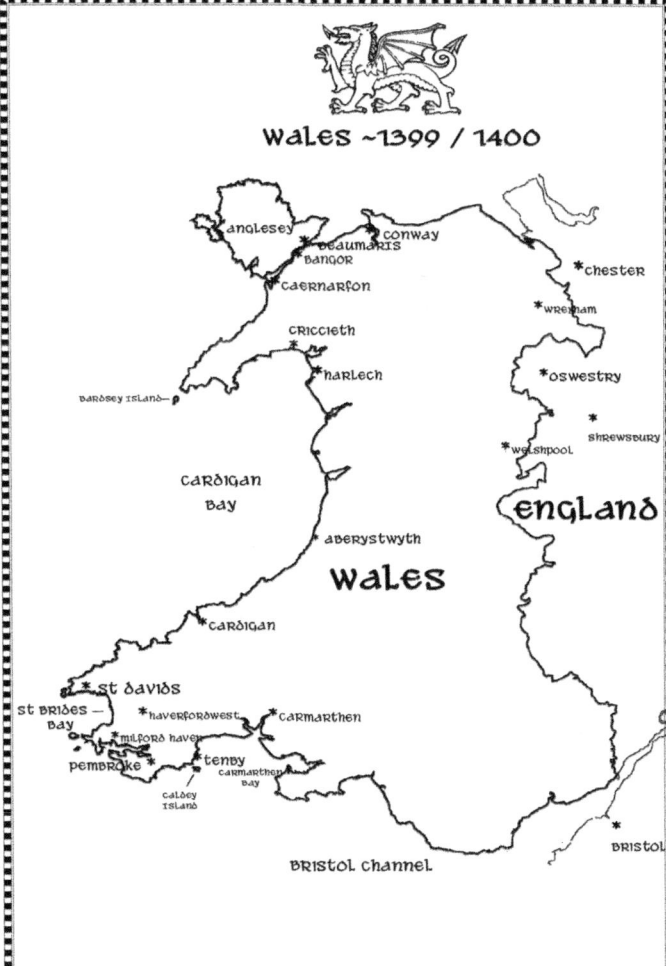

*AN INTRODUCTION TO THE SERIES FROM OTHER READERS*

*"Plunges the reader head on into an immersive tale of humour, murder and intrigue set in a gritty depiction of medieval England that's not for the fainthearted..."*

*"Medieval life is cheap, nasty and short, at least for some, for others, well, its all just a game to them..."*

*"The grizzled old mercenary Sir Roger Mudstone, you'll love to hate him, if that makes any sense?"*

*"A perfect medieval villain with a troubling talent for violence. He's the kind of man who'd sell not only his own grandmother but yours too..."*

*"Will, Bernard and Osbert, its like Cadfael has shuffled off this mortal coil and left three much stupider understudies, enjoy the ride..."*

# FREE BOOK OFFER

**Get your free copy of**
Death Of The Messenger
The Prequel to the
Draychester Chronicles

Visit www.westerbone.com to get exclusive discounts, news on upcoming releases **and a free copy of *Death of the Messenger*** , the prequel to the Draychester Chronicles series.

# OTHER BOOKS IN THE SERIES

## Available Now
Book 1 of the Draychester Chronicles

### Death Of The Official

## Available Now
Book 3 of the Draychester Chronicles

### Death Of The Anchorite

# 1

## OVER A BARREL

Will's head was crushed against the rough rock face of the cave roof. Water lapped around his neck and threatened to fill his ears. With each incoming wave of the sea, which had rapidly filled the cave, his head was smashed into the limestone. He couldn't move his arms or legs as he was strapped to an empty wooden barrel of Gascony wine. Fastened by the wrists and ankles with a thick iron chain that went right around the barrel, it allowed him virtually no movement. He was frozen, battered, and on the point of despair.

"I swear if I get free of this bloody barrel I'll never drink again"

"Don't be too hasty. It's not certain we're going to drown. Anyway, never is a long time."

Will peered incredulously through the gloom of the cave at the large man strapped to another barrel floating beside him.

"How are we not going to drown?" he asked his floating companion.

The big man looked upwards with his eyes and Will

followed his gaze. In the cave's roof was a square hole cut into the limestone into which a thick iron grill had been set. In the space above, a candle flickered. They could hear two drunken men arguing.

"I doubt the water rises much higher with the tide. If it did, the room above would be flooded and our drunken friends would get wet feet."

"If I don't drown I'll probably freeze to death."

They reflected on this for a minute before the big man said, "When do you think the tide will go out again?"

"I think it'd only just started to come back in when we set out along the beach."

The other man grunted.

"A few hours at most then?"

"A few hours…"

A voice called out from above, "Shut up down there."

"If I get out of here I swear I'm going to rip your head off," bellowed the big man, making his barrel rock violently.

"Shut up thief!"

The end of a wooden pole came jabbing down through the grill and poked the big man on his back. He was forced down into the water, making him splutter and cough.

When the pole had eventually retreated Will said, "Well that was stupid."

"Never claimed I was clever, just angry. If we do die down here, the bishop will probably have the merchant's house demolished. He'll be ruined."

Will said, "Well, that's a comfort. We'll still be dead of course. Tell me, how long have we been in this town?"

"A few minutes on the beach and then a few hours tied like this I suppose."

"So less than half a day and someone is already trying to kill us?"

The big man rattled the chains on his barrel. "I'd say it's a bloody good attempt, wouldn't you?"

"The bishop seems to have misinformed me about some parts of my duties," said Will. "Drowning wasn't mentioned."

"The duties of a bishop's official are many and varied."

"Yes, yes they are, I see that now…"

## 2

## ARRIVAL AT TENBY

Their arrival had been so much more promising. The voyage from Ilfracombe had lasted only a few hours. The distance was only forty miles or so across the Bristol channel to the Pembrokeshire coast. The three bishop's men, Will, Bernard and Osbert the clerk had set sail in the midmorning on the Margarete, a small cog that traded between Ilfracombe, Tenby and Bristol. The sea had been calm but Osbert, a poor traveller on land or water, had spent the majority of the time with his head hung over the side of the ship. It was just before sunset when they arrived off Tenby. Will and Bernard contemplated the view with the ship's master, John Corbet, a local of the town.

The setting itself was a natural sheltered harbour. The town, well built of lime and stone, looked down to the sea from on top of a dry cliff, one part coming down onto the waterfront where a curving stone pier bustled with activity. Defensive works fortified the head of the harbour and the isthmus joining the town to Castle Hill which jutted out into the clear blue waters. The town itself was surrounded by stone curtain walls, towers and heavily defended gates.

Their ship lay just off-shore in the bay on the north side of the town. The beach beneath the cliffs running around to the harbour was long and composed of fine golden sand. In the evening sunlight Will thought the town a fine and prosperous looking place. He turned to the master and said, "You can't take the ship into the quay?"

"Not yet, the tide has only just turned. A few hours more, and it'll be deep enough so we can tie up and unload. I can have you rowed to the quay if you want to go ashore now?"

"Can you land us on the beach instead?" said Bernard. "I've been too long on this damn tub, I need to stretch these old legs of mine before we walk up into the town."

The master laughed. "The journey was but a few hours, you'd make a poor deckhand," he gestured at a green-faced Osbert, "and your friend back there even worse."

Bernard grunted and said, "The sea and I are old foes, I seem to always be the loser."

Will looked towards Osbert. "As for our clerk, he gets sick crossing a bridge."

The master grinned. "I'll get one of the lads to row you in and set you down at the far end of the beach, good enough?"

Bernard nodded. "Aye that'll do."

The master looked at them shrewdly.

"I can recommend a couple of good inns in town, or perhaps you visit someone you know? I can have my man guide you. Perhaps the priory, you said you were bishop's men? Are you on your way to Saint Davids?"

Bernard wouldn't be drawn on their business. "I dare say we can find our own way my friend. I wouldn't want to put you to any trouble."

The master just shrugged as though losing interest and

called to one of his men to put the boat over the side and row them ashore.

As they sat in the boat heading to shore Osbert groaned and said his first words in hours. "I feel like I've not eaten for days. Everything that has passed my lips has gone back out over the side. Sea sickness is God's way of punishing me for some sin."

Will sighed and said, "I sometimes wonder if you're cut out for this life Osbert. The bishop obviously sees something in you but you make a miserable travelling companion."

Osbert give him a pitiful look and said, "I don't doubt that, I'd much rather be back in Draychester, but the bishop commands and I obey, as do we all."

Bernard said to the man rowing them in, "Drop us on the beach, then row our miserable friend here to the quay." He turned to Osbert and said, "Go up into the town Osbert and find our host's house and get some food inside you. We'll follow soon enough. You know who to ask for?"

Osbert brightened somewhat. "I do, I'll go gladly."

The small boat left Will and Bernard at the far end of the beach, looking back towards the quay and the way up into town. Bernard took his boots off and pushed his toes into the warm sand with a groan. "God's bones, that feels good. I grow too old for this Will, the journeying tires me more than in my younger days."

"Come on, you're beginning to sound like Osbert, let's stretch our legs, that'll cheer you up."

They began to walk along the empty beach. Here and there were piles of rope, fishing nets and what looked like some wine barrels. About half way along the beach, Bernard stopped by a barrel that lay on its side in the sand and thumped it speculatively. "Sounds empty. Still, if they leave stuff strewn around the beach like this, I'm not surprised the bishop's wine has gone missing."

Will pointed to a dark opening at the base of the cliff. "Perhaps they intend to store this stuff up there, looks like a cave or a passageway."

Barnard trudged up the beach to take a closer look with Will close behind. The light was now starting to fade. They couldn't see much in the gloom of the cave entrance.

"Looks like you're right," said Bernard, taking a step into the gloom and coming up against a stack of wooden barrels fastened together with iron chains. He bent down to look at something attached to a barrel and chuckled. "Take a look at this. I recognise this seal."

Will stepped into the gloom. Out of the corner of his eye he saw a sudden flurry of movement. Something heavy and incredibly painful came crashing down onto his shoulder, forcing him to the ground. With his face in the sand he heard muffled shouts and an angry roar that could only be Bernard. Still half stunned he was then dragged further into the darkness. A kick to the head completed his passage into oblivion.

## 3

## THE MERCHANT'S HOUSE

They floated in silence in the cave, contemplating an uncertain future. Eventually they heard raised voices again from the room above and the sounds of a brief scuffle ending in a distinct thwack and a yelp.

"Wasn't my fault father. I thought they were thieves!"

Another voice said, "What were they doing down there in the dark?"

There was another thwack and an even noisier yelp.

"You bloody fool. You two get that grate opened now."

There were a series of grunts and gasps as the iron grate was hefted up and away from the opening. Then a chubby white face appeared in the gap looking down at them.

"Bernard old friend. Is that you?"

"Don't old friend me Thomas Phelpes. I see age hasn't improved your wits. Let me guess, those two drunken sods up there are your sons?"

"They are. And I see that it is you Bernard. Is that someone else down there with you?"

Will rocked his barrel closer to Bernard's so he could gaze up at the ghostly face and said, "William Blackburne.

Perhaps we could dispense with the formal introductions and you could just haul us out of here?"

Bernard and Will sat in front of a roaring fire in the kitchen of the house of Thomas Phelpes far above the watery cave. Their clothes were drying next to the fire, and each sat wrapped in a thick blanket with a pot of ale and a chuck of bread and cheese.

Osbert sat on a three-legged stool directly in front of the fire, a sanctimonious smile playing around his lips as he regarded his bedraggled companions.

With his mouth half full Will said, "Tell me again, just so I'm clear, you don't always tie strangers to barrels and try to drown them? It's not some strange local custom?"

Phelpes grimaced. "I've said I'm sorry master William. The lads are on edge. What with all these thefts going on they let things get out of hand. The drink didn't help either. They'll be punished."

Bernard sneezed and shivered. "God's teeth, I believe I've caught a chill now. You'd better make sure they stay out of my way while we're here. If I see them, they'll bloody regret it."

Phelpes picked up the ale jug and filled Bernard's cup. "Here have some more ale and cheer up."

Bernard sneezed again.

"So how long has it been Tom, six or maybe seven years?"

"Ten since I came to live here. Eleven since I saw you last, at Bristol I think. The years have been good to me and the business. The bishop has always been a good customer and I hope I've served him well."

Will said, "Well he's not too happy about his last consignment I can tell you that."

"That's why you're here then young master William, you Osbert and my old friend Bernard?"

Bernard shrugged. "There's always more to it than that with the bishop. You know that Thomas. But let's start with the wine first. What's the story?"

Phelpes refilled his own cup and swirled the ale around before taking a sip. "It was a few months ago now. I received a letter from your bishop asking me to find some wine he could give as a gift to the king."

"So you found something special?"

He didn't answer directly but said, "You know anything of the trade that I carry out?"

"I know it's profitable," said Bernard gesturing at the room's rich wall hangings and fine tableware.

Phelpes nodded in acknowledgement. "We make a good living, and the bishop takes his fair share of the profits. His coin made all this possible and I owe him a great deal. The business isn't complicated. We carry corn and herring to Gascony, on the return we bring back wine. A lot of the trade goes through Bristol, but some comes through here. You'd be amazed at the volume we're shipping now. We're importing for most of the nobles and clergy in Pembrokeshire."

"This wine you purchased for the bishop, it was good?"

"The very best."

"And it's lost?" said Will

"Stolen more like," said Phelpes bitterly.

Will looked puzzled. "Why did you bring the wine here and not off-load it at Bristol? Surely that was the easier route, either to Draychester or to the king direct?"

Phelpes nodded. "It would have been, but in his letter

the bishop indicated the king would soon visit Pembroke. It seemed sensible to bring it here."

Will said, "We have heard nothing about the king coming to Wales."

Phelpes shrugged. "It's what I was told. I don't like to enquire too closely into the affairs of the nobles, not my place to. I try to mind my own business, but it's plain to everyone there're things afoot here and in the rest of Wales."

Bernard said, "I agree. As I said, always more to it where the bishop is concerned. But back to the wine..."

Phelpes nodded. "I'll tell you what I know. You can see how prosperous the town has become. Wealth breeds jealousy my friends, and this place is no exception. There's a feud been brewing here for years. It started about fifteen years ago, some men from the town took a Genoese ship just off the coast. She was brought into the harbour and two barrels of gold and other goods were unloaded."

"That was before you moved here?" Bernard asked.

"Yes, a few years before, but the tale's true enough. At the time, the king's commissioners were called in to investigate. That much is a fact."

"The old king required his share no doubt?" said Will with a wry smile.

"Of course. My understanding is he didn't see much of it and neither did some of those who'd helped take the ship."

Osbert listened with rapt attention. His face flushed from the warmth of the fire. "They were swindled out of their fair share?" he asked.

"Some thought so. The leader of the men who took the Genoese merchantman was a master of a local ship. Watts was his name, John Watts. He seems to have ended up with more of the loot than anyone else. If you'd met him you'd understand why, he's a hard-faced bugger and one you'd never want to cross. I know him all too well, come up in the world has John, he's the mayor of this fine town of ours now."

"An interesting tale Tom, but what's this got to do with the bishop's wine?"

"Hear me out Bernard. I'll come to that," said Phelpes.

"This feud you mentioned, it started then?" asked Osbert.

"Yes. It split the town, there's those in Watts's circle, and those who aren't."

"I take it you're not friends?" said Will.

"The two camps tolerate each other for the sake of business, but there's always something bubbling away under the surface. I try to keep out of it as much as possible, but it's hard not to take sides."

"And this feud shows itself how?" asked Bernard.

"Petty violence now and then, fights, the odd stabbing and broken skull. Interference and pilfering of each other's cargos when they think they can get away with it. As mayor, Watts's men collect the duty on goods being landed. Strangely, the tax he and his friends pay on their own cargos is far less than the rest of us."

"You think the bishop's wine has been stolen by Watts or one of his camp?"

"I do. No one else would dare touch it without his permission. He'll deny it, but it's not the first wine I've had go missing. It's been getting worse recently."

"Why do you think that is?" asked Will. "I thought you said you tried to keep out of things."

"Let's just say some of us have grown weary with the whole situation. We seek favour with the Constable of Pembroke to remove Watts and his cronies. These thefts, it's clear, Watts is sending me a message to keep my nose out of it."

Bernard sighed. "A pretty tangled web you're involved in Tom. Tell me does the bishop know what's going on here?"

"Some of it. You know he likes to be kept informed about these things and he's a powerful ally to have."

"Of course he knows," said William shaking his head. "I begin to see this isn't just about the wine is it Bernard?"

Bernard grinned. "Ah, if only it were that simple. Let me guess Tom, did the bishop plant the idea of removing the mayor from office?"

"He may have mentioned the matter in some of his correspondence," Phelpes said somewhat defensively.

Will shook his head again. "So, I suppose what we're supposed to do next is go and see Mayor Watts..."

"Is that wise? He sounds thoroughly ungodly," said Osbert nervously.

Phelpes snorted at Osbert's naivety. "Ungodly. Well, that's not the word I'd use boy. Let's be blunt, the man's a complete bastard."

## 4
## IRONS IN THE FIRE

Sir Roger Mudstone was hoping mad. Mainly because he'd just dropped a red hot poker onto his very expensive Cordoba boot. It left him with a sore toe and a smouldering hole in the shiny leather. The clerk who was supposed to be taking notes, suppressed a laugh behind an ink-stained hand. Even the prisoner who was tightly chained to the table by his hands and feet, couldn't help but snigger.

"Think that's funny do you?" Sir Roger hissed. He angrily retrieved the poker from the stone floor with his heavily gloved hand. "Let us see if you find this as amusing." He placed the glowing end of the poker on the bottom of the man's bare right foot and held it there. The man's bellows of pain were deafening and the stench of burning flesh made even Sir Roger feel slightly nauseous. When the man passed out, Sir Roger reluctantly removed the poker and placed it back in the hot glowing coals of the brazier. The heat and stench in the dark underground torture room were getting oppressive even for him.

"That'll be the third you've got through already this morning," said the clerk.

Sir Roger shrugged. "He's not dead yet, he's just passed out"

"That's what you said about the other two, they're still dead and neither uttered a word," said the clerk in a mocking tone.

Sir Roger slowly took the poker back out of the fire and waved it angrily at the clerk. "Would you like to replace him on the table? One more comment like that and I swear you'll be feeling this poker up your backside."

The clerk unimpressed by the threat just shrugged. "So far I haven't had to make any notes, not even a half hearted confession. Still, I suppose I've been spoilt. I've worked with some of the best in the business, professionals they were."

Sir Roger, who was notoriously thin skinned became incensed. "Are you daring to call me unprofessional? Have you any idea of who I am you little worm?" He advanced across the room towards the clerk who hastily retreated behind his desk. Sir Roger swiftly kicked the desk out of the way and pinned the clerk by the throat against the wall. He held the glowing end of the poker up to within an inch of the man's eye. The heat made the sweat run down both men's faces. Sir Roger spoke slowly and with bone chilling menace. "I've slaughtered a hundred such as you in a single day. I've terrorised half of christendom and burnt cities to the ground." Sir Roger dragged the clerk back to his desk by the neck and forced him down onto the three-legged stool. He placed the poker on the edge of the table where it started to burn a black hole into the surface. "If you want to leave this chamber with both eyes, I suggest you shut your fat mouth and just take the notes. Do you understand?" The clerk half strangled could only gasp out a garbled reply that Sir Roger took to be an acknowledgement.

Sir Roger turned his attention back to the prisoner. Picking up a pail of dirty water from the corner of the room he angrily hurled the contents over the head of the man. He spluttered into life with a groan.

"Sorry for the interruption. We had a slight disagreement about whether you were still alive or not. I won't keep you waiting any longer."

He carefully undid the chains attached to the prisoner's left foot and replaced it with a rope that led back to the rack at the end of the table. He did the same for each of the other limbs. The prisoner lay still and unprotesting, apparently exhausted. Sir Roger slowly began to tension the ropes by turning the rack. The prisoner groaned.

"Ah, still with us then are we?" said Sir Roger. He tightened the rack again, this time with more vigour. The man groaned again and muttered something Sir Roger didn't understand.

"Speak up man, its like you're talking a foreign language, I can't understand you."

From behind him the clerk said, "He's Welsh, he doesn't speak English. The other two were Welsh as well."

"They were? Well that's damned inconvenient considering I'm torturing him and I don't understand Welsh. Seems like we've got a dilemma then. We could just make up a confession? That's unless you speak Welsh clerk, do you?"

"No," he croaked.

"We'll you have turned out to be pretty bloody useless all round."

Sir Roger gave the rack another turn and was rewarded by a satisfying crack from one of the prisoner's legs. The man screamed in pain. Sir Roger laughed. "Looks like I've broken your leg. Are you sure you don't understand English?"

Sir Roger rubbed his hands together, bent over and really put his back into it. He forced the rack around another notch. There was an audible pop and Sir Roger realised that it hadn't come from the prisoner. He tried to straighten his back and was rewarded by an excruciating pain that shot down his spine and ended in his rump. His back was locked.

He shouted, "You little Welsh bastard! You've made me do my back in. I can't bloody move."

The prisoner briefly raised his head, open his eyes, and sniggered. Sir Roger roared with anger, then thought better of it when the movement sent another excruciating spasm of pain up his back. With infinite slowness, he turned to the clerk.

"Listen to me you worm. You'd better make sure this one stays alive. I swear to God I'll kill you with my bare hands if he dies. I'll be back to finish my work." He slowly and painfully hobbled his way over to the door. He opened it halfway and inched forward so his head was through the opening. He looked up the dark stairway to the chamber above.

"Travis," he bellowed, "Get down here, I need you now!"

His long suffering servant Travis appeared at the top of the stairs. "Are you finished already master? Is the poor Welsh man dead?"

"No, he's not bloody dead yet and why do I seem to be the last person to know that he's Welsh? In fact never mind, just get your backside down here and help me up the stairs. I've put my back out again."

As Travis made his way down the stairs he said, "I was

about to come and get you master. The mayor wishes to see you."

"About bloody time. I'd almost given up on Bebbington. Theres no loyalty these days Travis. A debt owed it seems is seldom repaid."

Travis thought Sir Roger should be the last man in the kingdom to moralise about unpaid debts, but he knew better than to voice his opinions to his master.

John Bebbington, Mayor of Chester looked at Roger Mudstone with considerable distaste. He'd got to know Sir Roger years before, when they'd both been mercenaries for hire on the continent. They'd fought in the same company for a time, and Sir Roger knew a few too many of Bebbington's secrets and indiscretions. Some secrets, it had to be said, were much darker than others and certainly none he'd want anyone else to know. He was a man of standing now, with a reputation to maintain. He'd not been keen to help the man, had even considered just having him and his servant pushed down the nearest well. He knew Sir Roger, fugitive as he was, wouldn't have just turned up at his door without taking precautions. Blackmail was a game Sir Roger played only too well. Reluctantly he'd given him the job of the interrogator, torturer would be a better name, in the city prison while he thought of ways to be rid of him. Sir Roger was technically outlawed. Bebbington wasn't sure of the exact details, but he'd heard that some very powerful people were upset. There was a price on Sir Roger's head. It'd been difficult to come up with a solution of getting rid of the man, but the situation in Wales had presented an opportunity.

"I think I might have a solution to your problem Mudstone."

"Don't you mean our problem?" Sir Roger asked with a menacing tone.

"I owe you a debt, but it was a long time ago, don't push me Mudstone," snapped Bebbington.

"I'm listening," growled Sir Roger.

Bebbington took a long drink from a goblet of wine, set it down hard on the tabletop and said, "There's conflict brewing again with the Welsh. The king is on his way back from the campaign in Scotland. The army is to go into Wales. There'll be a need for experienced men, hard men like you Mudstone, those who will get a job done with no questions asked and no mercy shown. For those with the right skills and the stomach for the job there's a pardon available for any outstanding crimes. I've no doubt you'll be welcomed with open arms. That's if I speak to the right people of course."

"A pardon, I like the sound of that. I'll need to see it in writing and duly recorded."

"I'm sure it won't be a problem. The king's desperate for men. You might be required to raise a company yourself. I'm sure I can supply you with some dregs from the city watch to start you off and you can have the pick of the scum in the prison."

"Sounds even better. I'll need some coin for expenses. A troop of my own men once more, it's strange how these things come around again."

"Yes, it'll be just like the old days for you," Bebbington said sarcastically. "As for the coin, I'll give you just enough to raise some men and be gone, it's the best I can do."

Sir Roger nodded and said, "So be it. Make the arrangements Bebbington, I grow tired of working in your dungeon."

"From what I hear the prisoners won't miss you."

## 5

## THE MAYOR

The bishop's men waited until the morning after their arrival before venturing out to find Mayor Watts. As they took their leave of the merchant's house they sought out Phelpes himself, but he was nowhere to be found, not in the central hall with its now cold fireplace, or the more private rooms behind. The house maid said they would probably find both her master and Watts on the quay, supervising the unloading of their respective cargoes. The air felt cold as they emerged from the merchant's house. At the front, on the ground floor, was the shop, from where Phelpes normally did business.

"Odd, I would have thought he'd have opened up by now, if not him, then one of his sons. Not like Phelpes to miss out on a day's business," said Bernard, studying the closed shutters thoughtfully.

The upper stories of the adjacent houses jutted out over the narrow street blocking the full strength of the morning sun. Osbert pulled his cloak tightly around him and said, "I have a bad feeling about this place."

Will looked at him in exasperation and said, "Please tell

me you aren't going to start this again Osbert. I'm not sure I can take your doom and gloom for weeks on end."

Osbert shrugged. "I am only saying I have a feeling about these things. Was I not proved right on our last trip on behalf of the bishop?"

From behind, Bernard clapped Osbert on the shoulder and said good-humouredly, "Well boy, I'm not sure you've got the second sight, but what you do have is the knack of stating the bloody obvious."

"And very bloody irritating it is too," added William grinning.

Osbert's only reply was a "Humph!" and he strode on ahead of them down towards the harbour.

As they descended the steep street, a steady flow of men and materials was heading the opposite direction up into the town. A cart, heavily loaded with barrels, squeezed past them, the horses straining against the weight.

The three of them halted halfway down the hill. A low wall kept the street away from the cliff edge and the drop to the harbour below. They were looking directly down onto the quay, which was alive with activity. There were three cogs tied up and unloading cargo. One was the ship they had arrived on the previous evening. The other two had presumably arrived overnight and had waited until high tide to come alongside.

A well-dressed man came up the hill at a fast pace. Will called out as he approached .

"A moment of your time sir?"

The man slowed and said, "Time's money lad and I dare say mine is worth a lot more than yours today."

"As I said, a moment only sir. Perhaps you can point out John Watts to us, we have business to discuss."

"Business is it? Better have your wits about you then, don't say you haven't been warned." He pointed a stubby finger down at the scene below and said, "He's beside the cog at the very end of the quay. You can't miss him, he'll be the one shouting at the poor bastards unloading."

As he turned away from them, a panicked cry came from the street above. With thunderous booms they watched as several barrels rolled off the back of the cart that had passed them minutes before. They began to roll and bounce down the street, quickly picking up a fearsome speed. The man they had been speaking to crossed himself and shot across the street into a narrow passageway.

"God's teeth!" cried Bernard, "Move yourself, now." One of his big hands shot out and pushed a slack jawed and petrified Osbert across the street towards a doorway that he quickly stumbled into. There was no time for William or Bernard to join him. The best they could do was throw themselves over the low wall and stand on a ledge at the edge of the cliff. One of the barrels thundered past where they had just been standing and continued downhill. The one behind caught the edge of the wall they were stood behind and disintegrated in an explosion of splintered wood and a shower of wine. It left them shocked and soaked but otherwise unharmed.

With shuddered breath, Bernard said, "I thought our time had come. A moment's delay and we'd be with our maker. You all right lad?"

William, white faced, could only nod. They stepped back over the wall into the street, carefully avoiding the splintered remains of the barrel. Osbert emerged slowly from the doorway across the street and came across to them.

He was about to say something but William just held up a finger to silence him.

"Just don't say it. You had a bad feeling from the start," said Will grim faced.

"What's happened to the other barrel?" asked Bernard.

Will nodded down to the bottom of the street where there seemed to be a crowd milling about looking into the water.

"I think it rolled all the way down and dropped into the sea by the side of the quay. At least it doesn't seem to have hit anybody."

"We've been saved from injury for some higher purpose. It's a miracle," said Osbert piously.

"We're bloody lucky that's for sure," Bernard replied.

Will looked back up the hill where they could see the now empty cart had come to a halt. A small man was stood next to it wringing his hands. "You think it was deliberate?"

Bernard shrugged. "I'm may be a cynical old bugger but I've been doing this a long time. Seems bloody suspicious to me. We're just about to go ask some awkward questions and we're nearly crushed to death. At the very least I'm going to kick that carter up the arse."

Will nodded and said, "The mayor can wait, let's get back up there." They set off back up the street at a brisk pace, Osbert as usual trailing behind them.

As they approached the cart, they could see the broken ropes that had been used to secure the barrels to the wooden bed of the cart. Will grabbed one of the ropes and studied the end. There was a smooth cut going about halfway through the rope and then the rest was frayed. Will held the end up to Bernard who took one look, strode to the front of the cart and grabbed the little man who he took to be the carter by the throat. He lifted him off his feet and brought the struggling man close to his face. He squeezed his neck in a vice like grip.

"You've got some explaining to do friend. I don't take kindly to someone trying to kill me. One of the ropes back there has been cut through."

"Easy now Bernard," said Will nervously, "you'll choke him before we hear what he's got to say."

Bernard relaxed his grip a little, and the man gulped some air. He spluttered, "I swear I didn't know. I tied them myself down on the quay, tight as could be. Done it a thousand times, never had an accident before."

Will said to the man, "Which ship did the barrels come off?"

"The Sweet Anne," he replied.

"Which one is that?" said Bernard shaking the man a little to speed up his answers.

His eyes bulging he gasped, "Johns Watts's ship, the one at the end of the quay."

"Did you see anyone hanging around the cart before you set off from the harbour?"

The little man struggled in Bernard's grip. "There's a hundred men unloading down there. Any one of them could have cut the rope. I wasn't watching, had no reason to."

"You work for Watts do you?"

"No master, it's my own cart. That wine was probably worth a good ten shillings. Watts will see me ruined for this, he only has to speak a word and no one will dare hire me again." The man seemed genuinely shocked at the turn of events and Bernard felt a twinge of guilt. There was no actual proof he'd done anything, and he was probably right, Watts would take some form of revenge for the loss of the wine.

He gave the man's neck one last squeeze and said, "If I find out later that you've been lying to us you're going to regret it. I'll make a point of seeing you dance at the end of my blade."

"I swear I did nothing master," the man said wide eyed. Bernard grunted and slowly released his grip and the man fell to the floor gasping for air.

Will said, "Well, I don't believe that was an accident any more than you do. The rope was definitely tampered with. The question is; on who's instructions?" They all looked down to the harbour and the ship at the end of the quay.

Osbert shook his head sadly and said, "I don't understand why the bishop keeps sending me to these ungodly places. I must have sinned badly."

"Come on, let's get this over with," said Will and began to walk down the street again, slowly followed by the others.

There was a boisterous crowd at the approach to the quay. The bishop's men joined the throng and pushed their way to the front. In the shallow water at the side of the quay two men were trying to retrieve the wine barrel that had managed to run the full length of the street. It looked relatively intact, but whether the wine was now tainted by sea water was another matter.

They watched as the two men finally rolled the barrel out of the water onto a slipway. The men strained to push it any further and were soon joined by two more. With a lot of swearing and grunting, the barrel was transported onto the quayside itself. The crowd surged forward and stood around the barrel.

A guttural bark, "Get out of my way fools," parted the crowd and a stocky man forced his way through. He was accompanied by two others who pushed the crowd back.

"Get about your business," snarled one of the others and the crowd gradually melted away. Leaving the three bishop's men, the barrel retrievers and the newcomers looking at each other wearily.

"What do you want?" said the man who was clearly in charge.

Will saw Bernard stiffen at the angry question. The man looked at Bernard and narrowed his eyes.

"John Watts?" asked Will.

"This is the mayor and you'll..." snapped one of the other men before his master cut him off with a heavy hand on his arm.

"I'm John Watts. I'm a busy man, what do you want?"

"We're the bishop of Draychester's men."

"I know who you are. I knew before you stepped off the Margarete last night. I make it my business to know what's going on in this town."

"The barrels that rolled down the hill, they yours?" said Bernard.

Watts shrugged. "What of it, an unfortunate accident, the carter has been careless and I'll see he's punished."

"It's lucky we weren't killed," said Will.

Watts smiled dismissively and said, "Luck's a strange thing, with you one day and gone the next." He sniffed and wiped his nose with the back of his hand. "So what is it you want? I don't handle the bishop's business. He favours others in the town as I'm sure you already know. I've work to do. I need to get this lot back to unloading my cargo."

"As you said, you seem to be the man who knows what's going on in this town. In which case you'll have heard of the theft of some wine that belongs to the Bishop of Draychester?"

"I've heard that fool Phelpes has lost it. Wouldn't be surprised if he's told you I've stolen it." His eyed narrowed "He has, hasn't he?"

Will didn't answer directly but said, "Well if it's been misplaced, I'm sure the bishop would appreciate your help locating it. You're the mayor, surely you have some idea of what's happened to it? Our bishop is not a man to cross."

"Are you trying to threaten me lad?"

"What he's asking is for you to do your damn duty as mayor," said Bernard menacingly.

One of the men who had helped rescue the barrel interrupted the verbal sparring and said, "The barrel has been damaged master. Look the top's bulging."

Watts sighed and said, "Better open it up, chances are its ruined with sea water now. I'll flay the back clean off that bloody carter."

The man began prying at the barrel top with his knife. The other soon joined him. As they forced the wood, the top suddenly popped off as though under pressure. Something white and puffy bobbed up over the rim of the barrel.

"What the hell is that in there?" asked Watts.

"It's a man," said one of his men, stepping back hastily.

"God's teeth. Empty it, empty it now," said Watts.

"What here on the quayside?"

"Yes. Turn it over now you fool. Do it."

The two of them pushed the barrel over on its side. A flood of blood red wine gushing out onto the quay, along with a bloated figure of a man who washed out and came to rest face down. Watts slowly bent down and grabbed the man's head by it's sodden hair and pulled it around so they could see the face. The right hand side was caved in, a mass of blood, bone and shattered teeth but there was enough left intact to recognise the man. Bernard whispered, "My God, it's Tom Phelpes."

~

Osbert looked down, grey and shaking at the sight of the sodden corpse lying on the cobbled quayside. "The man was a picture of health last night, now here he lies dead before us. Who in God's name would kill him in such a manner and place him in a barrel like that?"

"Now that really is the question isn't it?" said Watts grim faced. "You three stayed at his house last night, you're probably the last to see him alive."

Bernard said angrily, "What are you implying? That man has been supplying my lord bishop with wine for ten years. Poor Phelpes has been butchered in your town Watts. There'll be hell to pay when the bishop hears of this. I've fought in the wars and I've seen injuries like that before. It looks like a blow from a mace to me."

"So you admit that you're familiar with such a weapon then? I'm also sure you're familiar with the law. There'll have to be an inquest and I'm placing all three of you in custody while we wait for the coroner to get here."

"We're bishops officials, there'll be consequences if you detain us," said Will.

Watts laughed. "You've threatened me again lad. This is my town, and your bishop is far away. From what I see there's a murderer or murderers on the loose and you three are the prime suspects. Now you'll come quietly or the lads might have to make you. What's it to be?"

## 6
## IN THE GATEHOUSE

There had been a brief struggle on the quayside but at least twenty or so men of Watts were there unloading the vessel. They quickly jumped to the mayor's orders. Even Bernard, who was always quick to anger, recognised the overwhelming odds. They'd assumed they would be taken to the local lock-up which would no-doubt be a stinking pit like that of most towns. Instead, they had been roughly escorted back through the town to the northern gate and confined to a room over the gatehouse itself. They'd been bundled up the narrow stairs into the surprisingly spacious but sparsely furnished white washed room. There was a small table, four stools and, in the corner, a bucket. The stout iron bound oak door was locked behind them. Bernard looked around and said, "Watts isn't stupid, he's smart enough to do us no serious harm. Who would want the wrath of the bishop upon them? Confined here he can keep us away from what's going on. It could be days before the coroner arrives and an inquest is held."

Will nodded, "That's if Watts even sends for him of

course. Phelpes's death deserves more, I'm sure the bishop would want us to bring him justice."

"I've told you before Will, the bishop always looks after his own. This won't go unpunished however long it takes, he has a long memory does our master."

Osbert gave them a despondent look and opened his mouth to speak. They both said simultaneously, "Not a word Osbert!"

～

There were only two gates into the town on the landward side, the Western gate and the Northern gate above which they were now confined. The Northern gate was the bigger and more elaborate of the two. The gateway itself was between two round towers in the main wall of the town. Outside the gate were two flanking walls and an outer archway set at the end of them, through which the busy foot, cart, and horse traffic passed into and out of the town. There was a long-shuttered window in the room. It could be opened to give a fine view down upon the space between the outer and inner gateways. They had opened the shutters almost as soon as the room's door had been locked behind them. All three peered out. It was a long drop to the cobbles below.

"Reckon you could climb down from here Will?" asked Bernard speculatively.

"Only if I had a rope, it must be thirty feet down and it'd be a hard landing."

"How about the other way?"

Craning their necks around they looked up. There was twelve feet or so of stonework to what was probably a walkway above the room they were confined in.

Will said, "There's little in the way of handholds. The stonework looks in good condition, nothing to aid in a climb."

"The door?" said Osbert.

They walked over and studied the heavy oak door. There was a small iron ring used to open it from the inside. Bernard grabbed hold of the ring and tried to wrench the door open with his enormous hands. He pulled with the full weight of his body, his biceps bulging. The door didn't move at all. He tried pushing it.

"Probably a bar across the outside," he grunted. "There's no easy way out of here I fear."

"Where would we go even if we escaped? The whole town seems to be in Watts's grip," said Osbert.

Will went back to the window and looked down at the cobbles below. "We will need to use our wits. I take it they aren't going to let us starve up here. Someone will bring food and drink. Perhaps we can get more information on what's going on. No point in breaking out into the town only to be recaptured again. We're going to need help."

∼

During the long afternoon of the first day of their confinement, Will watched the squat figure of the gatekeeper collecting tolls at the outer gateway. Goods coming into the town for sale were taxed and from what Will could see there seemed to be as many carts leaving the town as entering. He presumed those leaving were carrying goods that had arrived at the harbour over the previous days.

As one cart, full of barrels, rolled by underneath he said to the others, "I doubt the bishop's wine is still within the walls of the town. There seems to be a never-ending stream of carts leaving."

Bernard stood up stiffly from the stool where he had been sitting. He wandered over to the window and looked down at the cart leaving through the outer gate.

"Be easy to load it on a cart and for it to disappear. Every barrel looks much the same as another. Who knows where any of it's going."

"Well they certainly do," said Will, pointing down at the gatekeeper and a little man perched on a stool in an alcove in the wall. "See the man on the stool. I've been watching a good while and I can see he's making a note of what's entering and exiting on the carts. He talks to every carter. Perhaps he knows if our wine left on a cart and where it was heading."

From across the room Osbert said, "Perhaps he does, but no one's going to let us out of here to question him."

Will smiled back at him and said, "Ah Osbert, glad to see your optimism is still alive and kicking."

Bernard laughed. "Well I hate to admit it but he's got a point Will. We're stuck up here until someone lets us out."

"Then maybe we can get the gatekeeper and his clerk to come up here to us?" said Will.

∼

"We're getting hungry up here man. Are you going to let us starve? We're bishop's officials you know." Will shouted down from the window.

"Aye well, you'll have to wait a while longer," the gatekeeper shouted back up. He gestured at the outer gate. "We'll be closing up soon. I've my duties to attend to yet, then I'll see if you're worth feeding."

"Osbert, have you got the bishop's money with you?" said Will softly.

Osbert nodded. "Of course, it's never left my person. They were rough with us but they took nothing but our knives. They wouldn't dare rob us."

"Well, bring it here then," said Will impatiently.

Osbert joined him at the window and handed Will a small leather bag which he produced from inside his tunic. Will hung it out over the window ledge and shook it, the coins inside jingling. He shouted down into the passageway. "We'll see you right gatekeeper. Why don't you and your clerk join us for some food and drink. We could do with the company, we've been shut up here all bloody day."

The man looked up and sighed. He eyed the money bag and finally said, "All right, all right, Watts has told me to keep an eye on you. God's teeth it isn't like we don't already have enough to do. Hang on to your stomachs, I'd not have you starve but you'll have to wait while we lock up. Don't get any ideas either. Watts has posted two of his men at your door. He'd string me up if you escape."

All three watched as the gatekeeper and his clerk started to close the gates and manoeuvre a great wooden bar into place to secure it.

Bernard said, "I don't object to filling our stomachs lad, but I take it you have some plan?"

"It's simple enough. Let's eat our fill and have a drink with those two. No doubt if we ply them with enough ale, we can free their tongues and learn something to our advantage. From what I've observed this afternoon, they must see almost every cart and its contents that pass in and out of the town. Not to mention everyone on foot or horseback."

Bernard grunted his agreement. "I'm hungry and I could do with a drink, it's a good plan."

Osbert said, "We must answer for every penny spent."

"And I'm sure you'll be keeping count as usual," said Will.

~

Half an hour or so later and the door to their room was opened. Two of the mayor's men stood just outside, they were well armed and wary looking. The larger of the two had a heavy-looking cudgel in one hand. "Now don't get any ideas lads. You'll just get a thrashing and we'll get it in the neck from the mayor."

"How long are you planning on keeping us in here?" asked Will angrily.

Osbert, arms folded and with a more miserable scowl than usual said, "It's an absolute outrage. We're on the bishop of Draychester's business, you've no right to detain us."

The big man just shrugged. "We're just following the mayor's orders. Soon as the coroner arrives from Pembroke, then you'll be free to go about that business, that's all I know. Now stand back, old Richard the Gate and his sidekick have brought you something to eat."

"Just bring the bloody food in, I'm starving," said Bernard.

The gatekeeper and his clerk pushed past the guards into the room. They carried a large wicker basket between them which they brought over to the table.

"My wife runs an inn, the Anchor, I sent for food, you'll not go hungry," said the gatekeeper.

Bernard said, "I should bloody well hope not. The mayor should feed us for free since he's detained us against our will."

The gatekeeper's clerk laughed. "You'll not see Watts dipping into his purse. Tight as a rat's arse that one."

The guards at the door laughed.

Bernard grunted and said, "Osbert, you'd better pay the man."

Osbert retrieved some of the bishop's coin from the bag beneath his tunic. He reluctantly counted out the pennies until the gatekeeper indicated he was satisfied.

Will said, "You'll stay for a drink? We've only had each other's company all day. As you can see Osbert's a miserable sod and Bernard's just old and twisted."

They all laughed except Osbert whose face remained stonily impassive. The gatekeeper looked at his clerk, who just shrugged.

"Aye well, what's the harm? I've never been one to turn down a drink."

The smaller of the guards at the doorway said, "And you'll not begrudge us a bite or two? Been stood out here all day we have."

Will exchanged a quick, satisfied glance at Bernard as the plan began to play out as he'd wanted.

"The more the merrier my friends, the bishop's money is always well spent," said Will catching Osbert's outraged stare.

Both guards came into the room closing the door behind them. The smaller one rubbing his hands in anticipation of food and drink. The larger of the two rested his cudgel against the wall in a corner of the room.

He said, "I'm John Rees, and this is Tom White. Watts's dogsbodies for our sins."

The gatekeeper introduced himself and the clerk. "Richard Seely, Rich the Gate some call me, and this is Owen the clerk."

"As for the gate, well I make a note of every cart that leaves or comes into the town through it. We charge each and every one."

The little gatekeeper's clerk was droning on and on. His life was full of endless scribbling, day after day. How it didn't send him mad Will couldn't understand, but the man seemed incredibly dull by nature. Still, he was starting to get drunk and Will had managed to drop in the odd question between his monologues.

"Then you'll know who moves what goods and to where?" asks Will.

"Been sat at that gate day in day out, come rain or shine these last twenty years. Seen some things in my time I can tell you that. I know everyone and everything that comes through our gate."

"Well then, cast your mind back a few weeks my friend. Do you recall some wine of Thomas Phelpes leave by cart? Unusual perhaps, maybe something out of the ordinary?"

The gatekeeper looked warily at his clerk, but then shrugged and said, "He'll of made a note no doubt, but if it's the stuff I think you mean then I remember it well."

"So there was something unusual about it?"

"Well, it were good stuff, the best I've seen in a long while. I know what's bound for some lord's table rather than some sweaty tavern. This were good enough for the Constable of Pembroke himself I'd say. But that weren't what were most unusual you understand."

"So what was?"

"It left and then it came back later the same day on a different cart. Owen, you saw it too?"

"I saw it. Recorded it all in the ledger."

"You didn't ask the carter about it?"

"I didn't. There was some funny business going on. After all this time, I know when to keep my nose out of other people's business. There are some folk within the walls you don't want to upset. The cart paid its due, Owen here recorded it in his ledger, and we said no more."

"It was Phelpes's cart that took it out? You knew the carter?"

"Was his cart all right, has one of his men take it over to Pembroke or Haverfordwest regular, so I know it well. Anyway, it was Phelpes's own son who was driving it, the younger one I think it was."

"Phelpes's son you say? And the inbound cart, who's was that?"

"That one were bound for Watts's warehouse down near the quay. There was some other stuff on there but it were the same barrels coming back in. I'd swear to it."

"So the wine is still within the walls?"

"I didn't say that, but if it's left here again, it didn't pass through our gate. It could have been shipped out again I suppose, you'd have to ask down on the quay."

"Is that all you've come here to Tenby for, to seek some missing wine?" asked the gatekeeper's clerk curiously.

"I've been asking myself the same question," mumbled Will.

Bernard changing the subject said, "I hear there's trouble coming from the north. The rumour is there's to be a campaign against this Glyndwr fellow who's been stirring up trouble."

"I've heard the rumours. The tale is he's fallen out of favour with our new king. That's where the trouble stems from. Or maybe he was never in favour, who knows, the nobles were always a bloody mystery to me. The fool is calling himself Prince of Wales now, the cheek of it. Gathered himself some local support. From what I've heard, any fighting is to be done way up north."

"So there are no Welsh in the town?" said Osbert nervously.

The gatekeeper shrugged. "A few only. You won't find many Welsh around here at all. Head north ten or fifteen miles and you'll find them. Many answer to the Constable of Pembroke, same as us, but they keep to their area to the north and we keep to ours here in the south."

"Theres never any trouble then?" asked Osbert.

"Always trouble brewing, they're Welsh we're English we don't get along. Still, there hasn't been anything serious around here since my great-grandfather's day. Burnt the town down to the ground back then they did. But don't worry lad, we've got ourselves some higher walls since those days." At this the two guards, the gatekeeper and his clerk all laughed uproariously.

Wiping his eyes the gatekeeper said, "Forget the Welsh lad. I'd be more scared about the Flemish in the town. They were settled here on the orders of the first King Edward. You'll still hear their tongue spoken down in some of the taverns. Now they really do hate everybody. Bloody rough lot they are, they'd run you through for a penny."

Osbert shuddered. "What a place. I knew we were doomed as soon as we stepped ashore. "

Everybody collapsed in fits of drunken giggling.

## 7

## TAKE YOUR PICK

The thin-faced man looked out through the iron bars of the small hatch set in the cell door. He said nothing.

"And this one, he looks harmless if a little pungent?" asked Sir Roger peering at the man whilst sniffing the air suspiciously.

"Aye, he don't smell too great, I'll grant you that," said the jailer, leaning against the wall. "Still, don't let the stench put you off master, this ones a Berserker."

Sir Roger's arm shot out and pinned the jailer to the wall by his neck. "I don't appreciate jokes, you take me for a fool?"

The man, red faced spluttered, "I swear master, he's a Berserker. Fought in the king's army against the Scots he did. Massacred scores. Well known in the town he is, give him a drop of the hard stuff and he's unstoppable. Took twenty men to bring him in here, banned from every ale house within ten miles, I swear it."

"He'd better be as good as you say Jailer, don't think you can pass off every lowlife in the place to us. I'm only looking for the exceptional. Believe me, I've a long memory for those who cross me."

"I swear he'll do you proud master."

Sir Roger released his grip and turned around to Travis who stood further down the dim stone passageway. "Make a note Travis."

Travis gingerly crept towards the cell door and drew a circle in chalk on it. The man within just stood looking through the bars with a vacant look.

"What's his name by the way?" asked Sir Roger.

The jailer still rubbing his sore neck just shrugged. "Don't rightly know, always known him as The Berserker, he don't talk much."

"Right lets move on, who's next?"

"Follow me and watch your heads." The jailer scuttled off along the passageway which started to narrow even further, the ceiling starting to lower at the same time. "Where in God's name are we going man?" demanded Sir Roger after a further five minutes of trailing after the jailer.

"Almost there master," he said turning a sharp corner which ended at an iron-bound oak door. There was no window in this one.

"We call this the pit. Had some real bad ones in here, I can tell you."

"Who's in there now?" asked Sir Roger.

The jailer rifled through a large set of keys he kept on a ring at his waist. He unlocked the door and pulled it open gently. "You'll like this one," he whispered.

The cell was pitch black. Sir Roger said, "I can't see a bloody thing in there. Travis, bring me that candle from over there."

Travis carefully took a spluttering candle down from a niche in the wall and handed it to Sir Roger who thrust it through the open doorway. Suddenly there was a strange gobbling sound like a chicken being strangled. In the dim light they could just make out a large figure chained to the back wall of the cell by the arms. What was most extraordinary was the battered knight's helmet he wore. His face wasn't visible as the visor was closed. Even Sir Roger was taken aback at the strange gobbling sounds coming from inside the helmet.

"Why the helmet?" he said softly.

The jailer grinned wolfishly. "The man's a cannibal, ate his wife, her mother and then started on the kids. Bites anyone who gets near him. Completely off his head. Remove that helmet at your peril, he'll have your arm off."

"How do you feed him like that?"

"Bloody carefully I can tell you," said the jailer. "Caught out one of my men last month, he lost three fingers handing over a bowl of gruel. He wasn't happy I can tell you, that's when we found that old helmet there. Stuck that on him and he's been as good as gold since."

"And the strange noises?" asked Sir Roger fascinated.

"God knows, done it since he was brought here, we call him..."

Sir Roger interrupted. "Let me guess, the Gobbler?"

"Right you are master," said the jailer.

"Travis, another one for us, make a note."

As the cell door closed Travis duly marked it with a chalk circle. Sir Roger said, "Im going to need more than just the Berserker and the one in there. They'll do for the specialist jobs of course. What I need is the everyday killers and in some quantity."

The jailer rubbed his chin thinking. "We'll I've got two sets of brothers down the other end of the jail. They've been here about a month. Nasty little buggers, none too bright mind you, but very nasty."

"Lead the way," said Sir Roger.

~

As they were making their way along the dim passageway, a hand suddenly shot out from between the bars of a cell door and grabbed Travis by the throat.

Sir Roger snapped, "Travis you imbecile, leave that man alone. There's no time to waste."

"Master he's choking the life out of me," Travis croaked struggling for breath.

The jailer chuckled. "That's no man, that's Maggie. I think she must like you Travis. Mind you, I wouldn't get too cosy, she's choked the last three of her husbands to death, that right Maggie?"

The hand released Travis from a death grip and a face appeared next to the bars with wild eyes and ragged hair. A mouth with blackened stumps for teeth hissed through the bars, "Shut your dirty lying mouth…"

Sir Roger looked back through the bars thoughtfully. "A woman could be useful. Especially if she's a killer as you say."

A tongue appeared between the blackened teeth of the mouth and flicked at them suggestively. She hissed again at the jailer. "Why don't you come in here and find out. I like a big strapping fella like you. We could have some fun…"

The jailer took a step back. "Oh she's a killer all right master. Wouldn't trust her an inch. She's more dangerous than some of the men in here. You sure you want to take her?"

Sir Roger nodded. "We'll take her. Travis, make a note."

The jailer shook his head in disbelief. "I hope you know what you're doing. I really do."

The women began cackling madly through the bars. Travis, on his hands and knees, crawled back to the bottom of the door and drew a chalk circle.

∼

"What is that smell? God's teeth it's making my eyes water." There was a round of sniggering from behind the cell door.

"I'd stand back if I were you," said the jailer unlocking the heavy oak door. It swung open, and the smell hit them like a solid wall. Sir Roger wrapped an arm around his mouth and nose and peered into the cell. There were four men each wearing leg irons fastened to the back wall with long chains. One man sat squatting over a bucket in the corner. He was laughing hysterically. Between peels of laughter he managed to gasp, "I've got the devil's dumplings in here. Want to see? Like giving birth it was."

The jailer, his own eyes watering said, "You're an animal Jones. I've a mind to give you a bloody good thrashing for that."

One of the other men said with a whine, "The slop you feed us in here, what you expect?"

Another, who looked like an older version of the man with the bucket said, "I haven't passed anything in a week, all bunged up with your slop. My brother seems to be making up for the rest of us though."

This set his brother off laughing again. Now sat firmly in the bucket he began to hop it toward the cell door the chain extending behind him. Sir Roger, hand clasped tightly around his nose, said to him, "What crime are you in here for?"

The man looked up at Sir Roger. "Depends who's asking?"

Sir Roger suddenly stepped forward and kicked the bucket from under the man. It clattered into the back wall, overturned and deposited its foul contents across the floor.

"Have a care master, I really wish you hadn't done that," said the jailer gasping at the stench. Travis backed down the corridor coughing. The jailer covered his mouth and nose and mumbled from behind his hand, "All of em in here are to be hanged. Rape, murder, thieving, I don't remember who did what, I doubt they do either. I do know the one who was sat on the bucket stole the mayor's finest mare."

The man now laying on the floor in the filth looked up and grinned with grimy yellow teeth at Sir Roger. He said, "Guilty as charged, it was a fine beast."

"So you stole Bebbington's horse?" Sir Roger gave an evil smirk. "I bet he wasn't pleased."

"Mad as hell," said the man.

Sir Roger turned to the jailer. "I'll take all four. Make sure you put a few buckets of water over them before you deliver. If they turn up smelling like that, you'll be taking them back."

"As you wish master, as you wish," said the jailer quickly shutting the cell door and locking it again.

"Travis," said Sir Roger gesturing to the door. Travis duly chalked a circle on the wood.

"Jailer, you know the arrangements?" asked Sir Roger

He nodded. "I do master and I'll await your instructions on delivery time and place."

Sir Roger grunted his satisfaction. "Enough, let's be out of here."

## 8

## BISHOP'S PALACE DRAYCHESTER

Once again Scrivener reflected on what an unusual man Jocelyn Gifford, bishop of Draychester was. Gifford was both a powerful noble and fabulously wealthy. A combination that, in Scrivener's long experience, was often accompanied by overindulgence, arrogance and stupidity. None of which could be levelled at Gifford. The bishop's clerk studied his master from across the low table. Gifford had once been a solider, and he had kept something of the warrior physique of his youth. He was still lean and fit, probably more so than some men half his age. Scrivener also thought his master one of the cleverest men he'd ever known. That's not to say he couldn't also be irritating and downright devious. But he was fiercely loyal to his household and retainers. Even rarer was that he chose not to surround himself with sycophants as did so many of the nobles of the kingdom. Scrivener sometimes speculated why Gifford had never made a bid for the throne himself. He had a claim via royal blood a few generations back and there were many who would have followed him. Perhaps it was safer to be one of the powers behind the throne rather than to sit on it. The nobles had a nasty habit of thinning their own ranks. Richard the previous king and his supporters had found that to their cost.

"You day dreaming Scriviner? What's on your mind?"

Scrivener focused his attention again and swiftly said, "I'm sorry my lord, I was just thinking of that wretch Mudstone."

"Ah, Roger Mudstone. I've not forgotten him either. You've had some news of him?"

Scrivener poured his master some wine and then poured again for himself. He swirled it around in his cup. "Perhaps my lord. There's a small hungry girl being fed in the great hall. Appeared this morning at our gate, with a monk, we're feeding him too. He's carried a message to us from the abbot of Whalley."

The bishop sipped his wine. "Well I'm sure we can stand the expense, how much can a small girl and a monk eat. So tell me, what does this message from Whalley have to say?"

Scrivener smiled. He knew his master lived for the intrigue. It was impossible for him to resist a good story, especially when it could lead to a man whose head the bishop had put a hefty price upon.

"It seems a consignment of salt on its way to the abbey got waylaid. This was high on the moors between Yorkshire and Lancashire."

"Mudstone," breathed Gifford.

Scrivener nodded. "I believe so my lord. It seems the girl worked on a pack horse team with her stepfather. They ran into Mudstone whilst crossing the highest stretch. He was with his servant, a man named Travis."

"Not a happy encounter I take it?"

"He killed the girl's stepfather and took her, the pack horses and their salt cargo to a moorland tavern. It's a place well known as a den of thieves. It was there he sold them all on."

"What, the girl as well?"

"Yes my lord."

"Then she did well to escape." The bishop pushed himself up from the table and ran a hand over his chin. "I think we'd better have a talk with this girl. Perhaps she has some knowledge of where he's headed?"

"She's in the great hall with the monk. I'm not sure how much she knows my lord."

∽

The great hall was the focal point of the bishop's palace. It was a fine space, tall with a timber-framed roof and high windows. There was a central hearth and down the length of the hall stretched three long tables with benches. It was rarely empty day or night. It took Scrivener and the bishop a moment or two to spot their visitors in amongst the throng. At the far end of the hall they could see a small girl, perhaps ten years of age. She was sat at the table with a small, jovial looking monk who was dressed in a rough greyish-white cowl.

"Whalley Abbey you say this monk is from?"

"Yes my lord," said Scrivener hesitantly. He knew his master had noted the white cowl of the monk. This identified him as a member of the Cistercian order. His master famously had little time for monks and even less for those who were Cistercians.

The bishop smiled at his clerk. "Don't worry Scrivener. I

can be quite civil when I need to be. Come on, let's hear their tale."

They made their way across the hall. As they approached the monk stood up. The bishop waved him back to his seat. "Continue with your meal my friend, we can talk as you eat. I'm Jocelyn Gifford."

The monk smiled nervously, sat down and said, "Thank you my lord. I'm Brother Gregory of Whalley Abbey. You must excuse us my lord, we've not eaten this well for days. It's been a long journey." The monk turned to the girl and said, "Anny, this is Bishop Gifford."

The girl, mouth full of bread and cheese said, "Hello your bishopness."

Gifford couldn't help but chuckle. "Well hello Anny. How's your food?"

"Best we've had all the way here your holiness."

The monk whispered to her, "Call him my lord or bishop child, he's not the Pope."

Gifford laughed again. "The good brother is right Anny. I'm only a bishop and I think my chances of becoming Pope are slim."

Anny considered this a moment and said solemnly, "I've come to think anything can happen. That's if you want it bad enough."

The monk said, "Anny! I'm sorry my lord, the girl is tired and somewhat wilful. She means no disrespect."

Gifford slid onto the bench directly opposite, and Scrivener sat down next to him. "Don't worry brother, let the girl speak freely. You know Anny, for one so young, I think you've got a clever head on those shoulders."

Anny gave him a bashful smile. Scrivener drummed his fingers on the table and said, "So brother, Tell us about Roger Mudstone?"

The monk's face turned stony. "Anny's stepfather was killed by Mudstone and his servant up on the moors above our abbey. They were carrying salt to us at Whalley."

The girl interrupted and said, "Travis didn't kill Tubby, that was Sir Roger. Travis never touched him."

"I'm sorry about your stepfather. If this Travis had no part in his death, then that'll be in his favour when we catch him and his master," said Gifford.

Anne shrugged. "I'm not sorry about Tubby, he wasn't much of a stepfather. Used to beat me something rotten he did."

"Anny!" said Brother Gregory warningly. He continued, "Mudstone sold her to another thief my lord. Travis, Mudstone's servant, helped the girl to escape. She seems to think she owes him something. Told her to seek help from the monks at Whalley. We heard about Mudstone's outrage in Sodham my lord and that he has been outlawed. Abbot Walter thought you might want to question the girl directly."

Scrivener thought it more likely that the abbot had heard there was a bounty on Mudstone's head. He would no doubt be eager to claim his share of it. Whalley, like many abbeys, was in the midst of an ambitious building programme. Funds were always needed. Still, whatever the abbot's motives, it could only aid in discovering Mudstone's whereabouts. Scrivener said, "Tell me Anny, before you got away from those bad men on the moors, did Mudstone say where he was going."

"Not sure. Asked me if I'd ever been to Lancaster with Tubby. That's a place where there are ships on a river by the town. Been there with Tubby a few times."

Scrivener and Gifford exchanged a look. "Are you sure that's what he asked child?" said the bishop.

"Of course I'm sure," said Anny. "Asked me if I'd been all the way to the sea. Said I'd been to a place with boats on the river called Lancaster. Not long after, he sold everything he'd stolen. Then him and Travis left me behind at the Moorcock with Hammo the Hand ."

Brother Gregory cringed. "I'm sorry my lord, she's rather direct. The Moorcroft is a tavern up on the moors, a nest of vipers can be found there. Hammo the Hand is their leader."

"Hamo only has one hand," said Anny helpfully.

The bishop smiled. "I believe what you say Anny, I really do and it sounds like this Hamo is aptly named." He turned to Scrivener. "So you think Mudstone has taken ship?".

Scrivener nodded. "Undoubtedly my lord. He's not going to rest long in Lancaster. He's gone there for one reason and that's to find passage. If he's any sense, he'll leave the realm. I'll send word to our people in the north. A man like Mudstone makes enemies easily. Somebody will know where he's gone, especially when there is money upon his head."

"I agree," said the bishop. "I'm sure you'll do what's needed Scrivener. Brother Gregory, I'm grateful that you came. You too young Anny. So, let me ponder how I can help the brothers of Whalley for their good deeds. And of course what's to be done with young Anny here. What are your thoughts Scrivener?"

Before Scrivener could answer Brother Gregory said eagerly, "I believe there is a price on Mudstone's head?"

Scrivener smiled knowingly. "Indeed, there is, although we need to catch him first. Don't worry brother, the information you've brought us may yet lead to him. The abbey will have its share. As for now, perhaps a gift of land my lord?"

The bishop nodded. "I think I know the very place

you're thinking of Scrivener. It would be a fitting gift. Let Scrivener here draw up the papers brother and he'll come find you later. Have you thought about what's to be done with Anny? Perhaps we should return her to her mother?"

The girl said softly, "Mums already got four younger than me to feed. She'll not be glad to see me back, not now that Tubby has got himself murdered."

Brother Gregory said, "The abbot thought possibly a nunnery my lord?"

"Let me think on it," said Gifford.

~

"It's the manor of Coxington you'll be wanting to grant to Whalley my lord?"

"Yes, of course. You disagree Scriviner?"

"Not at all my lord, it seems most appropriate in the circumstances. The manor was Mudstone's but has been forfeit to us now that he's outlawed. Still, it's practically worthless, although I can see your thinking, the land borders on the abbey at Ribsdale."

"Exactly," beamed the Bishop. "It neatly gets a worthless asset off our hands, rewards, at least in theory Whalley and irritates that idiot the abbot of Ribsdale. You know how these monks like to get the law involved. I'd wager the two abbots will be at each other throats over land rights or some such nonsense within the year."

"And the girl my lord? A nunnery?"

"She seems a bright little thing. I believe it would be a waste. Tell me, is my sister still in the north? I've not had a letter in some time."

"I believe she is on her way here, possibly within the week."

"I thought her intention might be as much. Well then, what better household to place the girl with? My sister takes in as many waifs and strays as do I Scrivener. She won't object if you put it to her in the right way. My guess is she won't be able to help herself."

"As you wish my lord, I'll do my best."

# 9
## THE BEASTS RELEASED

The light was dim in Mayor Bebbington's day chamber. The shutters were closed and the two candles placed on the table provided only a muted golden glow. He was suffering the after effects of a mind numbing migraine and his head was still pounding. He thought it was probably stress induced. It didn't help that Roger Mudstone sat opposite him. His old comrade-in-arms made his skin crawl. Sir Roger's man Travis leaned against the back wall in the shadows, head down, apparently more interested in studying his feet than their conversation. Bebbington poured some wine into his cup and tried to swill the foul taste from his mouth. A rolled up parchment sat on the table in front of him. He placed his hand on it and said, "I hope you appreciate the lengths I've had to go to in obtaining this Mudstone. You've upset some very powerful people. In particular, I hear the bishop of Draychester is after your head?"

Sir Roger shrugged. "I had a difference of opinion with him. He cheated me out of my inheritance, got my spineless late brother to gift it all to the church in his will. I'm confident I'll have my revenge. You know me of old Bebbington, I have a very long memory."

"Well all I ask is you leave me out of it. I've built myself a new life here. After this, I'll consider my debt to you is settled. Here take it." Bebbington thrust the roll of parchment across the table.

Sir Roger snatched it up and unrolled it. "So this is it. A pardon. Can't say I've ever seen one before. Doesn't look like much." He read it carefully before rolling it up again and placing it under his tunic.

Bebbington said, "It's enough to keep you from being locked up, at least for now. See my clerk before you leave. I've scraped together the coin you've asked for. Use it wisely, there'll be no more."

Sir Roger grunted in return. "My little band, where are we to exercise our talents?"

Bebbington took another long gulp from his cup. He knew he was drinking far too much. The past few weeks since Sir Roger had arrived had taken their toll. All the old memories of his time in France with Sir Roger's men were resurfacing. He could hardly meet the other man's gaze. Finally he said, "The Welsh are in revolt. They're led by a man named Glyndwr, he's apparently burnt the town of Ruthin to the ground and in response the king plans to punish the Welsh badly. Do the king's bidding in Wales and you'll be a free man."

"Well, well, that sounds promising, always lots of opportunities during a revolt."

"And I've no doubt you'll take all of them," said Bebbington.

Sir Roger ignored the barbed comment and said, "This man Glyndwr, you know anything about him?"

"A little. Most of these local Welsh landowners like

Glyndwr were followers of King Richard. He seems to have had some land dispute with his English neighbour, name of Reginald Grey, of Ruthin. Don't know him myself. Anyway, he's a fierce supporter of our new king. You can see where this is heading?"

"Ah I see, so it was a feud, understandable perhaps, but it's now a Welsh rising?"

"Yes. It started as a feud but it's gone much further. Glyndwr has pretensions, he's of old Welsh royal stock. His countrymen are flocking to his side. There's no love lost between Welsh and English. They've burnt Ruthin, but the unrest is spreading. I'm not sure Glyndwr can control what he's started."

Sir Roger's eyes were gleaming. He rubbed his hands with enthusiasm. "That sounds even better, the possibilities are intriguing."

"God help me, I'd rather not know what you intend Mudstone. My understanding is the king is bringing his forces down from the Scottish border. The army will be at Shrewsbury in a few days. Meet them there, you're expected. I take it you've chosen some men?"

Sir Roger smirked and said, "Oh yes, your jail has been most productive. I think I have what I need."

Bebbington suppressed a shiver and said, "I'm almost sorry for the Welsh. I remember your antics all too well from France. I've had nightmares about it for years."

Sir Roger shrugged with indifference. "Really? Well I've always slept quite soundly. Then again, you were always a little too weak for this sort of business Bebbington."

The other man smiled bitterly. "I still have some shred of humanity left, if that's what you mean."

"Exactly my point Bebbington, it makes you weak."

Bebbington poured himself another cup of wine, stared

down at the table and said, "Just leave the city with the scum you've collected Mudstone. Do it before nightfall. I pray to God I never lay eyes on you again."

∼

Sir Roger had assembled a motley collection of followers in a courtyard immediately behind the city's jail. He'd acquired six of the more disreputable members of the city watch, ordered by Bebbington to join him. During the previous evening a trawl of the worst alehouses in the city had already procured two dozen thieves and scoundrels. They were desperate for coin, wine and women. All of which he promised when they got to Wales. Some of them even claimed to have fought in the king's army before. Finally, in the late afternoon, his selection from the jail had been forced into a covered cart and chained to the wooden deck by their hands and feet. The covering was to conceal them from the city's prying eyes and the chains in fear of what they'd do to the rest of the party if they were free.

The loading of the Gobbler had proved the most difficult. He'd somehow managed to break free from the four men struggling to haul him aboard. There was a minor incident as he plunged down a side street, feet loose but his arms still chained behind his back. Fortunately it was turning dark, and the helmet clad figure was almost blind as he blundered down the narrow passage. He did manage to get his bare feet around the neck of the terrified old strumpet who sold herself nightly from the shadows there. It certainly wasn't the sort of customer she normally catered to and it took all four of them to pry his feet off her grubby neck. Her screams and the strange helmet clad grunting threatened to bring the whole street out. Sir Roger took care of her himself using a sharp little dagger he carried in his boot. They dragged the Gobbler back with some difficulty and manhandled him onto the cart.

"God's teeth he's a feisty one," swore Sir Roger. "Reminds me of my Father when he'd drunk too much ale. Quite like old times eh Travis, Travis?"

Travis sat petrified at the front of the cart unable to move.

Sir Roger shouted at him angrily. "Get down from there and give us a hand, we've not got all night. We need to leave before the curfew bell. Jump to it man."

They left the city by the Bridgegate. Sir Roger led on a fine horse he'd bought with Bebbington's coin that very afternoon. Travis drove the covered cart that contained the prisoners taken from the jail. Behind them on foot tramped the men the city watch had given up willingly, and the associated lowlifes Sir Roger and Travis had collected. More of Bebbington's coin had provided some battered but serviceable weaponry. They numbered thirty or so, not including the prisoners who were out of sight for now. As they carefully crossed the bridge over the River Dee, Sir Roger looked back on his grubby little band and grunted in satisfaction. He'd led worse in his time but they'd do for now.

∽

After spending an uncomfortable night camped by the roadside, they set off at first light. After an hour on the road Travis summoned up enough courage to ask, "Master, I'm not sure this is the right road for Shrewsbury. Perhaps we have gone wrong?"

"Don't ever question my sense of direction Travis. Besides, I never said we were going to Shrewsbury did I?"

"But if we're to join up with the king's forces, then we need to take the Shrewsbury road master. I think this one is heading directly into Wales."

"It never fails to amaze me how naïve you are Travis. That you've managed to live this long is a mystery. Now why on earth would I want to join the king's forces?"

"But the pardon master..."

"The pardon is a useful piece of parchment Travis, but that's all it is, a bit of parchment. I want more Travis. I want money, power, land, women. I'm not going to find that trailing after the king. I think there's someone much more deserving of our little band's talents."

"Who master?" asked a bewildered Travis. "I don't understand."

With his open palm, Sir Roger slapped Travis across the top of his head. He said exasperated, "Of course you don't understand Travis, that's because you're an inbred imbecile. I've no doubt your mother and father were brother and sister. Think fool, who else is there? We're going to join the Welsh of course. Now get a move on, we've someone to meet."

∼

Two miles further up the rutted road they found their guide sat on a rock. He was a slim, dark-haired little man, huddled in a grey cloak. His face was white and pasty with lifeless black eyes. Sir Roger brought his horse to a halt beside the man and said, "Madoc?"

The man gave the slightest nod of his head to Sir Roger. In a thick Welsh accent he said, "Follow my directions."

Then without another word he stood up and wrapped his cloak tighter around himself and put his hood up. He walked back to the cart, climbed up and sat down next to Travis who shrank away from him.

Sir Roger said, "A man of few words, eh? I was told you could lead me to Glyndwr's men. Disappoint me at your peril. I hope we understand each other?"

The man just looked at Sir Roger with his dull black eyes. He didn't say a word but lifted a limp arm and pointed down the road.

Sir Roger shrugged. "Let's move on."

∽

After an hours' travel during which it was impossible to get their guide to more than shrug or raise an eyebrow, they came to a halt. They had turned off what passed for the main road onto an even narrower muddy track. It ended at a small clearing in the middle of a thick wood. In the centre of the clearing sat a turf roofed cottage. A thin trail of wood smoke rose from the roof and hung in the still air like a mist. The surrounding woods were dark and oppressive. Sir Roger climbed down from his horse and stood in front of the cottage.

"You'd better have brought us here for some good reason Welshman. I'm inclined to give you a damn good thrashing just for the wasted time."

In a flat toneless voice, Madoc said, "There is a seer within, she knows where Glyndwr is."

"A seer," scoffed Sir Roger, "do you take me for a fool?" He grabbed hold of the Welshman and pushed him roughly through the heavy leather skin that was draped across the doorway. He drew his sword and barged his way in after.

∽

*Death Of The Vintner*

"God's teeth, what a revolting old hag," said Sir Roger.

At this Madoc sucked air through his teeth in reproach. "Speak carefully, Englishman. She's a powerful old woman. A Seer. Take care, a curse from her could doom all your future endeavours."

It was the most he'd said since they'd met. Sir Roger's hand shot out and grabbed the little Welshman by the throat and lifted him off his feet. His eyes bulged as Sir Roger started to throttle him.

"Frankly, I'm getting a little tired of your attitude Madoc, if that's even your name. I must have been mad to let you lead us here. I mean for God's sake, look at her!"

The Seer grinned at Sir Roger toothlessly and said to him, "I can speak English."

Sir Roger shrugged and said, "Then there's no need for this idiot to translate." He thrust his sword deep into Madoc's side. He quickly withdrew it and let the dying Welshman drop to the ground. He turned back to the old woman. "As I was saying, what a revolting old hag you are."

The Seer cackled. "Oh, that was right nasty, poor Madoc. Most men fear me, but not you, I like that. You would have desired me once, I was beautiful."

Sir Roger looked at her incredulously. "That must have been in my great grandfather's time."

"A long time before then young man. I've made many sacrifices to see into the future of men's affairs."

Sir Roger Sniffed the air and said, "Washing being one of them?"

She cackled again. "At least once a year I bathe in the sacred waters of Lake Bala."

"I'll have to take your word for that but I'm sure I can hold my breath for the time this takes. So, I presume I'll need to cross your palm with coin?"

A grubby hand shot out, and he gingerly deposited a small pile of pennies, carefully avoiding touching her skin. The coins quickly disappeared.

"Sit," she said gesturing to a pile of greasy sheep skins piled on the floor close to the fire.

"You jest with me hag. I paid a lot of money for this cloak, so I'll stand if it's all the same. Now you're going to tell me how to find Glyndwr."

The woman reached under her dirty rags and brought out a small leather bag drawn tight with a frayed string. She untied it, turned it upside down and shook the bag to free the contents. Out tumbled a jumble of chicken bones that fell to the dusty floor.

"Is that it?" asked Sir Roger in disgust.

The women held her hand up and studied the bones. She drew in her breath.

"Glyndwr. This will become more then he ever dreamed of, great victories, the English in retreat across the land, death and destruction. Then a great cause lost, defeat and despair."

"You can see all that in a jumble of bones? I could have taken the remains of my supper last night and done the same."

She glared at him. "It takes great skill to read the bones Englishman."

"So then, with this great skill you have, can you tell me where he will go?"

The women gathered up the bones into the bag, shook it and upended it onto the floor. The bones scattered across the dusty ground once again.

Sir Roger said softly, "What do you see old women? Tell me."

"He's burnt Ruthin already. I see his course, Denbigh,

Rhuddlan, Flint, Hawarden, Holt, Oswestry, Welshpool. Fire and death. Follow the path of destruction Englishman."

"Oh I will, where there's death and destruction there's opportunity. So, cast your bones for me old women, tell me what you see."

She shook her head. "Dangerous to see your own future. Be certain what you ask of me."

"Do it," he hissed.

She hesitated, then gathered the bones again and scattered them a final time across the floor.

"I see this place, you're stood over the body of an old woman, she's bleeding..." She gasped, looked up and began to back slowly towards the door.

Sir Roger smirked. "Well, well, old hag. I believe you truly do have a gift."

He lifted his sword and advanced on her, the bones crunching under his boots.

## 10

## THE CONSTABLE ARRIVES

Will's head was pounding. He very carefully opened one eye, but the room appeared to be in complete darkness. He vaguely remembered some of the previous evening. They'd drunk well into the night with the gatekeeper, his clerk and the guards. At some stage he'd fallen asleep with his head resting on his arms at the table. He could hear a chorus of snores and snuffles of what he assumed were his fellow drinking companions. Something had disturbed his drunken slumbers. He carefully pushed himself up from the table. The room had cooled off and his body was stiff. Once standing he could just make out a dim light from between the shutters covering the window. He stumbled over to the window feeling slightly nauseous and opened one of the shutters. His reaction to the cold air was to heave into the void. He ended with a large burp. Feeling somewhat relieved he looked up at the sky. It was still dark, well after midnight he judged, but nowhere near dawn. He looked down into the cobbled passageway. There seemed to be some loud shouting coming from outside the gate and some dark figures were heading through the inner gateway from the town into the passageway below. A ghostly face looked up at him. A voice called out, "Gatekeeper, is that you, where the hell are you? Look lively."

"What's the matter?" he called down softly, unwilling to wake his drunken comrades yet.

The voice called again, "Gatekeeper, Rich, where the devil are you, you silly old sod? Get up, get up now."

From the other side of the outer gate there began an incessant hammering, blows loud enough to wake the dead, reverberating through the still air.

"Hello, who goes there?" Will tried to shout, but all that came out was a parched croak. He stumbled back to the table, knocking over a stool with a loud bang. He found a cup with some drink still in it and swirled it around his mouth then headed back to the window.

"Hello," he croaked, "who goes there?"

The figure directly below shouted up, "Is that you Rich? We need to open the gate at once, the Constable of Pembroke's men are here."

"It's not Rich, wait," he croaked, "I'll get him."

Will turned back to the sleeping men. The quickest way was always the best. He hooked his leg around the table and pulled it away from them. There was an almighty crash followed by groaning and angry shouts.

∼

The gatekeeper and his clerk struggled with the huge beam across the main gate. Eventually they removed it and pulled back the iron-studded gate. Ten mounted men at arms led by a tall figure clad in chain mail burst through the gates.

"Is there no watch being kept in this town?" bellowed

their leader at the gatekeeper who had hastily backed against the wall.

"My lord..," he spluttered.

"Go and fetch Watts, now!"

The bishop's men and the two guards looked down on the scene from the upper chamber window.

"Who is that?" asked Bernard.

"The Constable of Pembroke that is," said one of the guards. "He don't look too happy."

"My lord," shouted Will into the gloom.

The constable peered up at them. "Who the hell are you?" he asked.

"William Blackburne my lord. My master is the bishop of Draychester. The mayor has three of us bishop's men locked away up here."

The man said in exasperation, "And your point is? Do you think I've time for Watts's petty intrigues man? The Welsh are in revolt. I've got other things on my mind."

"Truly I am sorry to trouble you my lord, we're on the bishop's business here. Watts has obstructed us since our arrival three days ago."

Suddenly Osbert was between them and he shouted down, "I have a dispatch from Bishop Gifford for you my lord."

The two other bishop's men turned to him with baffled looks. "You have a letter for him?" hissed Will softly.

"I do. My uncle Scrivener, the bishop's clerk, gave it to me before we left. It requests his help in our task. He said to give it to the constable if we came across him."

"And you didn't think to mention this to us before lad?" asked Bernard.

Osbert shrugged, "You never asked."

"Unbelievable," said Will under his breath.

They could hear the constable's heavy sigh from below. He shouted up, "God's teeth, do I not have enough troubles already." He shook his head and said, "Well then, I suppose you'd better get your arses down here. Far be it from me to displease his grace the Bishop of Draychester!"

Will turned to the two guards. "You heard the king's constable, you're to release us at once."

They were soon down in the passageway with the now dismounted constable's men and they all moved quickly away from the gateway down into the town itself. The constable led the way, evidently knowing the place well. They stopped outside the church.

"In here I think," he said. "Someone get some light going."

Before they could enter through the heavy oak door, they spotted a figure running up the steep hill towards them trailed after by the gatekeeper. Watts had evidently been dragged out of his bed as he appeared to be half dressed. The bishop's men couldn't help but smirk. When he drew near, he gave them a furious stare.

"Ah Watts, glad you could join us," said the constable.

"My lord I had these men locked up for good reason."

The constable looked at him wearily. "Frankly, I don't care, do you think I came here at this hour looking for them?"

"No my lord. If you'd sent word, I would have prepared a bed…"

∽

The constable finished reading the letter that Osbert had handed him. He sniffed once, seemingly satisfied, carefully folded it and placed it within his cloak. He looked at Watts expectantly.

Watts spluttered, "My lord, they're here to spy for Gifford, I know it. They came with a ridiculous story about searching for some stolen wine. No sooner than they arrive a man is found murdered."

The constable sighed. "Spy on what for God's sake? Your petty corruption here doesn't concern me and I suspect the bishop is even less interested than I. That is of course if you didn't steal his bloody wine?"

"You're accusing me my lord?"

"Don't take me for a fool Watts. I know what goes on here. If I find you've a hand in this, there'll be hell to pay. As long as the town makes me coin and you keep the peace I'm contented. Cause me a problem, and you'll be spending your days in the dungeons at Pembroke. Don't you ever forget you answer to me Watts and ultimately the king."

Watts shot the bishop's men a look of pure malice but then bowed his head to the constable and said, "My lord."

The constable swept his hands around and continued, "What you do within the town walls is your concern but leave Gifford's men well alone. Let them go about their business and let me worry about the good bishop as and when I need too."

Watts stared sullenly in resentment at the constable rebuke. Finally he bowed his head and said, "As you command my lord."

The constable nodded. "I'm glad we understand each other Watts. Now I have bigger concerns to think about. The Welsh in the north are in revolt. I need you to gather supplies at once. We're instructed to send them up the coast to Harlech in support of the king's forces. Now tell me, how many of your ships are in the harbour?"

"Revolt?" Watts said in surprise. Then gathering his wits, he said, "The Isabelle sailed last evening for Porthclais via Pembroke with goods for the bishop of Saint Davids. I've two other ships down at the quay my lord and I expect the Maud to arrive from Bristol this very afternoon. She's to return there shortly."

"She's not going back to Bristol anytime soon. I've a long list of supplies we need to find and send north for the king. I'll need all the ships available, there's no time to waste."

"But my lord," protested Watts, "I've made promises, contracts to be kept…"

Bernard interrupted them with what for him was a polite cough. The constable turned back to him with irritation. "Yes, yes, bishop's men," he flicked his hand at them dismissively, "be about your business, my regards to your master. Now as for you Watts, the king's needs are far greater than any contracts you've made, how long will it take to…"

The bishop's men hastily left the church. Watts gave them one last lingering look of hate before turning his attention back to the constable.

∼

They stood in the street outside the church. On the far sea horizon there was just the hint of dawn. Will said, "We'd better make the most of the time the constable is here. As soon as he's gone that oaf Watts will have us locked up again or worse. I'm not sure what's going on here but he's involved. As for Thomas Phelpes's son, we need an urgent word I think."

"What kind of son steals from his own father?" said Osbert.

"Get to my age boy and nothing will surprise you," said Bernard dryly.

"It seems likely he did a lot more than just steal. What's to say he didn't murder his father," said Will.

Osbert shivered at the thought.

Will continued, "Anyway we can't go accusing him at this time in the morning. We'll wake half the town up if we go barging in. Besides, we need cool heads for this."

Bernard ran a hand over his tired eyes. "You're probably right lad although my heart tells me to go break his door down and beat a confession out of him."

Will said, "I suspect most of the town is already awake after the constable's arrival. We need someone to make sense of all this. There must be a welcome door somewhere in this bloody town."

"There's a little chapel with some friars across there," said Osbert pointing to a narrow side street. "Carmelites I think."

Once again Osbert had surprised them both. "Don't look at me like that. I have eyes. I saw it when I walked up from the harbour yesterday whilst you two were getting drowned in Phelpes's cellar. I stopped to ask one of the brothers for directions."

Bernard looked at him thoughtfully. He said, "Friars? Well, I suppose it'd do no harm to speak with them. Never known a friar who wasn't a good gossip. Dare say we might get fed as well. Lead the way lad."

"And I've never known a man with such an appetite. Are you permanently hungry Bernard?" asked Will in jest.

"I think better when I've been fed lad, and that's the honest truth."

## 11

## AT WELSHPOOL

"Damn it," hissed Sir Roger. "Glyndwr's moving too fast for us. The town is well alight already."

They stood in amongst the tree line on the top of a low hill to the south of Welshpool. Travis looked at the billowing smoke, horrified by the scene unfolding in the town below. Even from here he could hear screaming. He croaked, 'Master the whole towns alight and the Welsh are cutting men down like wheat."

Sir Roger giggled like a small child. "Yes they are Travis, and the ones they aren't cutting off at the knees they seem to be driving back into the flames. They do seem to be an angry bunch." He sniffed the air excitedly. "Can you smell that Travis? Reminds me of burning pork fat. Anyway, we can't stand up here all day sightseeing."

He grabbed hold of Travis by the scruff of the neck and dragged him back into the woods, over the top of the hill and down the other side through the thick undergrowth. They emerged from the trees and came down to a muddy track where the covered cart sat containing the prisoners.

The rest of the men were milling around behind it and Sir Roger's horse was tied up nearby.

"Right you lot, it's time to get to work, don't get me wrong there's a lot of fun to be had too and loot of course. But we need to hurry, the Welsh will pick the town clean if we don't flush them out and fast. Remember, there'll be nothing left for us if you don't move your arses."

Sir Roger bounced into the saddle. He brought his horse alongside the one pulling the cart and gave it a whack from the flat side of his sword. The horse reacted by hurtling off up the track the cart bouncing madly behind. Travis clung on for dear life. Behind him he could hear an uproar of shouts, cursers and gobbling noises as the occupants of the cart were tossed about. Sir Roger galloped after the cart, his cloak billowing out behind him like the wings of a giant bird. The men cheered and ran after him brandishing a formidable array of deadly weapons.

They emerged from around the hill and thundered up the track towards the town. The smoke from burning thatch drifted toward them as they approached. Sir Roger managed to get alongside the cart and grabbed hold of the reins from a terrified Travis. He gradually brought it to a stop. There were several bodies scattered on the roadside directly in front of them.

Sir Roger looked towards the town. There was a continuous high pitched screaming, although who was making it he couldn't see. In between the flames, men with swords could be seen smashing down doors and disappearing inside. Men, woman, and children were tossed out into the street to be chased down and dispatched without mercy. There were some defenders in amongst the chaos, but other men on horseback were cutting them down ruthlessly.

"It does appear our Welsh friends are keeping busy,"

said Sir Roger rubbing his hands together in anticipation of what was to come. He drew his sword, flexed his arm and brought the weapon, with practiced ease, swooping around his head in a broad arc

Travis trembling like a leaf in the wind said, "I don't understand master. Are we with the Welsh or with the king?"

"Does it really matter Travis, we're mostly for ourselves. Although that could change depending on who we run into. Let's say our loyalties are fluid at the moment. There's no time to lose. Do you still have the wineskin I asked you to look after?"

Travis nodded and hands shaking rummaged under the rough wooden seat of the cart and brought out a leather wineskin. He climbed down from the cart and tried to hand it to Sir Roger. With his free hand Sir Roger cuffed him over the head. "It's not for me fool. We need it for the Berserker."

By now the rest of the men had caught up and came to a shuddering halt beside the cart panting heavily from the run. They looked eagerly at the town, their blood up and ready for the fight.

"My lord, do we advance?" one called out to Sir Roger.

He held his hand up. "Now easy lads. We need to even the odds a bit, in fact a lot." He grinned evilly and pointed at two of them. "You and you, get back there and get the Berserker and the Gobbler out of the cart. Careful, they bite."

A nervous laugh rippled through the men. In the end it took four of them to drag the helmeted Gobbler out. His hands were fastened behind his back with rope and a longer loop put around his neck. The noise from inside the helmet was unnerving. The Berserker by contrast came out meekly and stood there looking at them like a lost child.

"Come on, we're going into town. Point the Gobbler in the right direction, let the rope out a bit, and he can go ahead. Give the Berserker a sword but for God's sake keep the wineskin away from him for now."

They gathered behind the Gobbler, pushed him forward and slowly let the rope out. He surged forward the noise level coming from within the helmet increasing. They had to control him with the rope or else he would have been away from them immediately. The Berserker, an old sword pressed into hand, plodded alongside them placidly.

Travis stood paralysed next to the cart. As Sir Roger passed he said, "Stay here Travis and look after the cart. Don't let any of the others out and make sure you're here when I send for you, or by God you'll regret it."

Travis didn't say a word.

∽

The Gobbler was the first to disappear into the town. As they reached the beginning of the street, it had become increasing difficult to control him with the rope.

"Time to let him off the leash I think. Go do your worst," said Sir Roger. He cut the bonds tying the Gobbler's hands behind his back and the rope from around his neck. The man shot off like a hare and disappeared into the smoke. The only certainty that he was still somewhere up ahead were the increasingly bone chilling screams that rose above the roar of the flames.

"Who's got the wineskin?" asked Sir Roger. It was quickly passed forward to him. He took a long slow drink from it, wiping his mouth with the back of his hand when he was done. He looked around and grabbed hold of the

Berserker by the front of his dirty tunic and brought him close. The man looked back with dull eyes.

"Hello my friend, like a drink would you, eh?". Sir Roger pressed the wineskin to the Berserkers mouth and forced him to drink. There was a tiny flicker of life in the man's eyes. A hand came up and grabbed hold of the wineskin. He began to drink greedily.

"There that's better," said Sir Roger slowly backing away from him. "Back up if you know what's good for you," he hissed at the men behind. They hastily moved away. The Berserker began to stumble forward towards the town, sword in one hand, and wineskin in the other. They slowly followed. "Keep your distance," Sir Roger warned them.

From a side street, two men burst out with swords and shouted something at the Berserker in Welsh. In a blur he turned on them and let out a howl like a wolf. He was on them before they could even react. He sliced through the sword arm of the leading one and brought the sword back up and decapitated his companion in one fluid motion.

There was a collective gasp from Sir Roger's little band. The Berserker turned towards the noise which caused the men to freeze, even Sir Roger seemed a little apprehensive. Then a high-pitched scream came from further up the street and the Berserker pivoted and plodded off towards the noise.

Sir Roger chuckled. "Well that was money well spent, the jailor was telling the truth. He's as mad a one as I've seen in a long time. Let's see how long before those two flush out the Welsh. As for the English, God help them."

They started the advance, picking their way carefully between the wreckage and the slaughtered. Soon men began darting off down the side streets and through the open doorways. Sir Roger shouting, "Take anything of value and kill anyone who's still alive. Don't forget to search the dead. There'll be valuables, there always are. Spare no one, we don't need witnesses and for God's sake be quick about it."

∼

An hour later, and they started to bring the loot back to the cart. It was an impressive haul. The Welsh hadn't spent long enough in the town for a thorough search. Sir Roger's men were a lot more rigorous. He watched them emerge from the wreckage clutching their plunder. He'd be surprised if there was a single penny left in the place, every corpse having been picked clean. Sir Roger made it quite clear that the church was his and his alone to plunder. The Welsh had left it untouched, whether from fear of God or because they had orders to do so he neither knew nor cared. The main door, a heavy oak affair bound with iron, had been barricaded from the inside. Try as he might, he couldn't force his way in and he studied the structure for another entry point. Eventually he used a ramshackle shed built up against one end of the building to gain access to the thatched roof. He gingerly manoeuvred along the ridgeline until he came up against the tower. It was only ten feet above the rest of the roof. The stonework was rough, and he easily managed to scramble up and onto the top of the square roof. There was a trapdoor set in the centre. Before he opened it he paused to survey the carnage in the town below. He smiled grimly to himself, it was just like old times.

∼

With the trapdoor lifted clear, the top of a wooden ladder

was just visible. The interior of the tower was dark, but it didn't deter Sir Roger. He nimbly descended the ladder and found himself before a wooden door at the bottom of the tower, which he presumed led into the main body of the church. He drew his sword and slowly opened the door. The interior appeared empty but Sir Roger wasn't fooled, someone had barred the door from the inside. A lifetime of plundering had taught him where to seek the most valuable loot. In any town the church would usually provide the best haul. He advanced down the empty interior towards the altar. There was a tiny scrape and what sounded like an intake of breath.

"Don't be afraid," said Sir Roger softly. "My name is Sir Roger Mudstone, the Welsh have left. My men are finishing off the stragglers even now."

"You're English! Thank God!" said a weak voice from behind the altar table. An old man shakily stood up and rested his hands on the altar.

"Are you the priest of this place?" asked Sir Roger still slowly advancing.

"Indeed my son, I am."

"Are you injured Father, have the Welsh plundered the church?" asked Sir Roger anxiously. He came to a halt in front of the altar directly across from the priest.

The old man shook his head. "Never fear my son I'm unharmed. The Welsh did not disturb the sanctity of the church."

"Well, that is good news and jolly decent of them I must say. The valuables are safe are they?" asked Sir Roger pleasantly.

The priest pulled the altar cloth off the table and there sat underneath was a wooden trunk. "It's all here, safe my son."

"Excellent work father," said Sir Roger before he plunged his sword across the table into the priest's chest.

~

Sir John Cornwall, sheriff of Shropshire looked at Sir Roger's grubby and blood splattered band with some distaste. Fortunately, they'd managed to get the Gobbler and the Berserker back under cover in the cart before Cornwall had arrived. The Gobbler had proved somewhat uncooperative. They'd had to resort to bashing the side of his helmet in with a heavy wooden fence post. Sir John had arrived with the outriders of the English force two minutes after they'd thrown the unconscious killer headfirst into the back of the wagon. Under the circumstances, Sir Roger thought it better to keep the worst elements of his little band concealed. Sir John addressed Sir Roger with barely concealed contempt.

"So you're Mudstone. I've heard of you and your pardon. You were supposed to meet us at Shrewsbury two days ago."

Sir Roger shrugged. "We were heading there my lord. We ran into Glyndwr's men as they were leaving Welshpool."

"So you're telling me you headed directly through hostile territory? Why the hell didn't you come another way?" asked Sir John suspiciously.

Sir Roger held his hands up in innocence. "Forgive me my lord, but I understood speed was of the essence. We were too late to help in the defence of the town although we did manage to flush out some stragglers from Glyndwr's raid. The Welsh have massacred everyone and ransacked the place. They've even burned the church my lord."

Sir John shook his head in disgust only half believing Sir

Roger's version of events. "Tell me, do you think Glyndwr some sort of Welsh peasant Mudstone?"

Sir Roger shrugged again, this time with indifference. "I've not given it much thought to be honest my lord, other than to picture him on the end of my sword. If I run across him in person, I'll naturally try to either capture him or dispatch him. Do I really need to know anything more?"

Sir John said, "He's no fool, don't underestimate him. Do you know he studied law in London, at the Inns of Court? Seven years an apprentice. He served King Richard three years. From what I've heard, he's probably spent more time in England than you. Oh yes, your reputation in France precedes you."

"It's nice to know my work has been appreciated," said Sir Roger not hiding his sarcasm.

Sir John ran the back of his hand across his mouth and spat heavily onto the ground. "I've yet to hear anyone with a good word to say about you."

"I do what's required to get the job done my lord. I've seldom had complaints from those who employ me."

"I'd wager that's because most of them are probably dead. Under any other circumstances I'd see you dangling at the end of a rope Mudstone. But these aren't normal times. Let's say for what I've in mind for the Welsh you might be useful. If Glyndwr won't be brought to battle, then we'll just have to punish his people."

"Now that my lord is something I'm sure I can assist you with..."

∽

The English force under Sir John's command turned north westward. Sir Roger's band followed in the rear. Sir Roger tied his horse to the back of the now heavily laden wagon and climbed up besides Travis. After a few minutes traveling in silence Travis summoned up the courage to ask fearfully, "Did Sir John believe what you told him my lord?"

Sir Roger turned to his servant and laughed without a trace of humour. "Afraid for your neck Travis? You little weasel. Well, don't worry, you're safe for now. It doesn't matter what he believes. It serves Sir John's purpose to think the worst of the Welsh. He's looking to inflict some heavy retribution, and he knows I'm willing to do his dirty work."

Without knowing where the thought had come from Travis blurted out, "Don't we have enough master, perhaps we should flee now?"

Sir Roger swiftly grabbed Travis by the throat and whispered softly in the ear of the choking man, "You're thinking again Travis. What have I told you about thinking, fool? Have you any idea of the opportunities before us? We'll fill this cart with plunder ten times over before we're done."

The following day, the main army with the king and Prince Hal joined Sir John's forces. Sir Roger, on the orders of Sir John, was careful to keep himself and his men out of the way, hidden in amongst the baggage train at the rear of the English column. They marched onwards towards the Welsh coast and the heartland of Glyndwr's support.

The king's forces looted and burned along the way in an orgy of destruction. The king had succumbed to one of his periodic incandescent rages. For a time his anger overcame his good sense, and he extracted a terrible price on the Welsh.

## 12

## THE FRIARS

"This is it," said Osbert.

The little chapel of the friars stood down a side street. It was a humble-looking building, built of rough stone, but it was freshly whitewashed and looked well maintained. Will knocked on the sturdy door. He waited a minute or two. When there was no response he knocked again a little harder. Eventually the door opened a crack, and a voice said, "Give me a moment, I'm not decent yet." There was the rustling sound as someone got dressed. The door suddenly opened a little wider. A female figure slipped through, head down, face unseen, she dodged around them and was swiftly away down the street.

Will and Bernard smiled at each other. Bernard stuck his foot in the door and opened it a little wider. He put his head around the frame and said loudly, "Good morning brother, sorry to disturb you so early, we can see you're busy. We're officials of Bishop Gifford of Draychester."

The door opened fully and a small chubby friar peered out at them sleepily and a little embarrassed. He smiled and said, "Come in, the morning is chilly. Warm yourselves. I'm

Brother Howell. I've heard you mentioned about town. You've fallen foul of our good mayor I believe?" He gestured for them to enter.

"Unlike you brother, he's not the most welcoming of sorts," said Will.

The frier chuckled. "I try not to speak ill of anyone, but Watts is a hard man. As his stature has grown, I do believe the power has gone to his head."

"Human nature," said Bernard.

The friar turned to the big man and nodded. "Indeed, I believe it to be so my friend. How are you released?"

"On the orders of the Constable of Pembroke," said Will.

"Ah, I thought I heard some commotion earlier. I put my head out the door and saw the constable's men. That's generally the way of it with Watts. He overreaches himself and his master slaps him back down. You'll be here to ask about poor Phelpes I suspect?"

"He was an old friend, and of course he was agent to our bishop. We thought perhaps you could cast some light on what has gone on? Friars hear a lot of things I'm sure," said Bernard.

The friar sighed and said sorrowfully, "I knew him well. He was a generous patron of our little chapel here. You'll find him back there."

"I don't understand you?" said Will puzzled.

"They brought his body here from the quay yesterday," explained Brother Howell. He pointed to the far end of the chapel. There on a low table lay a figure wrapped in a white shroud. Around it burned some candles. They moved down the chapel and stood in front of the body. Osbert crossed himself and shuddered.

"You saw the body brother?" asked Will.

"Of course, I washed the corpse and wrapped it in the

shroud along with one of the other brothers. The injury was most severe. It was a killer blow I would have thought. I don't think he suffered much it would have been quick."

Bernard moved closer to the corpse. "When I saw the body yesterday brother, it looked like a blow from a mace. I've seen injuries like that in the wars with the Scots. You heard he was found in a wine barrel?" said Bernard.

"Of course, it's been the talk of the town. Some think it's a warning. Of course I wouldn't want to speculate," he added quickly.

"You're here on your own brother?" asked Will.

"There's three of us normally. Brother Stephen and Brother Cornelius are away in Haverfordwest."

"Tell me," said Bernard, "Phelpes's sons, what do you make of them?"

Brother Howell looked at him shrewdly. "Ah, I see where this is leading. Well I've known them since they were children. The their house is only a few streets away for us here. Do I think them capable of killing their father?"

"That's not what I asked, but do you?"

"The younger one, David, he's a pleasant enough lad. The older one, Richard, well he's had his troubles, harder to like. He's quick tempered and likes his ale far too much I fear. He also owes money all over town."

'To anyone in particular?"

Brother Howell shrugged. "I couldn't say, but he likes to wager and he seldom wins."

"A gambler then. A sore loser as well?"

"I suppose he could be called that."

"You didn't answer my question directly brother. Do you think he killed his father?"

"I believe most men are capable of murder if pushed far enough."

Bernard nodded his agreement. "True enough brother, true enough."

Brother Howell gestured back towards the other end of the chapel. "Come, let me get you something to eat and drink."

∼

An hour later and the day had well and truly begun. They were back before Phelpes's house in the lower part of the town. "You'd better open this door or I swear I'll break it down," shouted Bernard, the planks of the merchant's door creaking under the strain of his huge fists.

Will winced at the noise and said, "God's teeth Bernard, we need to be a little more discreet. Everyone is going to know our business."

Bernard just grunted at him and pounded on the door again. From inside a voice said, "All right, for God's sake. Give me a moment will you."

There was the sound of a bar being drawn back and the door opened. The younger of Phelpes's sons, David, stood pale and drawn, blinking in the early morning sunlight.

"Where's your brother?" said Bernard.

"He's not here."

"We need to talk to both of you about your father," said Will.

"He's gone I tell you. He won't be back," said David. He turned back into the house, leaving the door open.

"I've had enough of this," said Bernard barging through the door. They followed him inside.

The big man caught up with David by the shoulders and forcefully brought him to a stop. He shoved him over to a table and forced him down onto a low stool. He said, "Now you are going to sit there and tell us everything that's happened since we spoke with your father last. Start talking."

David put his head in his hands. "He didn't mean to do it. I was there, I saw, he just snapped."

"You mean your brother?" asked Will taking over the questioning. He gave a nod to Osbert who found from within his script a quill and ink and a small sheet of parchment. He started to take notes.

"We were drinking together again the cellar above the sea cave. Eventually father came down. It was late, and he told us to get to our beds. Richard started an argument, he always does."

"What was the argument about?"

"The same as always. He wanted our father to do business with Watts. He thinks we're on the wrong side of the feud in town. Watts is slowing killing our trade."

"Your father said as much. It's got that bad?"

"The trade was good up to two or three years ago. When Watts became mayor everything changed. Now you're either with him and his cronies or you struggle to do business. That's the plain fact of the matter. But father wouldn't listen, he was too proud and Richard has always been a hothead. Things just escalated."

"What happened?"

"Father accused Richard of stealing the bishop's wine and selling it onto Watts."

Will pressed him, "Is this what's been happening David? Is that what happened to the bishop's wine?"

Tears rolling down his face David said, "You don't understand. Richard was desperate. The fool has run up gambling debts all over town. Watts gave him no choice."

"Your father knew?"

"He suspected as much, Richard isn't discreet. After you turned up, it all came to a head that night."

"They came to blows?"

"Father pushed him off his stool. We'd been keeping a mace stood against the wall in the cellar since there's been trouble. Richard just snatched it up and swung it. I swear it wasn't planned. Father went down, there was blood everywhere."

"How the hell did he end up in one of the barrels?"

"We didn't know what to do. In the end I knew there was only one person who'd help us."

"Watts?"

"Yes, who else? I went and fetched him. He took one look at Father and got his men to take the body out through the cave and down to his building near the quay. I swear I didn't know he would do that with the barrel. He obviously wanted to discredit you."

"God's teeth what a mess this is. Where's your brother gone now David? Tell me the truth or by God I'll see you hang in his place," said Bernard.

Now ashen faced the man said, "Watts told us not to leave the house, and he'd take care of everything but I knew it was the end for us here. You can't trust a man like Watts. I urged Richard to flee. He's gone to seek sanctuary at the cathedral at Saint Davids, he left yesterday morning."

"Why not go to the church here?"

Osbert said, "Saint Davids is the most holy site in Wales. Three pilgrimages to Saint Davids are equal to one to Jerusalem. Perhaps only at such a place does he think he can save his soul."

David gave a hollow laugh. "It's not his immortal soul he was thinking of clerk, more his neck. I doubt Watts and his men would respect the sanctity of any church in Tenby. For what good it'll do him, Saint Davids was the better choice for my brother."

Osbert stating the obvious said, "No one would dare disrespect the sanctity of such a place."

"What do you think Watts will do now?" asked Will.

David shrugged his shoulders and said, "What a greedy man always does, he'll take advantage, he won't be able to help himself. The enterprise my father built has been ruined, Watts will swallow it whole."

"Don't underestimate the power of our own bishop in all this. He'll not be disadvantaged by anyone, that I do know," said Bernard.

"And the bishop's wine, what happened to it?" asked Osbert.

David turned to him with an angry glare and said, "Your master's bloody wine! I wish we'd never set eyes on it. I hope it's turned as sour as I feel."

Bernard with more tact said softly, "You might as well tell us everything David."

The man sighed and said, "Richard took the barrel out on the cart with one of our usual consignments. Watts owns a couple of hovels on the Pembroke road, about a mile from the town gate. The arrangement was to offload anything Richard wanted to sell there."

"So the wine was left there?" asked Will.

"Only for a short while. Watts is no fool, he took one look at the barrel and knew it was something special. It couldn't be passed off and mixed in with his own consignments easily. You could only get its true worth from selling it to a noble. He got one of his men to take it back into town on an inbound cart. He told Richard he'd been an idiot to steal it in the first place. "

"Why bring it back then, didn't he want it?"

"He wanted it all right, never doubt his greed, but he's cunning with it. Much easier to ship that along the coast alongside a cargo that's just arrived. To Pembroke or Porthclais, that's the harbour for Saint Davids. It's not as suspicious that way."

"Sounds like you've had experience?" said Will shrewdly.

David shrugged. "We've had the odd run in with a Breton Cogg or two over the years. Things happen, no point in looking a gift horse in the mouth."

"That aside, our wine has gone that route?" asked Will.

David nodded. "I'm sure it's been hidden away in the storage next to the quay. Watts has been waiting for the right time to move it again. Your arrival has forced his hand. One of his ships left last night, your wine will be well on its way by now. My guess is he's given instructions to send your wine onto Saint Davids. I'm sure it'll be to the bishop's taste. Ironic really, you being bishop's men."

Bernard slapped the man's face with the back of his hand knocking him from his stool. Will managed to get in between them before any more damage was done to David. Bernard shook his head in disgust. "I've a good mind to knock his teeth down his throat. He's as guilty as his brother. We need to sort this mess out before it gets any worse."

Will nodded and said, "I think we should go to Saint Davids, find our wine and catch up with David's brother."

Bernard grunted. "I agree." He stabbed his finger at David. "And you'll be coming with us, like it or not."

∼

"Brother Howell we need your help again," said Bernard.

"Ah, a friar's work is never done my son. God commands and I obey, so be it, what would you have me do?"

Will said, "We need to leave the town without Watts knowing. Can you help?"

"Well you can't go out the North Gate. I'm sure you've met the gatekeeper and his clerk? They're Watts's men. The West Gate will be easier."

Bernard smiled knowingly. "You've perhaps had occasion to leave town unobserved brother?"

Brother Howell gave a guilty grin. "Sometimes God's business requires discretion my son."

"So you know a way brother?" asked Will.

"I have several spare cloaks here, you could leave as friars."

Bernard rubbed his chin. "Bit obvious isn't it. There's normally only three of you here usually?"

"We come and go frequently. I walk down to the hospital just outside the West Gate most days. It's market day, there'll be a lot of folk coming and going via all the gates today. If you slip through one at a time over an hour or so I doubt anyone will give you a second glance. Just keep your head down."

Will said, "Well we can't just sit here. It's probably as good a plan as we have time for."

Bernard sighed then grunted his assent.

Osbert simply said, "It's a sin to falsely wear holy orders."

## 13

## ON THE PILGRIM'S WAY

A pale-faced David pointed up at the hillside and said, "We follow the track up to the Ridgeway. From there the road leads across country to Pembroke."

"The Ridgeway, is that the route the pilgrims travel?" asked Will.

"Yes, for those who head first to Pembroke. There's another route further north, but we stay on the southern path."

The road was flat at first but soon climbed steeply up through a wooded valley. From there it ran along the ridge of the low hills that lay just inland from the coast. To the left of them the sun sparked off the sea, which was a deep turquoise green. From the ridgeway the landscape was open either side of the road comprising the lush and fertile open fields of the villages of the south Pembrokeshire coast. In the morning sunlight Will thought it a fine county and the land well tended. He was glad to leave the troubles of Tenby behind its claustrophobic walls, at least for a while. The villages the road passed through were small, the cottages built with walls of earth with low thatched roofs and a hole to let out the smoke.

Their spirits, apart from the glum-faced David, were lifted by the warm sun. The weather had evidently been dry for days. The road was dusty and the mud surface baked hard by the sun.

"Hot work this, I may have to drink that bloody wine myself if we ever find it," said a grinning Bernard.

"Do you think it'll even be in a fit state to after all this time?" asked Will.

Bernard shrugged. "I'm no expert but wine like that doesn't keep well. It should have been on the noble's table weeks ago."

"He's right and I should know. You'll be lucky if it isn't like vinegar by now," said a mournful David.

"Then I expect the bishop will want us to seek some other recompense," said Will.

Bernard nodded approvingly. "Spoken like a true bishop's man. We can't come back empty-handed, wouldn't do at all. I can see you're taking to this role like a duck to water!"

Will laughed. "I'm still not sure what exactly my role is."

Bernard chuckled. "I've thought the same about myself lad for these last forty years. I've learned to make it up as I go along, it works for me.'

Osbert just shook his head in disgust, which made the other two start laughing harder.

～

Ahead of them in the distance they began to make out some figures walking. It soon became clear that they were heading in the same direction. After a few minutes steady plod they came up behind the travellers and recognised the dress of a party of pilgrims. There were some weary glances from the two figures at the immediate rear of the party of six or seven. Even on a sunlit day such as this, a traveller needed to have a care, the open road could be a dangerous place.

"A good morning to you pilgrims, how goes the day?" said a cheerful Bernard.

"Wearisome if I be honest," said the rear most man stopping and then mopping his brow with his hand. "This sun has left me fair parched. Spare a drop of ale perhaps, or some wine from one of your fancy flasks there?"

From up ahead a voice said, "Thomas behave man. Don't give him a drop sir. Start him off and he'll drink you dry."

A tall man with a bushy beard pushed through and came up to stand by the man named Thomas. He rested a withered hand on Thomas's shoulder. He wore a long, coarse cloak and carried a staff and small purse. On his head was a broad-brimmed hat with a shell-shaped badge. Will recognised the dress of the true pilgrim. The shell badge was worn by those who had travelled to the shrine at Santiago de Compostela. It was a journey undertaken only by the seriously devoted or the seriously rich. By contrast Thomas looked like any number of travellers one might pass on the road, somewhat road worn and giving off a faint waft of sour sweat.

The tall man looked them over with interested and said, "Good morning, Edward's the name. We're heading to Saint Davids."

As soon as he spoke there was the overpowering stench of bad breath. A strange aroma of meat and rotting fish.

The bishop's men took a step backwards. Bernard gestured at himself and the others. "Bernard, Will and that miserable looking one is Osbert, bishop's men". He jerked his thumb at David and said sharply, "He's David of Tenby."

The tall man's face lit up. "You're the bishop of Saint Davids men? Perhaps you'll accompany us?"

Will, half covering his nose and mouth with a hand, said, "The bishop of Draychester not Saint Davids is our master friend. We're bound for Pembroke first before Saint Davids."

With another pungent waft the tall man said, "Ah no matter. We started our journey in Wells. It's been nearly two weeks on the road now."

The two parties fell in alongside each other and they began to walk along the road again.

Will gestured at the tall man's clothes and hat and said, "This isn't your first pilgrimage I see?"

The tall man, Edward, smiled through blackened teeth and said, "It's the first to Saint Davids, but the third in this life my friend. Twice I have been to Santiago de Compostela"

Osbert said, "You seek a cure for an affliction perhaps?"

The tall man shook his head. "On the contrary, as you can see, God has rewarded my previous travels with good health but every man grows old. I seek sustenance for my soul."

Osbert looked at the man sceptically but pressed him further. "You'll have earned perhaps the same indulgence with this pilgrimage as if you'd been to Jerusalem?"

The tall man nodded and with a blast of putrid breath said, "Indeed, that's the ruling of the pope and with Saint David's blessing I pay it will be my last trip. With this pilgrimage my spirit is still willing, but the body grows weary my friends, but that's the way of the pilgrim."

"I hear the blessed Saint David himself would do

penance and stand up to his neck in a lake of cold water, reciting scripture," said Osbert.

The tall man looked at Osbert curiously and said, "Do you seek a cure at Saint Davids for some affliction also? A feebleness of the mind perhaps?"

Osbert gave the man an angry stare. Bernard barely suppressing a snigger said, "I can see how that would appeal to you Osbert. Maybe you can try it when we get to Saint Davids?"

Osbert glared at him and said, "Saint David was an extremely pious man, it's said he ate only bread, herbs and vegetables and drank nothing but water."

"In that case I doubt you're the stuff saints are made of my friend," said Will laughing, "you like your meat and wine too much".

Osbert ignoring the laughter said, "He performed other miracles. He was said to have been able to restore a blind man's sight and even bring a child back to life by splashing the boy's face with his tears."

"Yes, a worthy saint indeed," murmured the tall man apparently unwilling to discuss saintly virtues further. He was more curious about his new travelling companions. He gestured at David of Tenby. "And what of you, you go there as well?"

Before he could answer Bernard simply said, "He goes where we go at the moment. We do the bishop's bidding and now we also follow this one's brother who has gone to seek sanctuary at Saint Davids."

"And what crime does he flee from to Saint Davids?" asked the tall man curiously with a waft of his searing breath.

"Ah, well that would be murder" said William softly, his eyes watering under the onslaught.

"You do realise your brother will likely hang if we catch up with him?" said Bernard looking at David.

David said, "You know the law as well as I. No one can deny him sanctuary if he reaches Saint Davids and confesses his crime. He'll have forty days protection if he stays within the confines of the holy ground. Then he'll have to agree to leave the realm if he wants to live. The coast is close at hand, he can take a ship, Ireland is not so far. It's not uncommon, many have followed that path before him."

With some menace Bernard said, "That's if your brother makes it to Saint Davids."

"You think we've a chance to catch him up?" asked Will.

Bernard shrugged. "Anything is possible."

Will pointed ahead. "He's a day ahead of us at least, and I dare say he's not drawing attention to himself. He'll know that retribution is following him."

"Then he'd better make haste and so should we," Bernard said sourly.

"Retribution is for God and God alone," said Osbert.

Will shook his head sadly. "I think you'll find our bishop may disagree with you there Osbert."

~

As late afternoon grew into early evening, they approached the walls of Pembroke. The town, and the mighty fortress that dominated it, stood on a rocky limestone ridge at the head of a tidal river. They stopped just in front of the east gate.

Bernard said, "Well we know the constable's still in Tenby but I dare say we'll find a welcome at the castle and we need to seek the wine. There's a chance they could have unloaded it here."

"Do you think my brother could be resting here the night?" asked David anxiously.

Bernard said, "If he's any bloody sense he'll keep walking through the night."

"We're to seek shelter at Monkton Priory. I understand it's just across the river from the castle," said Edward, the tall pilgrim. "I dare say we will see you on the road to Saint Davids in the morning?"

Bernard nodded. "If we don't find what we're looking for here, which would be our lord bishop's wine," he pointed a finger at the downcast David, "and that one's murdering brother. I'm not hopeful on either account."

They entered through the town walls via the east gate, the castle lying at the other end of the ridge along the main street of the town. The pilgrims stuck off at a fast pace down the main street ahead of them. No doubt eager to find a bed and a meal before darkness.

When they were out of earshot Bernard said, "God's teeth. They should use that man's breath against the Welsh in the north. I've smelled sweeter dung. I'll not travel another mile with him."

Will grinned. "You'll have no argument from me there. Let's find the quay, someone will know if Watts's ship landed anything today. If we're lucky, it may still be here."

The quay lay on the north side of the town below the walls of the great castle. There was a cog tied up at the quay but David assured them it wasn't one of Watts. On the quayside beside the ship stood a few men chatting. As the bishop's men approached, they turned with curiosity to see what the newcomers wanted.

Bernard stomped up to them and said, "Did you unload any cargo from one of John Watts's cogs today?"

The nearest said, "Who's asking? You Watts's men are you?"

"Just answer the question man, we don't have time for this," said Bernard angrily.

Will stepped in front of him before the other man's frustration got the better of him. It had been a long day and they were all getting tired.

"We're the bishop of Draychester's men. The ship was carrying some wine that belongs to our lord bishop. We need to know if it was off loaded or not?"

The man shrugged his shoulders with indifference. "I wouldn't know anything about that. We took a couple of barrels off this morning onto the quayside, nothing special from what I could see, they should be up at the castle by now."

"And Watts's cog?" asked Will.

"She left this afternoon at high tide, been gone hours now, off down river. She'll be at Saint Davids tomorrow."

Bernard sighed. "David, you know what this bloody barrel looks like. I can't tell one from the other without opening and drinking the contents. We'll just have to go and take a look up at the castle."

∼

They left the quayside behind. As they were about to turn onto the street that led back into town, Osbert glanced to his right.

He gasped and said, "Look it's him". He pointed a boney finger at the bridge that took the road away from the town and across the river. They turned to look at a figure crossing the bridge. It was the wanted man, David's brother Richard Phelpes.

"God's teeth," hissed Bernard. "Come on, we'd better grab the bastard before he goes any further."

Before they could take another step, David bellowed, "Richard. Run brother, Run!"

Bernard turned and punched him in the side of the head. He dropped, like a sack of rocks, onto the cobbles unconscious.

Bernard said, "You asked for that." He then set off running down to the bridge, swiftly followed by the others. The figure on the bridge looked back towards them. There was a moment of horrified recognition and then he too set off running.

Half way across the bridge sat a two storey structure, a mill powered by the tide that even now was flowing swiftly under the building. The water passed under an arch directly below the mill. As Richard reached the open door, he darted into the dark interior and slammed the door behind him.

Bernard reached the door and pushed his considerable weight against it. The fugitive had somehow barred it, it groaned but didn't open. Bernard gave it an almighty kick, but it still didn't open. He started hammering on the door but there was no response.

Will said, "We might not be able to get in but he can't get away either. I don't see any other way out."

Bernard hammered on the door again. "Well I'm not willing to wait here all night for that turd to decide to come out. We need to get in there and drag him out. There must be another way?"

They looked over the wall of the bridge at the side of the mill. There was a window with shutters wide open, but there was no obvious way to get to it. The wall of the mill went down sheer into the water and the window was at least ten feet away from where they stood.

Osbert said, "It might be possible to climb out along the wall. I can see some handholds."

"You're offering to go out there are you?" said Bernard sarcastically.

"I can't swim," said Osbert.

They both turned to look at Will.

"Don't look at me," he said.

"I'm too big to get through the window," pleaded Bernard.

Will shook his head. "Of course you are. All right, just don't make me regret this…"

They gave him a leg-up onto the wall of the bridge. He clung to the gaps between the rough stone blocks and slowly started to inch out towards the window. He couldn't help but look down at the swiftly flowing water.

"Don't look down," said Osbert.

He licked his dry lips. "Just keep your trap shut Osbert. I need to concentrate."

Slowly he moved his feet along the gaps in the stonework and he eased his way along. Finally he was able to grab the edge of the shutter. With his weight on the wooden frame he was able to swing his feet onto the windowsill and he stood crouched in the window opening. He peered in. It was dark inside and the clatter of the hidden water wheel in the bowls of the building was deafening. Immediately in front of him was the swiftly revolving drive shaft. He couldn't see any sign of Richard Phelpes.

"Get in there and come open the door for us," shouted Bernard.

Will gestured rudely behind his back then slowly sat down on the windowsill and eased his way down onto the wooden floor of the mill. Once safely inside he slipped his way around the wooden drive shaft and found the main door. It had been secured with a heavy wooden bar, which he heaved out of the way with some effort.

"That wasn't so bad was it?" shouted Bernard above the din of the machinery.

"It wasn't you with his arse hanging out over the river," Will shouted back.

Osbert put his head through the door but quickly backed out again and mouthed, "I'll wait out here."

Bernard swiftly looked around the room. There we no obvious places to hide. Leant against the walls were sacks of grain. A rope hung down with an iron hook attached to the end. The rope led up through a trapdoor in the ceiling to the room above. Will realised it was a hoist for the grain. Bernard pointed to a ladder in the corner that led upwards to the next level. Will nodded and Bernard led the way up the ladder.

As Bernard reached the top of the ladder he saw a pair of booted feet hurriedly retreat across the room. Before he had time to look up, a bag of flour hanging from an iron hook came hurtling across the room and caught him a glancing blow on the shoulder. It spun him around and he lost his footing on the ladder. He slipped taking Will with him back down the ladder to the floor below.

Bernard heaved himself off the floor rubbing his shoulder.

"You all right?" mouthed Will still sprawled on the floor.

"The bastard's up there. Swung a sack at me," shouted Bernard above the din. "He's going to regret that. I need something to fend the sacks off."

Will looked around. There really wasn't much of anything.

He said, "How about the wooden bar from the door?"

Bernard strode across the room, dodging around the

main drive shaft. With one huge hand he picked up the heavy oak door bar. He made his way back to the ladder and started to climb cautiously.

With his eyes just above floor level he scanned the room. He saw a blur of movement and a bag of flour hurtled over his head with an inch to spare. He ducked as it swung back, hauled himself over the edge and rolled towards the wall. The sack was soon on its way back again. Only this time Bernard, now on his feet, fended it away with the wooden bar. Will got to the top of the ladder and threw himself over the edge and rolled over to the opposite wall.

This was the stone floor, where the grain was turned into flour, crushed between massive millstones that were driven by the main shaft. Around Will's head the grain was hissing down chutes from above to feed the revolving millstone. A heavy sack of grain swung gently on the end of a rope that vanished through trapdoors set in the ceiling. Their attacker was nowhere to be seen.

"The bugger must have gone up another floor," shouted Bernard, grim faced. "I'm going to tear him limb from limb."

"Just be careful, he's already murdered once, he's desperate," cautioned Will.

Bernard advanced to the next ladder and carefully started to climb. Will followed close behind. The noise level dropped considerably as they reached the next floor. There were several large grain bins, maybe twenty sacks of grain and a man, grey faced, propped against the far wall, blood oozing from a head wound. Will was momentary confused, it wasn't Richard Phelpes. Then he realised it must be the miller, this machinery didn't work by itself.

Bernard, with a furtive glance around, checked on the man. "He's breathing, knocked out stone cold though. I think there's only the floor above, nowhere else Phelpes can go now."

As if to confirm this, there was a creaking from above as someone walked across the wooden floor. Will looked at the boarded ceiling and said, "Promise me you won't just clobber him senseless. I'd prefer to see him hang."

"Depends on how cooperative he is lad. Come on."

As they emerged at the top of the ladder, they were confronted with an armed and belligerent Richard Phelpes. "You couldn't leave it could you. You and your bloody bishop. It was a barrel of wine, your master could lose a hundred more and not even notice."

In his hand he held the iron hook from one of the grain hoists.

"It's not just the wine Richard, you killed your own father. You think you can escape justice?" asked Will.

"That old fool. He never would listen to what was good for him. I'll hang, that's the only outcome. I'm better heading to Saint Davids, at least I've a chance if I make it there. Let me go, what use is my death to you?"

Bernard hefted the oak bar in one of his huge hands and slowly advanced. He said, "And the miller down below? I'd say there's a good chance you've permanently addled his brains. Don't you think he deserves some justice as well?"

Phelpes swung the hook towards Bernard. "Stay back. I won't tell you again."

"Put that down and I might let you live long enough to see justice done."

Richard swung the hook viciously at Bernard's head. He jerked back just in time and the hook embedded itself in one of the wooden roof beams. Richard tried to pull the hook free, but it was stuck fast.

Bernard smiled. "I think it's my turn now, don't you?"

"Try not to kill him," said Will.

Phelpes backed up, looking around desperately for something to defend himself. Bernard lunged forward with the wooden bar and struck the other man a blow on the shoulder. Phelpes cried out in pain and stumbled backwards against the far wall. As he fell, the wall revealed itself to be two wooden doors that allowed grain bags to be hauled up from boats on the river. They opened under his weight, and with a cry he plummeted through into the evening sunshine.

Before they even reached the open doors, they heard a splash as Phelpes entered the river directly below.

"God's teeth!" cried Bernard in frustration. "Will nothing go our way? The bugger had better drown because I swear I'm going to kill him before the days done."

Will inched cautiously towards the open doorway, stood on the edge, and looked down. "Seems he can swim, look he's making for the quay."

Bernard followed his gaze and sure enough Phelpes was half drifting, half swimming away from the bridge towards the quayside. A small boat suddenly started to move out into the river ahead of him.

"Who the hell is that in the boat?" said Bernard.

Will peered into the glare of the reflected sunlight coming off the river. "I do believe it's his brother."

"I thought I'd knocked him out cold. I must be losing my touch."

"Either that or he's as thick-skulled as his brother."

The figure in the boat intercepted the swimmer and proceeded to drag the man aboard. Bernard threw the wooden bar out the doorway in disgust.

"Come on, we need to get over there now."

～

Osbert had already wandered back to the quayside when they got there.

"Didn't you make some attempt to stop him taking a boat?" asked Bernard in exasperation.

The clerk responded angrily, "I was still on the bridge waiting for you two when I saw the boat go out. He was unconscious when we left him there. It must be God's will if they've evaded us. Anyway, why did you throw his brother into the river?"

Bernard snapped back. "I didn't throw him into the river fool, he fell."

Osbert gave him a withering look and pointed downriver. "Well I hope you can explain this all to our lord bishop when he asks you how the killer thief escaped justice."

The boat was now a dwindling speck in the distance, running with the tide. "Maybe we can take another boat and go after them?" said Bernard dubiously.

Will shook his head. "It'll be dusk soon, how will we find them? I'm as eager to see justice served as you my friend but no use us drowning in the dark."

"And I can't swim," said Osbert.

"Shut up!" the other two said in unison.

～

That night in their dingy chamber in the castle with Osbert snoring away Bernard said softly, "Much as I hate to agree with the whining brat he has a point. This isn't my finest hour Will, the bishop will think I'm getting too old for this and perhaps he would be right."

Will shook his head. "We've had some bad luck that's all.

We've got this far. The wine is still to be found. As for this murderous thief and his brother, well they'll make for Saint Davids that's for certain."

Bernard sighed. "I thought the wine could be here. You believe the constable's man when he says what was offloaded was their normal delivery?"

Will nodded. "I don't get the sense he was lying. I looked at the barrels as did you. I sampled it just as you did. Now I don't get the privilege of drinking the stuff the nobles quaff, but what I tasted was nothing special. It's not here Bernard, it's still on Watts's boat, headed for the bishop's palace at Saint Davids."

"I hope you're right lad, I really do."

# 14

# ANGLESEY

When they'd crossed to Anglesey, the burning and pillaging had continued unabated. However, the constant hit-and-run attacks of the Welsh had started to take their toll. The campaign had become further hampered by bad weather. The king was tired and frustrated, and his anger had subsided. He had withdrawn his forces to the relative safety of the castle at Beaumaris. The friary at Llanfaes lay close by. Sir John hadn't explicitly denied Sir Roger permission to attack it, but it was widely known that Glyndwr's current allies, the Tudors, had buried their ancestors there for centuries. Sir John prudently led his own forces past it unmolested. His reasoning had been not to stir up more trouble this close to safety. Sir Roger's mercenaries as usual were in the rear, theoretically guarding the baggage train.

Their master had ordered the place ransacked as soon as the lead troops with Sir John and the king had disappeared from sight.

With the occupants of the cart once again unchained it wasn't long before the good friars were fleeing in terror from their soon to be destroyed friary. At lease the ones who made it out of the small complex alive. It was twenty minutes before Sir Roger felt safe to enter the place himself. He found it was always best to let the Gobbler and company work out their frustrations first. He made his way in via a narrow gated archway. A grey cloaked figure was skewered though the chest with an iron bar which pinned him to the great oak door. His mouth hung open, his eyes wide in a death stare that vaguely disturbed even Sir Roger.

"No place to hang around brother," he murmured as he brushed past.

This was a place of the grey friars and it showed as he made his way through the ransacked buildings. There had been little of value before, now there was even less. Owning no property of their own the brothers lived by moving from friary to friary begging for the alms and gifts of benefactors as they went. If he was being honest with himself, Sir Roger's heart wasn't in it anymore. He'd had great plans for his little band of mercenaries, but the truth was the high point had been that initial raid at Welshpool. It wasn't like the wars in France where the pickings had been easy to come by. The Welsh didn't give anything up without a fight. Kicking through the burning embers of the friary he thought perhaps it was time for a change of tack.

He found his company in the remains of the refrectory. For their own safety they'd tied the Gobbler, his helmet dripping blood, to one of the stone pillars holding up the roof. He was gobbling softly to himself. Tied to another pillar directly opposite him was the Berserker who appeared comatose with his head slumped down.

One of the Jones brothers was sat in the corner with his arse hanging out, answering a call of nature. Sir Roger remembered the stench only too well. The other brother was laid flat on his back on one of the trestle tables, his companions pouring ale into his mouth from a large jug and cheering as he coughed half of it back up.

Sir Roger sat down wearily at the end of the table. After a minute he said, "The good brother hanging around at the front door, any reason you didn't just kill him?"

One of the men shrugged. "He refused Maggie's advances my lord, tried to run away. She don't take kindly to being turned down, do you old girl?"

There was a shriek of laughter from under the table. Sir Roger bent down slowly to find the only female, at least in theory, member of his company laying in the dirty rushes apparently drunk.

He sighed heavily. Had it really come down to this.

"So tell me, did you find anything of value at all?"

"Not as such my lord. These grey friars never have much coin. They do brew good ale though my lord."

"It looks like you have drunk most of it already."

One of the brothers plonked a jug in front of Sir Roger. He considered it for a minute. The contents were a cloudy golden colour. He sniffed it dubiously. "Tell me you haven't relieved yourself in this have you?"

"Direct from the good brother's barrel my lord."

Sir Roger took a long draw straight from the jug. "It's actually not bad, not bad at all."

∼

When Sir John and half a dozen of his knights walked into the refrectory, they found the place was in an uproar. Sir Roger dressed in one of the friar's cloaks, was parading up and down the trestle tables swinging a jug of ale in each hand. He was singing a particular filthy ditty that had been popular in some of the rougher establishments in his Draychester youth.

"Ah Sir John, so good of you to join us," he roared, spilling half a jug of ale across the table.

Sir John, outraged, spluttered, "You're a bloody disgrace Mudstone. Who told you that you could attack the friary?"

"What do you care? They're Welsh aren't they, friars or not, they're the enemy."

"You're a bloody fool Mudstone. If it was up to me I'd have you dragged out and strung up out there in the rain right now. What you and this scum you call soldiers have done is beyond belief. It's only been tolerated because you were useful, now you're just a liability."

"Scum they may be, I never claimed they were soldiers. So that's how it is now is it. One minute we're all friends, when you need me, but now I'm in the naughty corner."

"Shut up fool, and who the hell are they?" he said, pointing to the two figures tied to the pillars. The Gobbler let out his characteristic high-pitched hunting call in greeting. Even Sir John's battle hardened knights shrank back.

Sir John gazed at the figure with fascinated horror. "God's teeth, who is that?" He gestured to one of his knights. "Get that helmet off him."

The knight hesitated. Sir Roger waved a jug at Sir John. "Tsk, Tsk now I really, really wouldn't advise that."

One of the other knights said, "Shut up, you drunken fool."

"Name calling now is it? Well, that's low I must say," burped Sir Roger. "Anyway, if you insist on taking my friend's helmet off, don't say I didn't warn you. What do you say lads?"

There was a babble of replies.

"Who you calling a lad."

"Bad idea my lord, a very bad idea."

"Gobbler is uncontrollable without the helmet."

"Lost a finger I did, like a rabid beast he is."

Sir John nodded. "So he's the one is he? I've seen the aftermath of his rampages. What in God's name were you thinking of, bringing that creature along with us?"

Before Sir Roger's drunken mind could process a reply, Sir John draw his sword strode over to the Gobbler and shoved the blade through the visor right up to the hilt. It slid in with a sickening sound. There was a blood-curdling scream and a cascade of blood poured out the bottom of the helmet. The figure slumped down, held up only by the ropes around his waist.

Sir Roger wagged a disapproving finger and said, "Well, I must say that was uncalled for. I admit the Gobbler was a little unconventional in his behaviour, but he was a bloody good man. I dare say he's killed more Welsh than the rest of your knights here put together."

Sir John was red in the face now. He pulled the blade out of the Gobbler's ruined head and swung the bloody tip around so that it was an inch in front of Sir Roger's throat. "Don't say another word. I've had just about enough of you Mudstone. Your time here is over. Understand me when I say you'll be lucky if I don't see you hanged in the morning. The king will decide and let me tell you he's in a foul mood. Now have this rabble together in five minutes and make your way to Beaumaris or I swear I'll run you through myself."

∽

"God's teeth I detest this bloody country Travis. It never stops pissing it down," said Sir Roger, morosely waving his half-empty cup of wine at the leaden skies outside the chamber window. He'd been drinking for hours. Travis was sat as far away from him as was possible in the small room. He knew better than to make any reply when his master was in this sort of mood.

Sir Roger belched nosily and said, "At least when I was in France we actually got a summer. Place was full of the French of course but at least you could give them a good thrashing. They knew when they were beat, not like these Welsh. Eh Travis?"

He banged his cup down on the table making Travis jump. Sir Roger turned around and barked, "I hope you're bloody well listening to me Travis!"

"Always master," croaked Travis shrinking back towards the wall.

Sir Roger turned his attention back to the heavy rain falling outside the window. "The king's a fool if he thinks he can bring them to battle Travis. All they need to do is skulk about in the hills and come down once a week to harry us. They don't need to fight us out in the open, they just need to wear us down."

He sighed heavily. "That business at the friary was a mistake, it's just stirred them up even more. I tried to tell Sir John but nobody listened. My experience counts for nothing with these amateurs Travis."

Travis didn't like to think about the friary, his dreams had been filled with nothing else for days. His recollection of the events at the holy place differed markedly from Sir Roger's.

The door opened and one of Sir John's men-at-arms barged in.

"What the hell do you want, can't you see I'm drowning my sorrows?" barked Sir Roger

The man shrugged. "Sir John says to get your arse down to the great hall. You've new orders. I'd advise you make haste, he's not in the best of moods after that stunt you pulled at the friary."

~

"Do you want to hear the bad news first or the good news?" said Sir John.

"Do I have a choice?" asked Sir Roger sarcastically.

"The bad news is every Welshman in twenty miles is up in arms over the friary incident. No one is setting foot outside of the castle unless they're a fool or accompanied by a dozen men at arms."

"How is that any different from what it was last week?" asked Sir Roger.

"The difference Mudstone, and I hasten to add this is the good news, is that they all want to kill you specifically. The English they hate in general but with you I hear it's now something personal. You've desecrated a place close to their hearts it seems. You'll not be safe any place you find a Welshman."

Sir Roger shrugged. "Not the first time I've upset the locals and it won't be the last I'll wager."

"You arrogant bastard. It'll damn well be the last under my command. The king wants you gone. I tried hard to get you hanged."

Sir Roger's eyes narrowed, and he pressed his face close to Sir John, who took a hasty step back. "Now what sort of thanks is that for all I've done. I had a pardon in exchange for my special services. I held up my end of the bargain and more."

"I'm told there was some agreement made. If there is one

thing about Henry, it's that he always keeps his word. You've escaped with your life by the skin of your teeth."

Sir Roger belched, then scratched his arse and said, "And what do you propose we do now, as it seems we can't even leave the castle?"

"I'm not proposing anything. I'm telling you precisely what you're going to do. You and the scum you found in the jail at Chester are to take passage on one of the supply ships going back down the coast. The rest of your men you will leave here."

"That sounds positively the worst idea I've heard all day."

"The ship will be calling at Criccieth first. You're to leave your killers at the castle there, they're to reinforce the garrison. No one wants them roaming around here, they're worse than the bloody natives."

Sir Roger shrugged. "If that's your orders. I must say it's a waste. They were a talented bunch of lads, and maybe lasses although it's hard to tell..."

Sir John held his hand up to stop Sir Roger's drunken rambling. "As for yourself and your lackey here, you'll take the ship all the way back to Pembroke and await whatever other tasks the king commands of you. If I ever see you again, it'll be too soon."

"The feeling is mutual," hissed Sir Roger and without another word turned and left. A startled Travis scuttled after him with one fearful, backwards look at Sir John's rage filled face.

## 15

# DRAYCHESTER CATHEDRAL

Ralph of Shrewsbury sat on a stone seat set into the great west wall of Draychester cathedral. It was late in the day and at this end of the building only a few candles cast a dim golden light and Ralph was all but invisible. He had barely moved in his seat for a good ten minutes. His old bones were so used to the position they troubled him very little.

He broke wind silently. The old tale that you couldn't smell your own definitely didn't apply. He quietly chuckled to himself in the darkness. Farting was one of the few bodily pleasures he still enjoyed. This was one of his favourite places in the cathedral complex. It lent itself so well to the nasty little transactions he liked to indulge in.

He expected a visitor in a few minutes, but there was still a little time to just sit and contemplate. Ralph had lived a long time, and he supposed that most of the contemporaries of his youth in Shrewsbury were dead. Even here, where he'd spent so long, there were few left alive who knew him well and even fewer that knew his true nature. He'd meddled in other's affairs all his life, often for gain and more often these days just for the fun of it.

There was a flicker of movement in the dark. Ralph could make out a shadowy figure moving cautiously between the huge pillars of the cathedral. It slowly made its way towards him. He sat absolutely still and watched with interest. With a quick darting motion, the figure left the nearest pillar and slid itself onto the seat next to him. Neither of them said a word. Ralph, amused, sat and waited.

Eventually the figure whispered, "Master Ralph?"

Ralph turned slowly in his seat. "Were you expecting someone else?"

In the dim light he could just make out a look of confusion on the other's face. "Er, no. So it is you. I wasn't sure. What's that smell?"

"Smell? Ah, that would be old age my young friend, old age."

"It wasn't easy getting in here at this time of night. I can hardly believe my father used to do this."

Ralph said, "Your father was a talented man in many respects."

"Well, my father has been bedridden these last five years. I'm surprised you remembered him. He thought you were long dead."

Ralph nodded slowly as if considering the question. "As you see, I'm still alive."

"What is it you want of us?"

"Does your father still do business in Bristol with the Breton?"

The other man answered cautiously. "When the opportunity arises, we occasionally trade some goods. Not openly you understand."

"Oh I understand your business well enough boy. I need

you to pass on a message to the Breton. A request in fact. It'll be profitable for all."

At the mention of profit, the other licked his lips.

"My father said you always paid well, that's the only reason I'm here. He also said not to trust you. His exact words were that you were a devious old bastard."

Ralph chuckled softly, not in the least offended. "Your father is a very wise man." A leathery hand shot out from under Ralph's cloak and thrust a small leather purse into the other man's hand.

"What's this?"

"Payment. Deliver a message to your Breton friend, and you'll get the same again when you return with confirmation."

The man weighed the purse in his hand. "I'm not some messenger boy, there must be more to it than that?"

"Ah, I see you are truly your father's son. Then listen well. A cog will be sailing from Anglesey in a few days' time. It's stuffed full of spoils taken in the troubles with the Welsh. I'm sure the Breton will happily oblige and take the ship by force. Amongst those on board there's a man, a knight, his name is Roger Mudstone. All I ask is that Mudstone is to be put safely ashore in France, with or without his consent. The others on board, they're to be thrown over the side. You can come to some arrangement with the Breton to buy the cargo and share the profits. I'm sure you've done it before, only this time you'll be supplying the information to them."

"How do you know these things and to what purpose?"

"I know a great many things boy. The ship will make the trip. It'll be there for the taking. As to my purpose," he chuckled this time without humour, "I'm not sure you'd understand."

The other man looked down for a moment to conceal the purse under his cloak. When he looked up the space beside him was empty. He'd heard not even a rustle of the others' departure. Ralph had vanished into the gloom of the great cathedral as though he'd never been there.

The hairs on the man's neck rose up and a shiver ran down his spine.

## 16

## THE GOOD SHIP MYNION

"If it were my choice Travis, I'd never set sail on anything that looks so pathetic. I mean look at the bloody thing," said Sir Roger. Travis standing dejectedly by his side on the quay at Beaumaris silently agreed. He hated the sea, and the cog known as the Mynion, wallowing in the water below them, was not an impressive sight. If he knew anything about seafaring, which he didn't, he'd say she was dangerously low in the water. Her master, Thomas Goulde, looked up from the business of loading the ship and shouted, "Just stowing your goods Sir Roger. All safe and sound below. There's not a better ship on the king's business north of Bristol. The Mynion is a sweetheart isn't she?"

Sir Roger shouted back, "I think you'll find there are no other ships on the king's business north of Bristol. This stinking hulk is it. We don't have a choice."

Goulde shrugged his shoulders. "Well that's as maybe, I've always found her a sound vessel. Anyway I'm sure we'll all get along just fine. We'll be leaving within the hour."

"I know am going to regret this Travis but anything has got to be better than this dreary God forsaken country. I can't remember the last time I saw the sun, it's practically been pissing it down since we got here."

"It's such a small ship master. There's hardly a space to lay down with all the cargo we've crammed aboard. The men aren't going to like it, especially those you've had locked up in the hold."

With a snap of his wrist he cuffed Travis over the head sending him reeling. "Don't be a fool Travis. They can like it or lump it, do you really think I care? As for the ones chained up, only an inbred imbecile like yourself would believe we can leave them to roam the ship. They'd slit your throat before we were a mile out of harbour. Be grateful I'm looking out for your interests Travis, sometime I wonder why I bother."

Travis often wondered about that too. He stumbled towards the water, just regaining his footing at the last moment. He stood there on the edge of the quayside scowling down at the cog.

~

Sir Roger felt nauseous again. He wasn't sure he had anything left to projectile heave over the side. The Mynion had first headed north west to round the top of Anglesey. As they then headed south following the coast the sun finally broke through the low clouds. That was the good news, the bad news was they encountered a large swell. The Mynion seemed to wallow from trough to trough rather than making any attempt to cut through the waves. The bone jarring crashes from one trough to the next were taking their toll on the passengers. The fact the deck was awash with vomit didn't seem to bother Master Goulde or his crew in the least. They happily worked around the stricken passengers, the majority who had found a spot hung over the rails. Goulde himself was irritatingly cheerful.

"By God, its good to be on our way again eh Sir Roger? It's a fine day for it too." He bellowed.

A green faced Sir Roger winced at the volume of the other man's shout and said, "I've been shipwrecked once before and I'm damned if I'm doing it again. I'm holding you personally responsible to ensure I don't drown. It'll be a bonus if my cargo survives."

Master Goulde took it all in good humour. "Now, now, Sir Roger, we're making excellent progress. You'll soon get your sea legs. We'll be at Criccieth by tomorrow nightfall if we keep the good sailing weather"

"This is good weather?" croaked Sir Roger.

~

The following morning the Mynion rounded the end of the Llyn peninsula. The mainland was on their left and Bardsey Island lay to the right. The bell tower of Saint Mary's abbey on the island was just visible.

Sir Roger was crouched, back against the ship's rail, gray faced and miserable. Travis lay at his feet, moaning softly and periodically sticking his head up to vomit over the side. Master Goulde laughed at the state they were in. "Do you want me to put you down on Bardsey? I'm sure the monks at the abbey would pray for your soul. A man like you Sir Roger, I'd dare say you've got a few sins to confess. A pilgrimage would do you good."

Sir Roger managed to haul himself to his feet and staggered his way across the deck towards Goulde. He stood swaying in front of him. On any other occasion Sir Roger would have been inclined to cave the man's head in but he could only muster the energy for a nasty scowl and said, "You bloody smug bastard, can't you take us closer to shore, away from this swell?"

Goulde nodded at the shoreline where the waves could just be seen breaking against a rocky beach. "We're near enough as it is, we're only a mile out. Believe me, this is where we need to be. Close enough to see where we are, far enough out to avoid the dangers. There's many a ship run aground on this coast, I'd never put the Mynion in harm's way, she's all I've got."

Sir Roger wiped cold sweat from his brow. "God's teeth man, I'd rather be on the battlefield than stand another few hours of this."

"At least you're above deck, pity them below," said Goulde pointing to the hold.

"Don't worry about them, they're survivors. I'm more worried about my cargo."

"I hear you liberated most of it from the Welsh?"

"It's perfectly legal, the spoils of war."

Goulde raised an eyebrow sceptically and said, "I'm sure it is Sir Roger, I'm sure it is."

"Just get us safe to dry land, I'm fast running out of stomach contents."

Goulde roared with laughter, "You're a one you are Sir Roger."

∽

In the late afternoon they sighted the headland at Criccieth with its brooding castle towering over the small township below.

Goulde said, "The harbour's just to the east of the castle,

it's not much, just a stone pier. You'll be eager to stretch you legs."

Sir Roger looked up at the castle walls.

"Who's in charge here?"

"Ah, well that would be the constable, Edward Trumwyn, good man, no sense of humour though. He can arrange to have your men in the hold taken off. I need to go ashore first, I have some letters to give him."

"No doubt instructions from Sir John Cornwall about my men?"

Goulde nodded. "He said as much to me when he handed me the letters. Trumwyn's already got a hundred Welsh prisoners up in the castle. Don't suppose he'll welcome more men to feed even if they are supposed to be allies. Wouldn't surprise me if he locks them up with the Welsh."

"My advice, if he's any sense, would be to stick them in the dungeon. That's if he wants to avoid a riot. I'll tell him myself. I'm coming ashore with you."

"Has anyone ever told you you've a cold heart Sir Rodger?"

"Now what heart would that be Master Goulde?"

∼

They made their way up from the harbour quay to the castle which was dominated by its twin towered gatehouse. As they drew closer Sir Roger noticed the place was in disrepair. The stonework was impressive but overgrown with vegetation. There appeared to be a tree growing on top of one tower. As they passed through the great iron studded doors Sir Roger pushed a finger half way into the rotten wood.

"God's teeth. The place will fall within a week when the Welsh attack and believe me Goulde they will attack."

Goulde shrugged his shoulders. "And I'll be at sea God willing. You don't plan on pleading with Trumwyn to stay with your men do you?"

Sir Roger chuckled humourlessly and shook his head. "Are you mad? They'll all be dead within the month and I'll be long gone by then. Glyndwr won't stop until he's taken the whole of Wales. His kind of fighting is the worst kind Goulde."

"How's that?"

"He fights for a cause. The only thing I fight for is silver and gold."

∽

The constable's quarters were on the second floor. Trumwyn sat hunched on a three-legged stool in the centre of the chamber, a half empty goblet sat on the floor in front of him.

He greeted Goulde gruffly and eyed Sir Roger curiously. He took the letters from Goulde and read them in silence as the other two stood somewhat awkwardly in front of him.

Finally he looked up and said, "I've heard about you Mudstone, nothing good either. Why the hell Sir John landed me with your men I don't know. I've got trouble enough with the Welsh we've got locked up. There's little enough supplies for the men we have. I don't suppose you've brought me any supplies Master Goulde?"

"My orders were to bring Sir Roger's men here and then take Sir Roger and his man Travis on to Pembroke. I'm sorry but we've no supplies for you."

Trumwyn nodded. "Well, even with your reputation Mudstone, I could use another experienced leader." He looked down at the letters and said, "Still this is counter-signed by the king himself so I don't have much choice in the matter."

~

The hold on the Mynion hadn't been opened since they'd left Anglesey. There'd been plenty of shouted curses and moans over the past two days so Sir Roger was pretty sure there was still some life down there. He left the actual opening of the hatch to two of Goulde's men. They slid back the thick iron bolts and heaved the heavy oak hatch to one side. The smell that wafted up from the open hole was disgusting. Sir Roger and Travis were forced backwards away from stench.

"God's teeth that's ripe," said Sir Roger his eyes watering. He gestured to Goulde's men, and they lowered a short wooden ladder into the hold. He slowly inched forward and arm covering nose, he shouted down into the darkness.

"All right lads, we've arrived. Get yourselves above deck, there's food and lodgings up at the castle. Get going, we need you out of there."

A dirty hand shot over the edge of the hatch and slowly pulled its owner up onto the deck. It was one of the Jones brothers. He was wild-eyed and dripping with filth from the hold. Sitting on the edge of the hold he looked at Sir Roger and croaked, "You stinking rat. If you think any of us are going anywhere without our fair share of the booty you'd be wrong."

Sir Roger walked over slowly, his hand over his nose and mouth. His foot darted out and pinned Jones's hand to the deck. As if from nowhere Sir Roger produced a wicked-looking dagger which he pressed into the man's neck just enough to draw blood. As Travis and Master Goulde looked on horrified, he used his heel to grind the man's hand into the deck. There was an audible crunch as Jones's finger's broke. He howled with pain. Sir Roger used his foot to nudge the man over the edge and he fell with a sickening thud back into the darkness. Sir Roger edged closer to the hatch and shouted down into the dark, "I think you forget that I decide who gets what and when they get it. Maybe I should just leave you all down there in the bilge? No? Then get up here now."

One by one they came up from the dark. They stood in a rough semicircle facing him, dirty clothes dripping and eyes filled with murderous intent. The injured Jones brother stood cradling his hand. A thin trickle of blood ran down his forehead from a swelling that was already the size of a duck egg.

Sir Roger with forced cheerfulness said, "Come my old friends there's no need for all this unpleasantness, we're all comrades in arms here."

"Comrades in arms," shrieked Maggie. "We've been locked in that sinking hold for two days. You dog, I want my share and I want it now."

There was a chorus of agreement.

"Give us our due now."

"You're a lying, treacherous bastard."

"God help me I'm going to enjoy killing you."

One of them poked the Berserker with a grubby finger. "Even this one wants his share now, that's right lad isn't it?"

The Berserker stood unresponsive, eyes completely vacant.

"I don't take kindly to threats," said Sir Roger.

The uninjured Jones brother looked round and spotted an iron hook with a short length of rope fixed to the bottom of the mast. He tugged it free, and wrapping the rope slowly around his wrist, said to Sir Roger. "I'm going to rip your innards out from crotch to throat. Let's see how brave you are when your liver's hanging from the end of this hook."

Sir Roger backed up a few steps. A brief smile played on his lips. He put his hands together and cracked his fingers, then moved his shoulders and neck from side to side to take away any stiffness. He sighed heavily and with one fluid movement he unsheathed his sword and said, "Tempting though it is you'll excuse me if I don't take you up on the offer. I think I'll just kill you instead."

For a brief moment there was uncertainty in Jones's eyes but then the red mist descended on him. With ever increasing speed he began waving the iron hook around in figure eights. He bellowed and ran directly at Sir Roger who held his ground until the last possible second before sidestepping. As he did, so he brought the blade down on the other mans outstretched arm. With hardly a judder it passed cleanly through the flesh and bone just below the elbow. Jones's lower arm fell to the floor, the iron hook still grasped in the hand, embedding itself into the deck. A fountain of blood cascaded from the stump splattering everyone around. Jones, open-mouthed, dropped first to his knees, tried briefly to stand then fell face down onto the deck. Sir Roger calmly wiped the blade on the fallen figure's back. He pulled the hook and arm from the deck and slung it casually over the side.

"Who's next?"

Maggie gave him a mainly toothless grin and flicked her tongue between the two remaining blackened stumps in appreciation. "Gawd, that were a fancy move."

There was a sudden glint of sunlight on metal as a dagger appeared briefly in her hand before she hurled it directly at Sir Roger's head. He saw the movement and jerked his head to one side. The knife missed his ear with an inch to spare and vanished over the side.

Sir Roger flexed his arm and made a few practice strokes with his sword. "Let's stop playing games. I'm giving you a last chance to leave with your lives. So, what's it to be?"

Maggie licked her dry lips with a rough black tongue. She met Sir Roger's gaze and suddenly saw past the arrogant man to the madness that ran to his very core. It chilled her to the bone, draining the fight from her in an instant. She'd not felt this sober these past ten years. Slowly letting her breath out she said softly, "Come on my lovely lads, let's get off this stinking tub."

"He's killed my brother and ruined my hand," hissed the injured Jones glaring with angry red eyes at Sir Roger.

Maggie, never taking her eyes off Sir Roger said, "Believe me, he'll chop you down too. No point in being a martyr, but suit yourself, I'm not going to stop you."

Finally she dropped her gaze, grabbed the Berserker by the arm and dragged him over to the side of the ship. She pushed him up onto the stone pier and climbed up after him. The others, with a few muttered curses, swiftly followed. Jones, his injured hand hanging by his side, was the last off, dragged up onto the pier by the others. He looked back at Sir Roger and said, "I swear I'll kill you if we meet again."

Sir Roger shrugged and said, "I'm already looking forward to it. Better make sure the Welsh don't kill you first." When they had staggered off up the stone pier towards the castle Sir Roger finally sheathed his sword.

"Travis," he shouted, "where the devil are you, you little worm? Travis."

Travis slowly emerged from under a pile of old ropes. He stood shaking before his master.

"Clean that up," said Sir Roger pointing to the bloody body lying face down on the deck.

∼

Master Goulde shook his head. "You know Mudstone I've rarely seen a man make so many enemies in such a short space of time."

They were standing at the stern of the Mynion watching Criccieth castle slowly fading into the sea behind them. As they'd departed they could hear a barrage of insults being hurled from the castle.

Sir Roger nodded. "My father, curse his mouldering bones, said I had a talent for it."

"I take it you weren't close?"

"We loathed each other."

"Ah. He was perhaps disappointed with your sins?"

"Not him, he was a devious, conniving, vicious, cold-blooded killer. I'd say if he actually gave it a thought he approved wholeheartedly. He taught me one thing though."

"What's that Sir Roger?"

"It's the strong who survive in this world Goulde. The weak and the stupid are there to be preyed on. It's the natural order of things."

Master Goulde gave him a sideways look and caught a glimpse of the madness in Sir Roger's eyes.

## 17

## SAINT DAVIDS

The bishop's men had left Pembroke by boat on the morning tide. She was considerably smaller than the vessel they'd travelled to Tenby in. A good size for river work, and fast with it, but she gave her passengers an uncomfortable ride in the open waters of Milford Haven.

Osbert, green faced, was in a foul mood. "We could have made our way overland via Haverford, this is madness."

Bernard snapped, "Stop whining boy. It would have taken two days by land, with luck we'll be there by nightfall."

Will nodded and said, "He's right Osbert. We need to make up some time. The sooner we sort this mess out the sooner we can head home."

Osbert said, "How I miss my place by the fire and my soft bed. I dare say I'll never see Draychester again. We're all going to drown out here. I just know it."

Bernard said sarcastically, "Don't worry Osbert, our good bishop won't let you escape that easily boy. He'll have put a good word in for us with Him above. There's a lifetime of work to be had out of you yet."

From the choppy waters of Milford Haven, they headed north across St Bride's Bay. Osbert sat lodged under the rail, still green faced and cantankerous. It was a glorious day and a southerly wind had them making good progress. Will and Bernard sat at the front of the little vessel exhilarated by the speed and spray. It was impossible for them to be miserable on such a day and the gloom that had descended during the previous days slowly lifted.

Above them, in a cloudless sky, seagulls shot past carried effortlessly on the wind. Will looked at them enviously. "To be able to fly free like that, what I wouldn't give."

Bernard chuckled. "Aye lad, miracles of God's creation they surely are. Pity we serve a more earthly master."

"You think we'll ever catch up with the bishop's wine? It seems the closer we get to it the further away it becomes."

"It's led us a merry dance that's for sure. I feel this time it's within our grasp."

"And Richard Phelpes?"

"Him too lad, him too."

"If he seeks sanctuary in the cathedral, he's likely to go unpunished."

"God will always punish a murder," said Osbert, who had been quietly listening between hanging over the side.

Bernard nodded. "He's right, for once. Nothing goes unpunished lad. If not in this world, then in the next. Anyway, not a lot we can do about that for now. If Phelpes seeks sanctuary, well let's just say these things have a way of working themselves out."

Will said, "Then let's not disappoint the bishop. We need to find this wine and soon."

Will looked at Osbert hanging miserably over the side and felt a twinge of guilt. He tried to distract him. "Tell me about the bishop of Saint Davids Osbert. What are we to expect?"

"Bishop Mone? A favourite of old King Richard. By all accounts he's been keeping his head down these last few years. King Henry isn't the forgiving type."

"Are you saying he won't object when we ask to riffle through his cellars?" said Bernard.

"I'm sure we will be accorded the assistance our status dictates," said Osbert before turning back to dry retch over the rail.

Will sighed. "You're starting to sound like your Uncle Scrivener, he talks in riddles too. What you mean is our welcome may be frosty, but he'll feel obliged to help?"

Osbert wiped his mouth on his sleeve and said weakly, "If only for the sake of his own skin. He'll want to keep our bishop happy and himself out of mind of King Henry."

Will laughed. "Osbert, I've said it before, you never cease to amaze me."

"You two may treat me as a fool, but I spent my entire childhood around my uncle Scrivener and the bishop. I've seen how the bishop uses my uncle to keep track of friends and enemies both. There's good reason, the more you know the safer you are."

"Osbert I've never really taken you for a fool," said Bernard gently. "You may be insufferable sometimes, but I know Scrivener sees something of himself in you. That's why you're here with us."

∽

There was still an hour or two of daylight left when they reached their destination. It was a brisk walk of half an hour up from Porthclais harbour to Saint Davids. The cathedral and bishop's palace were enclosed by a high wall that ran around the entire complex. The wall was punctuated by four gates. The bishop's men felt strangely at home amongst the throngs of pilgrims and others heading towards the main gate. The atmosphere was familiar to them from their own cathedral at Draychester. It was a mixture of nervous expectation, holiday and religious experience. They soon reached the large pointed arch of the east gate that led into the cathedral close. A sturdy gatehouse with a tower guarded the actual entrance, which was itself flanked on the right by an even higher two-storey tower.

"It looks more like the entrance to a castle," said Will. As they passed through, all three glanced upwards and saw that more defensive gates could be dropped down to secure the entrance.

Bernard nodded approvingly, "No expense spared by the looks of it."

There were two men on duty at the gate, not interfering with the flow of pilgrims and other visitors but keeping a watchful gaze. The trio stopped in front of the older of the two. Will rummaged under his tunic and pulled out the seal he carried on a thin leather strap around his neck. He held the seal out in one hand. The man gave it a cursory glance.

"We're officials of the bishop of Draychester. We have business with your own bishop."

The man gave them all a more searching look this time and said gruffly, "All three of you bishop's men are you?"

Bernard nodded. "Myself for many a long year, these two but a few."

The man nodded back and said, "You'd better make your way to the palace then. Down the steps and on past the cathedral, cross over the river, the entrance is on the side, you'll see it. Don't expect the bishop to be up and about yet."

"It's nearly nightfall," said Osbert shocked.

"Aye well, he's taken to his bed. Not been the same since the old king lost the throne. That right Harry?"

The other gatekeeper nodded. "Some days we do guard duty down at the gatehouse at the palace. He don't get up until evening most days. Hardly leaves the precinct, only other place he's been these last two years is the bishop's palace at Lamphey. You'd better ask for his clerk, Thomas."

∼

As they moved away from the gatehouse they looked down on a small valley. It was like a green bowl containing the cathedral and bishop's palace. A small stream divided them, the palace being on the far bank. A flight of worn stone stairs flanked by stone walls led down towards the cathedral. However, it was the bishop's palace that attracted most of their attention.

They could see two main ranges at right angles to each other and all raised on vaulted undercrofts. To top it off was a distinctive arcaded parapet. The stonework was of alternate purple and yellow. It was a startling effect given the bright whitewashed surrounding walls.

"God's teeth, this isn't want I expected. Even the king would be envious of such a palace," said Bernard.

Will said softly, "The cathedral is fine to be sure but from what I can see no finer than our own at Draychester, but I agree, the palace is fit for a king."

Osbert gazed down at the buildings below. "If not fit for a king then for a prince bishop, for that is what Bishop Mone was in all but title."

Will said, "I'd wager he's not happy about his fall from favour at court."

"That's what being a noble is all about lad. It's a dangerous game to play, especially when you've backed the wrong side," said Bernard.

Will sniffed. "Well, it doesn't look so bad to me, he's still living in splendour isn't he?"

Bernard shrugged. "Who knows how long that will last? Perhaps the king is happy to leave him here, his power ebbing away, or perhaps he'll have him replaced. So what now lad? Do we seek our missing wine first, or do we seek its thief and murderer?"

"You think Richard Phelpes and his brother David beat us here?"

"I think we have a few hours. We made good progress and came direct from Pembroke. I doubt they tried to come this far in that bloody rowboat. Still, we should check any who have sought sanctuary at the cathedral in the last few hours."

"There would be more than one?"

"You'd be surprised lad. There's always those seeking to escape justice. In Draychester it's not unknown for there to be three or four sanctuary seekers in a week. Of course they aren't all murderers like those we seek."

"If he's not in the cathedral, then maybe we should watch the main gate from outside the walls. Once he reaches the cathedral, we can do no more."

"Actually that's not strictly true," said Osbert. "I believe the custom here is that he has to reach and touch the high altar first."

"And then?"

"Well, he doesn't simply get granted sanctuary. There's a process, the coroner will need to be summoned. He would have to confess to the crime in the coroner's presence, whether he committed it or not. Only then is he under the protection of the church."

Bernard said, "So we could drag him out of there anytime before that?"

"Only in theory," said Osbert.

"I can't but think that Bishop Mone would disapprove of us manhandling someone seeking sanctuary once they had entered the precinct, let alone from within the cathedral itself," said Will.

Bernard chuckled. "You're probably right lad. I suppose that would be pushing our luck, but it's going to be hard to stop him reaching the cathedral."

Will nodded. "With the number of pilgrims coming through here he could easily disguise himself with something as simple as an old cloak. Once he's under the protection of the church what then Osbert?" asked Will.

"He's got forty days to sort his affairs during which he can't leave the cathedral. He'll have to swear to leave the realm by the nearest port and never return. Everything he owns is then forfeit to the crown."

Bernard sighed and said, "Well, there's only a short time before they close the main gate for nightfall. No one without proper business will be allowed through until morning. If he's not in the cathedral already, it'll be tomorrow before he makes his attempt. Let's at least go and check inside."

They made their way down the steep stairs to the cathedral. A steady stream of pilgrims was making their way in the other direction, their pilgrimage complete at least for today. They entered the cathedral by the south door, which led into the nave. The first things they noticed were the sloping floor and the outward lean of the massive purplish grey stone pillars. Each pillar was linked by a semicircular arch to the next.

"Amazing," said Will gazing upwards, "is it just me or are those pillars leaning outwards?"

"It's no illusion," said Osbert, "The whole place is built on marshy ground. Apparently they skimped on the foundations as well. Then of course there was the earthquake in old King Henry's time, that didn't help."

"How do you even know these things Osbert?"

"I talked to one of the Bishop Mone's clerks once, when they visited Draychester. Clerk to clerk, it's surprising what you learn."

They gazed at the carved stone screen at the front of the nave. It was a fine piece of work.

"We need to find someone to ask about our fugitives," said Bernard.

Osbert led them around the stone screen and along the south aisle. They passed an elaborate tomb with the effigy of a bishop lying on top. The sides covered with carvings of the apostles. Will stopped to take a better look.

"Osbert?" he asked.

"Bishop Gower's final resting place. Spent his coin on the bishop's palace and a lot of what you see around us."

Will nodded. "I understand, he who spends the most coin gets the best tomb."

Osbert gestured to the east end of the cathedral. "Saint David was a humble man by comparison."

A small crowd of pilgrims was gathered before the richly decorated stonework of Saint David's shrine, patiently waiting. Three niches along the base allowed them to kneel before the shrine and each was allowed their turn for a minute of two. Depending on their affliction, some had to be helped by their fitter companions. A few wore hoods and had bandaged hands which Will took to be leprosy sufferers. Candles burned above their heads, casting a golden glow. As the three of them approached, they all recognised the familiar smell of overpowering bad breath and its owner Edward. The pilgrims before the shrine were the same as they'd accompanied on the road to Pembroke. Will hoped for all their sakes that Saint David cure Edward of at least this affliction even if he were unaware of it himself.

Two men stood apart from the pilgrims, occasionally tapping one on the shoulder if they took too long in front of the shrine. They looked to be in charge.

Will approached the nearest and said, "A minute of your time friend."

The man held his hand out palm outwards. "You'll need to wait awhile yet, soon as these good folk are done. There's just enough time for you before the gates are shut on the precinct." He looked at Will and the two stood behind him and said, "Or if it's some special private prayer time with the good saint you're after, well I can arrange that too. Perhaps you're wanting to make a donation now?"

Will smiled. "It's not about the shrine we ask my friend. We need to speak to someone about two sanctuary seekers?"

"Ah, well why didn't you say so, who's asking?"

"Officials of the bishop of Draychester."

"Well, in that case, you'll need to speak to the sub-dean. He's up in the chapter house. Take the staircase from Saint Thomas's chapel." The man pointed a boney finger towards the north transept.

~

They made their way up a narrow spiral staircase and emerged into a light and airy room located directly above the chapel below. On one side were two stone seats set into the wall. A plump figure sat on one, apparently asleep, his head leant back against the stonework. There were wooden benches running along the other walls. Otherwise the chamber was bare. As they approached, they could hear the man's snores.

"Do you think this is him?" asked Will.

"There's no-one else here. Osbert give him a poke," said Bernard.

"Why me?" asked Osbert in a whisper.

Bernard just glared at him. Osbert glared back and then gently tapped the man on the shoulder. If anything, the snores just got louder.

"God's teeth," said Bernard, and none too gently flicked the man's right ear.

The man's eyes flickered open, and he brought a hand up to his ear. "Who are you?" he asked sleepily.

"We're from Draychester, bishop's men."

The man stifled a yawn. "Sorry, must have nodded off. Draychester is it, well you're a long way from home. Went there myself once, got drunk as a lord in some tavern. The days of one's youth, eh."

"Are you the sub-dean?" asked Will.

"For my sins I am. My names Nicholas Byset, how can I help you?"

"Has anyone claimed sanctuary today?" asked Bernard.

The sub-dean looked at then nervously. "You're not seeking sanctuary for some crime yourselves are you?"

Bernard getting impatient said, "Of course not. We ask after some fugitives from justice."

The sub-dean shook his head. "In that case the last was two days ago. Did you happen to see the old crone near the main door of the cathedral? Smashed a skillet over her husband's head. Walked all the way from Carmarthen by all accounts."

"Her husband is dead?" asked Osbert.

"No, but he's got a bloody sore head." The sub dean laughed at his own wit. "He turned up yesterday asking after her. I've said to the old girl that she hasn't murdered anyone yet. She should patch things up with him and go home. Think she prefers it here though."

Will smiled indulgently. "So no real sanctuary seekers then?"

"Oh there's a couple knocking about the cathedral. A lad from Haverford, a cobbler's apprentice, stole a purse of silver pennies from his master. The other one is a miller, not sure where he's from, he's been caught adding chalk to the flour."

"Why?" asked Osbert curiously.

Will gave him a withering look. "You've led a sheltered life Osbert. You can bulk the flour out with chalk of course, it's an old trick. I imagine he's not very popular with his neighbours."

The sub-dean chuckled and said, "They were all for lynching him, they probably would have if he hadn't made it here first. So, are you looking for someone in particular?"

Bernard answered. "Two brothers from Tenby. One of them has murdered his father, the others involved up to his neck."

"A murderer you say, well I would have sent for the coroner at once in a case like that, but no one has sought sanctuary against a murder accusation for weeks. It's usually an idiot involved in a drunken brawl who ends up putting a dagger in someone's guts."

"In this case it's a little more complicated." Will briefly described the circumstances.

The sub-dean leant back in his seat. "I'll tell you

honestly, the bishop takes his obligations regarding sanctuary seriously."

"And that means what exactly?" said Bernard.

The sub-dean suddenly lost all his joviality. He leant forward towards them. "Bishop's officials or not, he won't take any interference from you lightly. Just a friendly warning my friends, I'd let events involving these two brothers take their natural course."

∽

They left the cathedral by the south door, crossed the small river by a wooden bridge and found themselves at a gatehouse on the north side of the bishop's palace.

"Your turn," said Bernard gesturing to the door and back to Will. He used an ornate iron ring on the great oak door to give three hard knocks. They stood there for a minute with no obvious signs of life coming from the other side of the door. Before they could stop him Bernard, impatient as usual, used one of his huge fists to pound on the wood.

From behind the solid oak came a muffled voice. "All right already, can't a man take a piss without being disturbed?" The great door of the gateway slowly opened inwards dragged by a thin man with a bushy white beard and damp boots.

He gave them an appraising look, wiped a hand on his tunic, and said by way of an explanation. "Can't take my ale these days. Goes in one end and straight out the other."

Will explained who they were. "We need to speak to Thomas the bishop's clerk."

He nodded and gestured them through the door and said "Swords and daggers you need to leave here. The bishop don't allow anyone to go armed in the palace. We got just the spot for them." He removed a large key he wore around his neck on a leather strap. He used it to open a big oak trunk sat in a nook in the wall just inside the gate. "In there if you please."

Will deposited a battered dagger and Osbert something that looked like an old tooth pick. Bernard took somewhat longer to relinquish his stash. The guard watched in amusement as he removed numerous weapons from about his person. "You always go about with that amount of weaponry big fella?"

Bernard grinned. "You can't be too careful my friend. The open road's a dangerous place."

The guard locking the trunk grinned back. "Too true. Right, follow me. Oh, and close that bloody door behind you."

Bernard turned around and used a huge shoulder to push the door closed. The gatekeeper led them out into a large courtyard and the three bishop's men gawped at their surroundings. The gatekeeper stopped for a minute to let them take it in, a smile on his lips. "First time here? Impressive ain't it?"

There was an arcaded parapet that ran along the top of all the buildings around the courtyard. It was decorated with a chequerboard pattern of purple and yellow stone blocks. The rest of the walls were whitewashed, the contrast was quite dazzling even in the fading light.

"Must have cost a pretty penny," said Bernard, gazing up.

The gatekeeper nodded, "Aye well, old Bishop Gower were one for show and every bishop since has spent nearly as much even if they couldn't afford it." The corbels that supported the arches were decorated with a bewildering number of carved figures. There were lions, monkeys, dogs and birds with the odd mythical figure and human head.

"It's a vulgar display," Osbert whispered to Will, "hardly fitting at the same place where Saint David takes his rest."

"This is all about a show of power Osbert. I'm sure you understand that. You can hardly deny that our own bishop does the same?"

Osbert sniffed with disdain. "At least he does it with more taste."

The gatekeeper said, "Thomas will be in the bishop's hall, he works from a little table in the corner." He led them to the left, out of the courtyard, and up a short flight of steps through an elaborate arched doorway into the hall on the first floor. A man sat on a stool at a low table scattered with documents. He held a quill in his hand.

"Bishop of Draychester's men here to see you Thomas."

"I take it you've left the gate unattended again?"

"You know Hugo is sick, only me on duty today. If you'd lend me one of the kitchen lads at least I'd be able to go take a piss once in a while." With that he turned on his heels and stalked off without a backwards glance.

"I'm sorry about that. He's a grumpy old sod at the best of times. Welcome. My name is Thomas Fitzwilliam, bishop's clerk."

∽

"Wine you say?" asked Fitzwilliam.

"Yes, wine that rightly belongs to the bishop of Draychester," said Bernard.

"And you're implying that we've somehow stolen this wine from your bishop?"

"No, as I explained…"

"Because I assure you I keep meticulous accounts."

Will said, "We're not implying you had any knowledge of the theft."

Fitzwilliam slightly red in the face said, "All our wine comes from reputable merchants who either the steward or myself have dealt with for years."

"One of those would be Phelpes?" asked Bernard.

"The Phelpes, of Tenby, of course."

Bernard smiled and muttered, "So now we're getting somewhere."

"You've had a shipment recently?" asked Will.

"We've had several consignments of wine in the last few days. Some by sea, most by cart from Carew. Though I think only a few casks would match the quality you've described. It's all recorded in my ledger."

"Can we see the wine that was delivered?"

"It will be in the undercroft now under the great hall. We'll need to ask Baldwin, the cellarer. This is highly irregular. I think perhaps I should consult with the bishop first. Normally I'd ask the steward, but he's away in Bristol ordering supplies."

'We'd be happy to talk to the bishop, but we could just take a look first. There'll be no need to bother him with this at all if the wine is not there."

Fitzwilliam looked at them for a moment, then sighed heavily and said, "Perhaps you're right. The bishop is not in the best of health. All this business with the new king has affected him greatly. You'd better talk to Baldwin."

∼

Fitzwilliam led them from the bishop's hall down an internal stairway and along a passage that led into the undercroft directly below the great hall. They followed him through a series of storerooms. There was an astonishing amount of food supplies crammed into every nook and cranny.

"Are you planning for a siege?" asked Bernard amazed at the shear quantity and variety.

Fitzwilliam shrugged. "It's soon the feast of Saint Matthew. We're expecting many guests."

The three Draychester men exchange glances. Feast days were a more modest affair at their own bishop's palace. They found Baldwin the cellarer rolling empty casks out of a storage room. At first he seemed somewhat bemused by their questions then became increasingly angry.

"Phelpes himself came here about two weeks ago. Said he'd got hold of something special that the bishop would appreciate."

Will said, "This would be Richard we're talking about?"

"No, it was David, not that hot head Richard."

"You're sure it was David?"

Baldwin said exasperated, "Of course it was, I know him well. He stood here in front of me in the undercroft not two weeks ago. Said he'd received a shipment from Gascony at Tenby, the best quality. There was a barrel available. I accepted."

Bernard cried out, "I knew it! That bastard. He's been lying about this all the time. He was in it as much as his brother, right up to his scrawny neck. I should have beat the truth out of him when I had the chance."

Will held his hand up for calm. "The wine, it was expensive?"

Baldwin nodded. "The best wine always is."

"So you didn't have to ask permission from the bishop or the steward?"

"They trust me to use my discretion when it comes to wine."

Will turned to look at Fitzwilliam. He nodded in acknowledgement.

Bernard said, "So you don't take the occasional inducement to buy a particular cask or two?"

Baldwin turned red and spluttered, "How dare you."

Bernard shrugged. "No one would blame you. A few coins here and there, no harm in indulging yourself a little now and again, eh?"

"I assure you nothing like that ever happens."

Bernard sniffed. "Well, I suppose we'll just have to take your word for that."

Will said, "So, show us the cask. I'd like to actually set eyes on the stuff, we've been chasing after it for days."

Baldwin pointed to the back of the storage room. "It's back there. I'd thought about taking it out for tonight's meal in the great hall."

Bernard snapped, "No you won't, not after all the bloody effort that's gone into finding it. It's coming back with us."

Fitzwilliam said, "Well you'll have to talk to Bishop Mone about that. You can't take it out of here without his permission. And what about Phelpes? He sold us stolen goods."

Bernard gave a harsh laugh. "I wouldn't worry about him. Selling stolen goods is the least of his worries. It's the conspiracy with his brother to murder their father that's more worrying. Still, we're expecting both of them shortly."

Fitzwilliam said, "I don't quite understand?"

Bernard pointed to the back of the room. "Never mind. Lead the way Baldwin, let's take a look at this bloody wine."

"This is it?" asked Will dubiously.

Baldwin the cellarer placed a hand on the cask and nodded. "This is the one."

"You're sure of that?" asked Bernard.

"It's from Gascony all right. See this mark here, that's a customs mark from Libourne. A lot of wine is shipped from there. This other mark, that's a vintner named Couraud. Had a few casks with his mark over the years, it's always quality stuff, the best."

"Fill us a jug," said Bernard.

"Are you sure? If I open it, I can't guarantee it won't be like vinegar by the time you get it back to your bishop."

"We need to be sure it's what those marks purport it to be. Do it, fill a jug."

Baldwin went over to a wooden bench in the corner of the cellar and returned with a wooden spigot, a glazed jug, and two wooden goblets. He removed the bung from the cask, catching the spurt of wine in the jug and expertly inserted the spigot. He drew off some more wine and filled up the jug. He poured a generous measure of the rich dark red liquid into the two goblets, took one himself and handed the other to Bernard. Baldwin sniffed the wine in his goblet and then gently slurped, savouring it on his palate and simply said, "Now that's quality."

Bernard looked on in amusement and then took a long swig, sloshed the wine around his mouth and drew it back and forwarded between his teeth and said, "Christ's bones, that's not bad, not bad at all."

Baldwin looked at him with disgust. "Not bad, is that all you can say? That's one of the finest wines you'll taste outside of Gascony itself. I'd be surprised if there were more than two or three casks of this in the whole kingdom."

Bernard shrugged. "All the more reason it should be with its rightful owner then. Have a taste of this lads, see what you think."

Will took the goblet from him and drank deeply. "Nice, very smooth. So this is what the nobles drink, eh? I could get a taste for this stuff, not that I could ever afford it."

Osbert took the goblet from him and sipped it cautiously then nodded his head in appreciation and said, "Perhaps we can finally plan on going home now?"

∽

Fitzwilliam led them back to the bishop's hall. "Wait here. I'll go and see if the bishop is up and about yet. He soon returned and led them away from the hall and into the bishop's private chambers. They were luxuriously furnished with brightly coloured tapestries of hunting scenes draping the walls. It was clear the bishop didn't spare any of the worldly pleasures on his own comfort. They found Bishop Mone sat in a comfortably padded chair next to the fireplace, a goblet of wine held between pale hands. He was not a young man, his lank hair was thin and receding and his face looked drawn and grey. Gesturing with a trembling hand that they should sit he said, "How is Bishop Gifford?" He didn't bother to hide the insincerity in the question or wait for a reply. "I hear he's great friends with the king?"

Clearing his throat nervously Will said, "Indeed my lord, I believe they have known each other since their youth."

Bishop Mone nodded. "Really. I don't know the king well myself. I haven't been at court for some years and perhaps I spent too much time at Westminster in the past."

"I'm sorry to hear that my lord. I'm sure Bishop Gifford would ask me to pass on his best wishes to you."

"Hmm. I'm sure he would. He's a shrewd man your master, he picked the winning side a few years ago. Let's hope he continues to enjoy such good fortune or perhaps he'll too be confined to his own bishop's palace at Draychester."

Will coughed nervously again. "Ah, forgive me my lord, but I wouldn't like to speculate on matters above my status."

The bishop smiled without humour. "A wise man. Keep your head down and your mouth shut, eh? I don't blame you. So to other matters, I hear you like to wander through my wine cellars?"

"The wine my lord, it's a delicate matter, perhaps..."

Bishop Mone held a hand up to cut him off. "Well of course you must have it back. I'd hate to think I was depriving your master or indeed the king himself of their wine. "

The three bishop's men gave each other furtive glances, hardly believing it would be this easy. Finally Bernard said softly. "I'm sure Bishop Gifford would ask me to thank you for your kindness my lord."

"Quite. Well, I've instructed Baldwin to ensure it's put back on the first cog going south. You've no objection to that?"

Bernard replied, "On the contrary my lord. If we can also take passage with the boat back to Pembroke and perhaps onwards to Bristol that would be ideal."

"Well, that's settled then, if the master of the vessel agrees. As to the Vintner, Phelpes I believe, there's some ongoing unpleasantness?"

Bernard answered. "The father is dead my lord, murdered by one of the two sons, they have both fled justice. We believe they will seek sanctuary here at the cathedral."

"So I've heard from my clerk Thomas. As a favour to your own bishop, I'll have the gatekeepers keep a watch for them tomorrow. If they're spotted, they'll be denied entry through the gate and be detained outside the precinct. The gatekeepers can send for you then and the town watch can deal with them. I can't make any promises mind. If they make it into the precinct and the cathedral, then my hands are tied. I won't withhold sanctuary to any man, it's church law as you well know."

Bernard bowed his head. "My lord, you are most kind, it's all we can ask."

The bishop grunted. "You can all join me for supper and you can tell me more of your illustrious master and of your quest for his wine. I fear I've become starved of any real news."

∼

Sir Roger stood on the raised platform to the rear of the cog and peered at the coastline. He turned to Goulde.

"You'll put us off at Saint Davids Master Goulde."

Goulde looked at him with surprise. "My instructions are to deliver you to Pembroke not Saint Davids."

Sir Roger turned to him again and glared. "Never the less, you'll put in at Saint Davids. I'm not asking you, I'm ordering you."

"You forget I'm the master of this ship."

"That can easily be changed, don't tempt me."

Goulde looked at the other man shrewdly. "And what will I tell the Constable of Pembroke? I've letters for him, they'll mention you for sure."

Sir Roger shrugged. "Tell him I've gone to Saint Davids to do penance for my sins. It may take me some time."

"You'll want us to unload your cargo. I'm not to take it on to Pembroke for you?"

"No. The trunks stay with us."

～

With the Mynion tied up against the quayside at Porthclais, Master Goulde swiftly unloaded the three large trunks from the hold that were Sir Roger's. Travis got the distinct impression he couldn't wait to be gone. The quay was almost deserted apart from some poorly dressed children fishing for crabs. Gould shouted up from the cog. "St Davids is up the road, about a mile and a half. If you give one of those lads a coin, I'm sure they'll go and ask for a cart for you."

"No need to waste money, I'll send Travis," said Sir Roger.

Goulde just said, "I'm away before the tide turns."

Sir Roger sat down on one of the trunks and nodded calmly. "Give my regards to the Constable of Pembroke."

Goulde didn't bother replying, and the ship was soon pulling away from the quay. Travis gazing after it said, "Will Sir John and the King not be angry that we've disobeyed their orders master?"

Sir Roger smirked. "Out of sight out of mind Travis. Did you really think that I was going to sit in some damp Welsh castle for the next year? I'll stay in the background for a while. Anyway, they'll have their hands full with the natives soon enough."

Travis had serious doubts that Sir Roger could ever bring himself to stay in the background. He knew better than to voice his concerns, that way lay pain. "Then what are we to do here master?"

"Well, to start with I rather think I'll enjoy the hospitality of the bishop of Saint Davids. After all, I have a pardon signed by the king himself. You'd better get up to town, hire a man and a cart and get back down here. Don't hang about, you know I don't have much patience."

"I'll need some money master."

Sir Roger looked at him angrily. "It's always the same with you isn't it Travis, money for this, money for that. It's never ending." Eventually he sighed heavily and dug out a bulging leather bag from under his tunic. He opened it carefully and shook out three silver pennies into his palm. He tossed them to Travis and said, "Negotiate carefully, if it costs more than two pennies I'll beat the extra out of your hide."

Travis took the money without a word and started to trudge up the hill away from the harbour. Sir Roger lay back on the trunk and enjoyed the last of the evening sun.

～

The creaking of the cart arriving woke Sir Roger from a deep sleep. He stretched and got up a little stiffly from the trunk he'd been lying on. Sir Roger stifled a yawn and regarded the sorry-looking donkey and decrepit cart with a distinct lack of enthusiasm.

"Is this the best you could find?" he asked exasperated. Travis held the donkey's head and looked at his master without answering, knowing better than to offer any excuses.

Sir Roger walked over and cuffed him around the head. "Just get these damn trunks loaded up on the cart. If the bloody thing collapses, you'll be carrying them up there on your back."

Sir Roger stood and watched as Travis struggled with the three heavy iron bound trunks. He didn't offer any help but gave plenty of unwanted advice on the best ways to manhandle them. Eventually they were laid on the rough wooden planks of the cart. Its wheels splayed out precariously under the weight.

"Well I'm not walking and I'm certainly not sitting in the back," said Sir Roger. He gave the donkey a dubious look and then sat down heavily on its back. It let out a deep sigh.

"Lead on Travis. I'm hungry, no time to waste."

Travis tugged on the worn leather harness around the donkey's neck. It looked at him with utter contempt and stood rock solid. Sir Roger pulled out a wicked-looking dagger from under his leather tunic. The donkey glanced back at him then miraculously sprang to life and began the long trudge up the hill the cart swaying behind it.

~

"Who did you say you were?"

"Sir Roger Mudstone."

"And you're on pilgrimage?" said the gatekeeper, looking dubiously at the donkey and cart. Travis stood beside the cart keeping his mouth shut. He wasn't surprised the gatekeeper had doubts, but Sir Roger was usually persuasive.

"That's right. I'm sure a generous donation to the cathedral will see us in the guesthouse."

The guard sniffed, wiped his nose on his sleeve and asked, "What's in the cart?"

Sir Roger lost his patience and grabbed the man by the throat, lifting him off his feet in the process. The other gatekeeper, who was resting against the wall on the opposite side of the gateway, retrieved a long cudgel from a niche in the stonework and ambled over.

"I'd put him down if I were you sir." He said it with respect but also with menace. He thumped the cudgel into the palm of his hand to emphasize the point.

Sir Roger glanced at him with contempt but slowly eased the pressure on the other man's throat. He reluctantly released his grip and wiped his hand on the man's tunic. He turned to the other gatekeeper and said, "I've been on the king's service in the north and these trunks are the property of his majesty. I'm seeking a few days' rest and prayer for the good of my soul before we continue on to Pembroke. Do I need to give any more of an explanation to a mere gatekeeper?"

The man looked at Sir Roger appraisingly. He glanced at Travis and the cart. He didn't believe a word of it but it wasn't his place to say so. Finally he gave a nod. "There's no need for any bad feeling sir. Wouldn't be doing our job if we didn't ask." He stepped aside and pointed ahead. "Straight down the road, cross the river. As you can see, the bishop's palace will be right in front of you. The gatehouse is around the right-hand side."

Without another word, Sir Roger barged past. Travis gave the two gatekeepers an apologetic look, grabbed the reins of the donkey and set off after his master. The donkey sighed and plodded after them, the cart trundling along behind.

"You just can't help some folk," croaked one of the gatekeepers massaging his crushed neck. He gazed after the cart descending the road down into the valley. "He's a wrong-un for sure."

The other man shrugged. "For two pennies a day I'd say

it's not our problem. You're going to have one hell of a bruise there."

There were further questions at the gatehouse to the bishop's palace which Sir Roger this time overcame with a generous donation of coin. The cart got a curious stare but Sir Roger hurriedly got Travis to unload it in the fading light. A lad was given a coin to take it and its tired donkey back into town. Another exchange of coin with the hostler gave Sir Roger a comfortable chamber in the pilgrim's guesthouse on the west side of the courtyard. Travis had to make do in the guesthouse's main room with the other servants and less wealthy pilgrims. He was glad to be away from Sir Roger and his surroundings were comfortable enough.

∽

"I've heard of you Mudstone and looking at this pardon I'd wager the king has made good use of your services these past months."

Sir Roger forced his thin lips into a passable smile. "The Welsh have proven most stubborn Your Grace. It's been necessary to persuade them to comply with the king's rule."

"Persuade you say," said the bishop with distaste. "Yes, I've heard that you can be very persuasive." He decided not to dwell on the rumours about the man. "You'll join me for supper Mudstone? I've a few other guests tonight, three of the bishop of Draychester's men. Perhaps you'll know them. I do believe I had dealings with your father or perhaps brother some years ago in Draychester. You are from Draychester originally aren't you?"

Sir Rogers's left eye twitched in a most alarming fashion. Bishop Mone did a double take, unsure if the man was having some sort of fit or not. Eventually Sir Roger rasped,

"Three bishop's men you say? Is one of them a huge ugly hulk of a man, the other an annoying redhead and the last a thin weasel of a clerk?"

"I'm not sure I'd describe them in exactly those terms but indeed those sound like the same."

## 18

## THE GREAT HALL

Later that evening, Thomas Fitzwilliam, the bishop's clerk led the Draychester men back out into the courtyard. "The bishop doesn't get about much these days, he'll be glad of your company at supper. He was a great supporter of our old king. Relations with the new king have been somewhat strained. There's a knight here as well, Sir Roger Mudstone, down from the fighting in the north. He'll be joining us."

Bernard leant forward and with one giant hand clasped Thomas's arm in a vice like grip and brought him to an abrupt stop. The clerk gaped at Bernard in alarm.

Bernard shook his arm. "Did you say Roger Mudstone? Tell me man, is that who you said?"

Thomas stuttered his answer. "Sir Roger Mudstone, yes, he arrived earlier with his servant, a man called Travis. Is there some cause for alarm? I've heard rumours about him. The Welsh hate him with a vengeance, they say he's done some unspeakable things. He has a pardon with him signed by the king."

"I can't believe that lying, conniving, murderous bastard

is here. Osbert run down to the gatehouse and fetch my sword."

Will said, "Hold fast Osbert. We can't start some blood match here within the cathedral precinct."

Bernard snorted. "He burned a priest alive lad. I watched with my own eyes. Our own bishop has placed a price on the arrogant bastard's head and by God I'm going to enjoy removing it from his shoulders."

Will said, "Thomas you've seen this pardon yourself? It's real?"

"It's genuine all right. I examined it myself and it bears the king's own seal. Whatever he may have done in the past, he's been pardoned by the king himself. The bishop will not welcome violence within the precinct, this is a place of God."

Osbert, looking at the extravagant display of wealth represented by the buildings around the courtyard, gave a derisory snort.

"When did he arrive?" asked Will.

"Not long after you. He came to the gatehouse as a pilgrim, he and his man Travis. He said he'd been in the north fighting the Welsh with the king and wanted to spend a few days for the good of his soul here at Saint Davids. They had a cart with them with three heavy trunks. I've given him a chamber in the guest house."

∼

They entered the great hall via a staircase leading from the courtyard. Will was immediately impressed with the sheer size of the hall and the wooden-beamed roof. He was used to the rather gloomy hall at Draychester but here there were three large windows on either side that made it light and airy. A cheery fire burned in the centre, the smoke rising up to a central louvred opening in the roof. Most astonishing of all was a great wheel shaped window in the gable wall. As they trailed after Thomas, Bernard gazing up at the window said, "Now there's something that cost more coin than the three of us will see in a lifetime."

Osbert nodded and said, "It seems to me to be ungodly for a bishop to flaunt such wealth."

"I take it your won't be turning down his food though?" asked Will sarcastically. Osbert just glared back.

At one end of the hall was a raised table where the bishop could entertain the more important visitors. Down the length of the hall, either side of the hearth, were two long trestle tables where the rest of the guests could be seated. At the other end of the hall was a wooden screen that presumably shielded the stairs to the kitchens below.

At the top table servants had already spread the cloths, setting steel knives, silver spoons, dishes for salt, silver cups, and mazers. At each place was a trencher, a thick slice of day-old bread serving as a plate for the roast meat that was to be served. Thomas gestured to one of the servants and ewers, basins, and towels were produced for hand washing. "I can't believe we're sitting down with that animal," whispered Bernard as they made their way towards the table.

And there sat Sir Roger, already slouched nonchalantly in a chair, slowly sipping from a goblet of wine. His gaze was fixed on them with a frightening intensity. He raised the goblet to them slowly in a mock toast.

"Well, well. If it isn't the Bishop of Draychester's churls. I'm surprised your master lets you roam this far from home."

Will placed a hand on Bernard's arm. "If this was the other way around your advice to me would be to stay calm.

There's nothing we can do at the moment, at least not here in Saint Davids. The man has got a pardon from the King himself."

Bernard glared back at Sir Roger. "I don't care if he's got a pardon countersigned by the bloody Pope. He's a murdering, conniving bastard, who deserves to dangle at the end of a rope."

"Keep your voice down," hissed Will.

They took their seats to the left of the bishop. Bernard sat at one the end of the table looking back along it to where Sir Roger sat at the opposite end. In the middle were the bishop and his clerk Thomas. Will sat down next to the bishop and Osbert squeezed in between him and Bernard.

The big man whispered, "Whatever he's been up to in Wales, you can be certain it's only been to the benefit of himself."

Osbert shrank down in his seat as though he could somehow slip out of Sir Roger's sight altogether. "I wish I'd never come here. Look at his eyes, they're dead, he has the devil in him for sure. He'll murder us all before the night's out. We're doomed." His hands were shaking as he picked up his wine goblet, spilling a good portion down the front of his tunic.

"Osbert, get a grip," whispered Will angrily. "He's hardly going to attack us here in the hall."

"If he so much as breathes on any of us tonight, God help me, I'm going to rip his heart out," growled Bernard fidgeting in his seat.

Will sighed and said, "Have a drink and calm down. This will be the best food we've eaten in a month. I for one intend to enjoy it whether our murderous friend across there likes it or not."

⁓

After grace was said a procession of servants bearing food began to emerge from the other end of the hall. First came the bread and butter, followed by Baldwin and his assistants with the wine and ale.

"I hope Gifford feeds you well in Draychester," said Bishop Mone. "A good meal is a godly thing but it must be balanced in the correct way, isn't that so Thomas?"

Thomas looked at the bishop of Draychester's men and said somewhat apologetically. "My lord has made a study of good digestion."

The meal started with the appearance of a bowl of apples. The bishop of Draychester's men shifted uncomfortably in their seats. Bishop Mone's eccentricities were becoming apparent. Will said diplomatically, "Although Bishop Gifford's table is excellent my lord, I'm sure we'll have much to enjoy here as well."

"Indeed. Well, I'd start with the apples," said the bishop. "I always work from light to heavy, gives me bad guts otherwise. Still, feel free to suit yourself."

⁓

"Before Wales, where were you Mudstone?" asked Bishop Mone not really interested but trying to make conversation between his obviously hostile guests.

"In the north, I had some business to attend to. Before that Draychester and abroad, mainly France. I was there for many years."

"What brought you back?"

"My brother died. I came back to claim my inheritance."

Bernard gave an ironic laugh. Under the table Will stamped on the big man's foot.

"You find something amusing my friend?" asked Bishop Mone turning to Bernard.

"I knew his brother briefly," said Bernard, warming to his tale. "Very generous to the cathedral in Draychester. I'm sure Sir Roger will tell you as much himself." Bernard grinned maliciously at Sir Roger.

Bishop Mone said, "Ah, where would we be if not for those of such a generous disposition towards the church."

Sir Roger spluttered into his wine which brought an even bigger grin to Bernard's face.

With considerable will power Sir Roger simply said, "My brother was a difficult man my lord. He didn't always appreciate the interests of his family."

"Ah yes," said Bishop Mone with a wistful sigh, "Families, well we can't choose our parents or siblings can we? For good or bad we're stuck with them."

More food arrived at the table, lettuce, cabbage, purslane and herbs with chicken and kid goat.

Bernard gazing at Sir Roger with unconcealed hatred said, "Why don't you tell us about your brother's bequests to the church Mudstone? I'm sure the bishop would be interested to hear."

"I think not," said Sir Roger through clenched teeth.

"Come, come don't be bashful Sir Roger," said Bishop Mone, now intrigued.

"Let me enlighten the bishop for you Mudstone," said Bernard. "His brother left everything to the cathedral at Draychester except for some worthless manors in the north. The brothers loathed each other. Sir Roger kept one manor, the other he gave away to the cathedral. Not long after he attempted to burn that one to the ground. The priest of the place was roasted like a common hog. I saw it with my own eyes."

Bishop Mone looked at Sir Roger in horror and said, "Is this true Mudstone?"

Sir Roger jumped to his feet thumped the table, pointed at Bernard and roared, "You worthless, stinking, son of a whore. I'm going to gut you like the pig you are and send your innards back to your conniving bastard of a master."

Bishop Mone paled at the ferocity of the outburst. Bernard, much to Will's horror slowly rose from his seat, leant forward towards Sir Roger and hissed, "I wouldn't waste a piss on you if you were on fire. My own bishop has placed a price on this piece of dung's head."

"Gentlemen, please!" said Bishop Mone alarmed. "You're to be civil to each other while your under my roof. Sir Roger carries a pardon from the king himself. He's been on the king's service against the Welsh. His past sins and crimes have been set aside."

Bernard slowly sank back into his seat as did Sir Roger. "Mudstone's sins may have been set aside by the king my lord but not by me. I doubt whether our own bishop sees it that way either. This man burned a village and caused a priest to be burnt alive. I was there."

"So you say. Nevertheless, I'll have no violence between any man within the precinct or indeed within Saint Davids itself. You'll keep your quarrels for elsewhere."

Bishop Mone didn't attempt to make any more small talk with his visitors. He settled into a murmured conversation with his clerk Thomas and a little while later arrived the pork and beef with more vegetables and nuts.

Sir Roger sat at his end of the table slowly sipping wine his stare fixed on the three Draychester men. Will and

Osbert studiously avoiding his gaze, Bernard returning it with an equal ferocity.

Bernard said, "Look at him sat there, not a care in the world but us. I'd wager he's been on a murderous spree through Wales."

"Surely even our own bishop won't go against the king's pardon," said Will.

Bernard said through gritted teeth, "There are ways and means lad. A dark night can hide many things, who can say what might happen to the man."

Osbert shivered. "I for one wouldn't want to be anywhere near that devil on a dark night. He means to do us harm that's for certain."

Bernard slapped his hand down on the table, shaking the dishes. "Then we should strike first."

Will looked around in alarm. "Keep calm for pity's sake. Bishop Mone will have you locked up."

Only Sir Roger seemed to have noticed. He gave them a thin sneer. Will said thoughtfully, "There is something we could do without actually putting a dagger in his guts, at least for now. Those three trunks, I'll wager it's his plunder from Wales. He'll have picked the poor Welsh clean, the man's got a craving for wealth and all that it brings."

Osbert said, "Are you suggesting we rob him?"

Will shrugged. "I'd hardly call liberating a thief of his ill-gotten gains as theft."

Bernard chuckled. "He'd be as mad as hell. I can imagine his face now. It's clever, he can hardly claim he's been robbed else he'd be admitting he stole it in the first place. We take the coin from him and he'll follow where we lead."

"That servant of his, Travis, will know the truth of what's in the trunks," said Osbert.

"Don't worry. I'll beat it out of the miserable worm," said Bernard.

"Have a care," said Will. "Mudstone will likely kill the poor sod if he thinks he's been betrayed."

Bernard shrugged. "Travis made his choice a long time ago." He turned to Osbert.

"Osbert, regardless of what happens tonight, in the morning I need you to watch for the Phelpes brothers. I spoke to Thomas the bishop's clerk earlier. There's a room directly above the main gate where you can watch from the window. You know what they look like. If you spot them approaching the gate, you're to tell the gatekeepers."

"What do you mean, what's going to happen tonight?"

Will who had half an idea of what Bernard intended said, "Hold fast on your anger my friend, Mudstone can wait awhile yet."

Bernard smiled and simply said, "Humour me lads, I know what I'm about."

~

A large selection of cheeses had arrived at the table. Bernard said in a very loud voice, "How's your arse Mudstone?"

Sir Roger leant forward in his seat, his face erupting in a red flush of embarrassment and outraged anger. Bernard was pleased with the reaction and he took up the theme enthusiastically.

He said to Bishop Mone, "I only ask, you understand my lord, because the last time I clapped eyes on Sir Roger I'd just fired a crossbow bolt into his backside."

Bishop Mone looked between them alarmed and somewhat angry at the sudden eruption of hostilities once again. He held up a hand and said, "Please gentlemen hold your tongues, I grow weary of it, let things be whilst you're under my roof. I'll hear no more of this dispute."

Ignoring the bishops' plea Sir Roger said in a strangled voice, "That was you?"

Bernard grinned. "It was. I was aiming for your head mind. Still it was a bloody good shot for the distance. I'll wager you couldn't sit down for a month."

Sir Roger jumped up, the chair clattering to the floor behind him.

"You worthless turd. I'm going to gut you like an over ripe hog." He drew a slender dagger from under his tunic, squeezed round the end of the table and advanced on Bernard.

Bernard, still seated, smiled at him indulgently. "I'd like to see you try."

Bishop Mone stood up and pointed at Sir Roger. "Sit down now. There will be no more of this, put that weapon away at once."

Sir Roger never taking his eyes of Bernard said, "Shut up old man, this isn't your business."

Bishop Mone outraged shouted across the hall to the servants who had all stopped what they were doing and stood transfixed. "Fetch the guards and call the watch from the town. Do it now."

"Get up pig, so I can gut you," said Sir Roger to Bernard.

Bernard smiled again and said, "I don't think so," and then hurled his goblet of wine at Sir Roger's head. The goblet missed but a trail of wine splattered down the front of Sir Roger's tunic. He howled with rage and charged forward. Bernard jumped up and pushed the table over directly in his path. There was a cascade of pots and food that had Sir Roger's feet slipping from under him.

"Damn you," he shouted, enraged and scrambling to keep on his feet.

Bernard bent down and picked up a large earthenware jug. He hefted in one of his huge hands and thinking to use it as a club advanced.

Sir Roger snorted with contempt "You intend to do me harm with a jug?"

Before Bernard could answer, Sir Roger darted forward thrusting the blade at Bernard. The big man twisted to one side the dagger slashing through the tunic on his upper arm and drawing blood. He swung the other arm around and crashed the jug into the side of Sir Roger's head. It shattered and Sir Roger stumbled back momentarily stunned.

"There's your answer," said Bernard. He looked at his bloody arm and continued, "And it's going to take more than this scratch to stop me from tearing your head off."

Sir Roger sneered at him. "Will it be enough when this dagger is buried in your guts?" He came at Bernard again, thrusting the knife towards his stomach and forcing the big man to retreat down the hall. As he slowly moved backwards, Bernard desperately glanced around for a weapon he could use.

One of the guests sat mesmerised, a piece of chicken skewed on a small knife frozen on its way to his mouth as he watched the fight. Bernard snatched it out of his hand as he came level. He flicked the chicken at Sir Roger face. As the enraged man tried to batter it away, Bernard plunged the sharp little blade into the back of his hand. Sir Roger cried out in pain but he didn't drop the dagger. Bernard grinned at him and said, "Ouch, I bet that hurt."

Sir Roger used his other hand and pulled the blade out with a grunt. A thin trickle of blood left the wound and ran down his fingers. He flicked it away and a fat little man sat on one of the side tables got a crimson sprinkle across his front. He gasped at the sight and slumped his head onto the tabletop in a dead faint.

Sir Roger now with the dagger in one hand and the small blade in the other hissed, "I have two blades now and you have how many? Ah, that would be none." He swung the dagger towards Bernard's face whilst thrusting the smaller blade towards his middle. Bernard backed up again and took a quick glance behind. He was almost at the wooden partition at the back of the hall. It shielded the entrance to the stairs that led down to the kitchens.

Servants and guests scattered around them as he continued to dodge Sir Roger's lunges. Bernard reached out an arm and grabbed a wooden platter from the table. A dish of sweet pastries flew into the air as he turned it sideways to use as a shield. He brought his arm around and battered Sir Roger with the platter, his opponent's dagger embedding itself deep in the wood. He tried unsuccessfully to tug it loose. All the while Bernard continuing to push the platter forward and downwards trying to crush the other man into the floor using his sheer bulk to advantage. Sir Roger strained against the weight and tried to slash at Bernard's legs with the smaller blade. At the last second before his own legs buckled Sir Roger threw himself sideways out from under the platter. He sprawled on the floor, gasping for breath. With the sudden loss of resistance Bernard toppled forward and planted his own face into the rush-strewn planks. Sir Roger scrambled to his feet and came at him with the small blade clenched in his bleeding hand. Bernard gasping with exertion rolled to one side under a table before the other man had time to thrust the knife into his back.

"Damn you bishop's man," roared Sir Roger, "why are you making this so hard."

Bernard popped up from the other side of the table. He stood there with the table in between them and leant on the wall for a second to catch his breath. He grinned at Sir Roger. "I'm enjoying this. It's been a good while since I've had such a scrap. Truth is, I think I may be getting a little old for it. A real man would have dispatched me by now."

Sir Roger reached down and pulled his dagger loose from the wooden tray and pointed it at Bernard. "God help me I'm going to skin you alive you son of a whore."

Bernard shrugged. "Well, anything's possible, you can try I suppose." With that he grabbed hold of the end of the table and thrust it around to keep it between himself and Sir Roger then darted into the doorway in the wooden partition behind. Servants pressed themselves to the narrow stone walls of the little corridor as he barged past shouting, "Out of my way." He clattered down the stairs emerging into the kitchen below.

Sir Roger wrenched the table out of the way, dived through the doorway and plunged down the stairs after him, his feet hardly touching the steps in the process.

The kitchen proved to offer a much better selection of weapons than the great hall. Everywhere he looked, Bernard was spoilt for choice. Shocked serving staff and cooks looked back at the wild-looking figure before them.

"Get out of the kitchen now," he roared, flailing his arms about for effect. They didn't wait for a second order and bolted en-mass through the entryway into the storerooms of the undercroft.

On a tabletop in front of him were three small bowls of steaming fat that one of the cooks had ladled off the top of a stew. As his opponent clattered down the stairs, he hurled them at the opening. Sir Roger emerged from the doorway and was rewarded with a splattering of hot fat that caught him across the chest and neck. He howled in pain, dropping the dagger to the floor as he fought to scrape the sticky fat off his bare flesh, burning his hands in the process.

Bernard laughed at him. "You lucky sod, I was aiming to take your eyes out." He reached over to the fire and pulled a large iron skillet from the embers. It was empty apart from the greasy residue of whatever had been cooked in it earlier. He held it in one hand as though it was a bat and grunted in satisfaction. Sir Roger charged at him like an enraged bull. Bernard sidestepped and caught him a glancing whack on the shoulder with the skillet that sent his opponent spinning away.

Bernard grinned. "That was fun. Want to do it again?"

Sir Roger scrambled on the work surface behind him and found a bowl of unbroken eggs. He started hurling them at Bernard who defy deflected each one with the skillet. A shower of broken shell and egg yolk splattered the white-washed walls of the kitchen and Sir Roger in equal measure. Bernard laughed.

An increasingly frustrated Sir Roger said, "You think this a game you turd? I'll teach you some manners yet."

Over the fire was an elaborate spit composed of a long iron rod threaded through two iron hoops embedded in the fireplace. In the corner was a small trembling figure, the spit boy, pressed into the stonework, terrified. Sir Roger pulled the boy out of the corner and held him as a shield in front, an arm pressed around the boy's throat. With the other hand he wrenched the iron rod from its fittings, cursing as the hot metal burnt his hands. He now had a formidable weapon.

"Leave the child be, this is our fight," said Bernard.

It was Sir Roger's turn to laugh. "Sentimentality will be the death of you, whore son."

He thrust the rod forward, barely missing Bernard's head. Bernard resisted retaliating with the skillet for fear of harming the boy. He looked at Sir Roger with contempt. "You cowedly worm," he spat.

Sir Roger pressed forward, jabbing the rod repeatedly at Bernard, forcing him back. Again and again he jabbed dragging the boy with him. Finally, Sir Roger had Bernard against the wall of the kitchen. He pulled the rod back for the final killer thrust. The spit boy promptly bit into the fleshly part of Sir Roger's upper arm leaving a bloody imprint of teeth. Sir Roger roared in pain and flung the boy aside.

Bernard shouted, "Run boy," and then with all the force he could muster, swung the skillet with both hands and smashed it into the side of Sir Roger's face. Sir Roger was lifted off his feet and went headfirst into a side of beef that hung from an iron hook in the ceiling. His momentum took it down onto the floor with him in a lover's embrace. He rolled over with it pinning him to the ground. He moaned once, struggled to lift it off himself but his strength was spent.

Bernard took a dirty cloth from the worktop, wrapped it around his hand and took a hot iron out of the fire. On the opposite side of the kitchen Sir Roger lay groaning and spitting teeth. Bernard held up the iron to him and said cheerfully. "I was looking forward to some mulled wine but I think this can be put to some better purpose."

Sir Roger stared back with bloodshot hate-filled eyes. "You wouldn't dare," he mumbled from the ruin of his mouth. "The bishop will have you hanged if you kill me."

Bernard nodded. "I'll wager you're probably right, the

bishop will have me strung up if I dispatch you here. But don't worry. I'll just have to be patient. I'll leave you with something to remember me by."

He walked over and placed a knee on the side of beef pinning Sir Roger to the floor. He stared down at him and said, "I'm not much good with my Latin. Just a smattering here and there. I do know the word for dead, it's Mortuus." He proceeded to use the hot iron to burn a letter M onto Sir Roger's left cheek up close to his nose. When the other man had stopped howling, Bernard said, "It's the first letter of your name as well, that'll be handy."

There was a clattering from the stairs and six heavily armed men emerged into the kitchen. Swords drawn and levelled they surrounded Bernard who still had his knee on the beef. One of them looked down at Sir Roger who had now passed out and said, "I hope you haven't killed the sod. The bishop is already angrier than I've seen him in years."

"He's still breathing, just," said Bernard wearily getting to his feet and dropping the still glowing iron.

"What the hell is that on his face?" asked another.

"He had an accident," said Bernard. He didn't resist as they tied his hands together behind his back and shoved him towards the stairs.

∽

Sir Roger lay unconscious in the courtyard at Bernard's feet. Two of the gatekeepers, swords drawn, were either side of the big man. Bishop Mone stood in front of them with more armed men called from the watch of Saint Davids. The courtyard was full of curious onlookers, pilgrims from the guesthouse, servants and canons from the cathedral. Osbert and Will stood close by, worried at the turn of events.

Travis was knelt down beside Sir Roger checking his battered master for signs of life. The M burnt into Sir Roger's cheek was now an angry red raised welt.

"Is he dead?" asked Travis somewhat hopefully.

"Afraid not," said Bernard.

Bishop Mone red faced and shaking with rage said, "Did I not warn you. It's outrageous, your bishop will hear of this, do you hear me?" He pressed his face up close to Bernard's, who merely blinked back at him.

"Well have you nothing to say man?" he spluttered.

"I'm sorry my lord. You saw yourself, I was provoked."

Thomas the clerk, worried for his master's health reached a hand out to the bishop's shoulder. "My lord, please let me deal with this. I beg you, don't exert yourself."

Bishop Mone spun around and almost spat in the clerk's face. "Just get them both out of my sight. They're to be on the next ship that leaves Porthclais. I don't care if it's going to Ireland or the bloody Holy land. Do you hear me? You'll put them on board. As for now, lock them up in the gatehouse dungeon."

Thomas said, "I'll see to it my lord. Now please, I beg of you, exert yourself no more."

The bishop, his rage suddenly subsiding and weariness taking over, simply said, "I'm too old for this. Have I not earned the right to a peaceful old age? I'm to my bed. Do not disturb me until tomorrow evening at the earliest."

He turned his back on them all and slowly walked off towards the bishop's hall and his private chambers. Thomas looked at the guards and said, "You heard the bishop's orders. Stick them in the gatehouse dungeon. It'll be better for everyone if we manage to get rid of them sooner than later. I've no idea what boats are in at Porthclais but it'll have to wait for tomorrow now."

The two gatekeepers dragged Sir Roger away by his feet, not taking too much care how many times his head banged across the rough courtyard. At the gateway to the bishop's palace they were joined by two of the yard lads who grasped Sir Roger's arms and between them they hauled him off past the cathedral and up the steps towards the east gatehouse of the precinct.

Bernard hissed at Will, "Get over to the guesthouse and find those trunks, there'll never be a better time."

"What about you", whispered Will.

"Don't worry about me lad, it's not the first time I've been locked up and it won't be the last."

He was soon being pushed along in the same direction as Sir Roger flanked by several members of the watch.

Will tapped Osbert gently on the arm and they slipped away toward the guesthouse.

## 19

## TREASURE IN THE GUESTHOUSE

The undercroft below the guesthouse was dark. Although Will had taken a candle from their chamber it gave out only a feeble glow. The space was a graveyard of all the things you might need again but never would. There were woodworm ridden tables, split buckets, bits of old rope, broken chairs and a hundred other abandoned items.

Will leading the way around the various obstacles in their path said, "I doubt they've cleaned out down here for twenty years."

"Are you sure you know where you're going?" asked Osbert dubiously.

"I parted with a penny to one of the yard lads earlier. He says there's a locked storeroom against the back wall. Mudstone had the trunks dragged all the way down here and into the storeroom. Locked it himself."

"And he's given you the key?" asked Osbert sarcastically.

"I don't need the key my friend, you'll see. Ah, here we are."

Will held the candle up and looked at a thick wooden

door, secured with a lock. Osbert tried the latch, but the door was solid. "It's no use, we're not going to be able to get in there. Even if we do, we're never going to get them out of here without being seen."

Will fished under his tunic and brought out a short little iron pick.

"What's that?" said Osbert curiously.

Will gave him a look. "Sometimes I wonder about you Osbert I really do." He pushed the pick into the lock with a practiced hand and within a few moments he had the door open.

"I forget you have a criminal past," said Osbert.

The room was small, no more than a pace or two long and the same across. The three chests were stacked on top of each other against the stonework of the back wall of the undercroft.

Osbert said, "They look like the chests in the cathedral at Draychester."

"That's probably because he's looted them from a church."

Osbert was outraged. "How can he commit such a crime? It's sacrilege?"

Will shrugged. "I don't think Mudstone was thinking about his eternal soul while he was massacring the Welsh with axe, sword, hammer and bow. Anyway, do something useful and help me move this one onto the floor."

Between them they lifted the top trunk of the three down. It was a simple oak chest bound with iron hoops with a lock. Will swiftly got to work, and the lock was soon opened. He lifted the lid and found it was stuffed with bulging leather bags. Slowly lifting one out he weighed it in a hand then loosened the drawstring around the top and poured silver coins into his other hand.

Osbert's eyes bulged, he licked dry lips and said, "Are they all full of coin?"

Will returned the coins to the bag, bent down and picked another bag up and handed it to Osbert. "See for yourself."

With shaking hands, Osbert poured silver coins out into his own palm. "Dear God, there must be a king's ransom in there, all robbed from the Welsh."

"Not all from the Welsh. I'd wager some it is English silver as well. I don't think Mudstone cares from which side of the border he takes it"

"What now?"

"Let's see what's in the others."

They lifted another chest down beside the first and Will picked the lock. At first sight the contents were somewhat of a disappointment. They looked like a pile of dirty linen rags. Will reached in and found there was something wrapped within each rag. He lifted one out. It felt heavy. Unwrapping the rag he caught the glint of gold in the candlelight. In his hand sat a plain gold cross. He unwrapped another heavy bundle and out came a silver plate. "These have been taken from some church."

Will slowly emptied the chest and a steady pile of precious objects emerged. When he finished, he opened the last chest and found it perhaps a third full of loose pennies.

Osbert shivered. "Put it back Will, put it all back, it's cursed. I'm scared for our souls if we take this from him."

"Rather it's with our bishop and let him decide its fate than with Mudstone. God alone knows what mischief he'd get up to with this wealth. "

"Promise me you'll take nothing for yourself, you'll burn for it if you do."

Will with a shiver himself turned to Osbert and said, "I

don't think I've ever been less tempted my friend. This is blood money if ever there was. We'll deprive Mudstone of it but its fate is in the hands of Bishop Gifford. Perhaps he'll hand it over to the king, perhaps not. At least it won't be our decision to make."

"What will we do?"

"Empty as much as we can and fill these chests with something else to give them a bit of weight. We'll start with that chest full of coin bags."

Osbert said, "There's a cart full of cabbages and turnips in the yard. I saw it earlier. They were filling some sacks with them and loading them up onto it."

Will smirked. "I'd like to see the bastard's face when he opens the trunk and finds it full of cabbages. We need to drag some of those sacks down here, we can swap the vegetables for Mudstone's loot."

∼

The chests were tightly packed with alternating layers of turnips and cabbages then stacked back on top of each other. Will locked each one and also the door of the storeroom leaving everything as close as possible to how they had found it.

When they were done they dragged the heavy sacks of Sir Roger's loot to the bottom of the stairs and stood panting wondering what to do with them.

"We can't hide these easily, what are we to do?" asked Osbert.

Will thought for a moment then shook his head. "You're wrong, we can hide them in plain sight in amongst the other vegetable sacks on the cart. Just make sure we find out where it's going."

"I already know that, it goes to the bishop's palace at Lamphey."

"You'd think one palace would be enough," said Will.

"By all accounts he hardly ever leaves here now. Lamphey was his retreat during the summer months."

"Why am I surprised? Anyway, it doesn't matter as long as the cart takes them away from here. They can be retrieved before they get too far."

"How long do you think Bishop Mone will keep Bernard and Mudstone locked up?"

"I'll talk to Thomas the clerk tomorrow morning. Perhaps the bishop's anger will have cooled by then. God forbid he puts Bernard on a ship to Ireland. With luck, the only ships in harbour over the next day or two will be heading to Pembroke. I'm sure they'll be glad to see the back of us all."

"What can I do?"

"You Osbert, can follow Bernard's instructions and watch for the Phelpes brothers tomorrow. There's still a debt to be settled there."

∼

The following morning, Will sought out Thomas, Bishop Mone's clerk. He found him at his little table in the bishop's hall. He looked up from his scattered papers and said, "Before you ask, which I know you're about to, I believe your friend can cool his heels in the bishop's dungeon for a while longer yet. "

"Then the good bishop is still angry?" asked Will.

"His anger has cooled somewhat but not enough that I dare let your friend out, as much as I might want to. It'll do him no harm for a day or two. By the look of him it won't be the first time he's been locked up and I'll make sure he's well fed."

"And what of Mudstone?"

"The same. I've said as much to that servant of his, Travis I think he's called. There'll be a ship either late today or tomorrow. When it leaves, you're all to be on it. The same goes for that hothead Mudstone."

"You think it's wise both of them on the same ship?"

"I'm to instruct the master to make sure they are chained up below until you reach Pembroke. After that I wash my hands of any responsibility. You can see the bishop is not a well man and I won't let him be disturbed further."

"I'm sorry Thomas, truly I am, that was never our intention. Mudstone bears a grudge against my lord, Bishop Gifford, it would have come to this wherever our paths had crossed his."

Thomas simply sighed as though all the cares in the world were on his shoulders. "I don't doubt that my young friend and if all the rumours are true about him, you'd be wise to stay out of his way."

## 20

## GIFFORD AND SCRIVENER

Bishop Gifford of Draychester sat down opposite his old friend. He sipped from his wine goblet and watched Scrivener sort through the piles of parchment, notes and letters which littered the table. Eventually he nodded towards the papers and said, "Your nephew Osbert seems to be perhaps over dutiful?"

Scrivener lifted his gaze and smiled. "He does seem to be following his instructions to a degree most would find insufferable. He takes after my sister," he said dryly. He continued to sift through the growing mound of correspondence. "He'll have used up most of the allowance for the trip on messengers and couriers alone. I've only been passing on the more relevant details to you my lord. I fear the state of his feet and the current cost of pies in Tenby would be a distraction."

Gifford chuckled. "On the contrary my old friend, it's always good to know the price of a pie. The feet, I agree, I could do without knowing about."

Scrivener gave him an indulgent smile, rubbed his eyes tiredly and said, "Aside from the sheer quantity of his output, which is somewhat overwhelming, he has actually passed on some useful information. The boy has a keen ear and a keener eye. You agree we need to act on this unfortunate business regarding Phelpes the vintner? Perhaps officially a strongly worded letter to the Constable at Pembroke Castle to rein in the mayor of Tenby?"

Gifford rubbed the rough stubble on his chin in thought. "I agree our official action is to send a messenger to Pembroke with our concerns. Now, unofficially of course, the mayor's ships could suffer an unfortunate impounding at Bristol. Unpaid customs duties, that sort of thing. As for the man himself, I suppose he could sustain a very painful and debilitating accident in Tenby harbour. Nothing fatal, we don't want to upset the applecart entirely."

Scrivener grinned maliciously, "The mayor is far from blameless in all this, it seems clear to me he encouraged the rift between Phelpes and his sons and the theft of the wine. A few broken limbs perhaps my lord? The handling of cargo is a risky and dangerous occupation after all."

"By all means, that sounds quite appropriate and can I just say what a nasty and devious mind you have Scrivener."

"Ah, you're far too kind my lord. I'll make the required arrangements. Shame about the elder Phelpes, Thomas as was."

Gifford rolled the wine around in his goblet. "Indeed, the man certainly knew his wines, if not his sons. Have we heard any news about the murdering siblings?"

"Not yet my lord. Even with Osbert's impressive scribbling we are days behind the events by the time dispatches reach us."

Gifford's eyes sparkled. "What an adventure Scrivener. Bernard is as solid as a rock and those two lads will have some tales to tell when they get back. Oh to be young again, eh my friend?"

"I'm sure they'll be enjoying every waking moment my lord," said Scrivener with only a trace of the irony he felt.

Gifford turned to face the fire and stared into its flames in a contemplative mood.

"Tell me old friend, have you felt something strange in the atmosphere here in Draychester recently? I can't quite put my finger on it, just a feeling somebody meddles in our affairs somehow."

Scrivener looked up sharply from the papers, concern in his eyes. "You think we have a spy amongst us?"

Gifford shrugged. "I'm not sure. As I said it's just a feeling I get sometimes. You know me of old, I'll always use my brains but sometimes you need to listen to your gut as well."

Scrivener poured himself some wine and said, "I know of the obvious spies and informers of course, and I feed them what they want to hear. They serve us better untouched. Every noble household has them."

Gifford nodded, "I don't doubt you keep a tally of the worms amongst us Scrivener. They serve their purpose I agree. No, this is something different from a mere spy, malignant, evil perhaps. I've had the feeling only a few times before, always in battle. All I ask is that you stay vigilant old friend."

Scrivener nodded and said firmly, "Always my lord, always."

∾

Scrivener simply knew the man as "The Rat". Oh he knew his real name, but he'd thought of him as "The Rat" for so long no other name had any meaning. When he wanted something of a dubious nature done in Draychester itself, the man was invaluable. The Rat if not friends, was at least acquaintances with some of the lowest and most unpleasant characters that skulked the city streets. He could go places and do things that Scrivener couldn't.

They were meeting in an ill-lit alehouse close to the tanner's quarter. The landlord kept a quiet corner free for Scrivener on request, and the ale was just about drinkable. As for the rest of the clientele, well they knew how to mind their own business.

Scrivener rested his chin on his hands and softly asked the Rat, "If I were looking to interfere in the affairs of the nobles who would I go to in Draychester?"

The Rat looked somewhat bewildered. "Well, that would be you master of course."

"Discounting me. Who would you approach?"

The Rat rubbed a hand over his rough stubble. "Depends what the job was and how much coin was involved. Things to do with the nobles are always dangerous and expensive."

"Oh this would be dangerous stuff all right and plenty of coin would change hands."

The Rat looked at him curiously. "Well, I suppose that would be narrowing it down a bit. And you say this isn't you asking master?"

"No forget me, pretend it's before our good bishop and myself came here. This person paid well, but he was devious, mean and certainly a dangerous individual to know. Maybe something strange about him, a touch of evil some might say."

"Evil? Before you came you say?"

"Yes, think back."

The man shuffled uncomfortably in his chair. Scrivener said, "I can see you want to say something. Spit it out."

"A long time ago, in old Bishop Thorndyke's time, there might have been somebody like that around."

"What do you mean might have been?"

"It was a long time ago, and I was just a lad you understand, learning the trade."

"Get to the point."

"Old Bishop Thorndyke, he didn't like to get his hands dirty in this sort of business. I would run errands for him sometimes. I'd take a message up to an alehouse at the crossroads out on the east road."

"I know the place."

The Rat looked at him in surprise, "Wouldn't have thought you'd know about such a place, you hobnobbing with the nobles and such."

"I didn't say I've been there myself. I do however know of its reputation."

"It's a shite hole, was then and is now."

"So I've heard. Who is it you'd meet there and what kind of messages did you take?"

The Rat glanced around as if uneasy and leaned in closer. "Used to be this friar who'd hang around town. Never seemed to do much of anything really, he was just always there if you know what I mean. Anyway, Old Thorny would send me to meet him at the alehouse every few months. I'd pass on letters and such. Sometimes I'd hand over coins, sometimes I'd collect a payment. Old Thorny was up to all sorts of no good in those days. Devious sod he was."

"So this friar was the man you feared?"

"No, not him, he was just doing the same as me. His master was the one pulling the strings."

"So who was his master?"

"Once I followed the friar back from the alehouse. It was a stupid thing to do, but I was just a lad and curious. Still, I was good even then and I swear he never saw me. By the time we got back to the city it'd gone past the curfew bell and the gates were shut."

"I take it that didn't stop you getting back in."

"Of course not, there are ways and means as you well know. The friar didn't have any problems either. He was never a real friar that much I do know."

"You followed him into the city itself?"

"I did. He slunk along the back alleys like a thief. I could barely keep up with him."

"And where did he lead you, this pretend friar?"

"To the cathedral precinct. There's a hole in the wall where the cooks throw out the scraps from the kitchens. I've used it many a time myself after dark. You need to be nimble on your feet and not mind the smell."

"Once within the precinct walls he went to the bishop's palace?"

"No, he went into the cathedral and I followed. The Compline prayers had been said. The place was mostly dark apart from the candles at the shrines. He went and sat on that seat set in the wall halfway up the nave. He waited what seemed an age."

"I know it. Not a place I'd choose to sit in the dark."

"I was hidden behind one of the great pillars. Close enough to eavesdrop and if needs be, to swiftly slip away. Truth be told I was desperate for a piss and I'd made my mind up to leave."

Scrivener couldn't help but laugh. "So before you emptied your bladder, what happened?"

"Suddenly there was another figure by the friar's side. Hooded he was. I swear I didn't see him arrive, and I never saw his face. One minute the friar was on his own the next he had company. I could tell he was surprised he jumped a good foot."

"You heard what passed between them?"

"I heard the friar pass on what Old Thorny had told me to tell him. Some intrigue so long since concluded, I forget the details. There was an exchange of coin, both seemed satisfied. The friar left first, I remained behind the pillar. I had it in mind to follow the hooded fellow and discover who he was."

"And so?"

"As the friar passed me I slid further around the pillar. When I moved back around, the hooded man was stood right there beside the pillar. The hair stood up on the back of my neck. I'm not ashamed to say I near wet myself."

"You being ready for a piss anyway," said Scrivener with a smirk.

"Now don't mock me master, you weren't there, and I was still a young lad in those days."

"Go on then, indulge me, what did this mysterious hooded figure have to say?"

"He grabbed my arm. Bloody painful it was, I would have run if I could have. His hand was cold and leathery, an old man's hand I reckon. He said I was too curious for my own good and if I wanted to play this game, I'd need to be more cautious."

"You still didn't see his face?"

"Kept his head down the whole time. His face hidden by his cloak."

"What did he sound like then, a noble perhaps?"

"No, not a noble. Cleric I'd say, I can't be sure, but that's what my gut told me. Just something about him; and his cloak was good quality but not something a noble would wear."

"Is that it, that's all he said to you?"

"Well he pressed a coin into my hand. For my trouble he said. Oh, and he farted."

"He farted?"

"Proper old man's fart, stank it did, he chuckled about it then he was gone."

"You didn't try to follow?"

"Of course I didn't, I was bloody terrified."

"You've not come across him since, or the friar?"

"Let's just say I didn't go seeking him out then and I haven't since. You need to know when to leave things well alone in this game, at least if you want to stay alive. Makes me shudder just thinking about him even after all this time."

"And the friar, what became of him?"

"You might well ask. Not long after he ended up down that deep well at the end of Pennygrope lane."

"A bad end. You helped him on his way?"

"Not me. Old Thorndyke might have ordered it I suppose, or maybe the hooded man himself. I don't know who did it and I wasn't stupid enough to go asking about it either. It was no accident though. When they hauled him out, it was obvious someone had bashed his head in before he entered the water."

∼

The Rat hurried away from the meeting. Scrivener's questions had unnerved him. He hadn't thought of the hooded man in years yet his feet brought him to the entrance of a dark passageway behind the marketplace. This was the alley where he'd watched the friar's broken body being carried from. He remembered the sopping wet corpse with its caved in head only too well. Pennygrope Lane, as its name implied, was a place where a penny could buy you some company at any hour of the day. He stopped and peered into the gloom. He could see two dark figures pressed up against a wall. Business seemed as brisk as ever. A woman's voice called softly, "Won't be a minute my love, we're nearly finished. Just wait there and I'll be with you shortly. Get your penny ready."

The Rat smiled and whispered back, "Long time since I needed to spend money down Pennygrope Lane my girl."

He chuckled and moved away into the brighter space of the marketplace. As he made his way home, he wondered if he should have told Scrivener everything. The hooded man's fart, as ridiculous as it sounded, he'd smelled it since. Scrivener would have laughed in his face, but the more he thought about it, the more he knew it was true. If only he could remember where.

## 21

## ON WATCH

Osbert was tired. He'd been watching from the window of the gatehouse for hours. For most of the morning the sun had been streaming into the room above the gate. It was warm, and he was getting sleepy. He'd come with a meal of bread and cheese and now that he'd consumed the lot his eyelids felt heavy. He rested his head on his hands on the windowsill and tried to focus.

At first he'd been watching every arrival at the gate, looking for the Phelpes brothers. But, truth be told, there was a constant stream of pilgrims and others with business in the precinct passing through the gate below. The very nature of pilgrimage meant many were disfigured and covered their faces, all seeking a miracle cure at the shrine of Saint David. He'd tried his best, but he wasn't sure he'd even spot the Phelpes brothers if they were stood in front of him. All they'd need to do was cover their faces with a hood. The only way would be to pull the cover from every disfigured soul seeking entry. He shuddered at the very thought.

Outside the gate, as at every cathedral in the land, stood a mix of professional beggars, souvenir sellers and hawkers of pies with fillings of dubious origin. The pilgrims had to run the gauntlet of these unofficial guardians of the gate before they could pass into the precinct.

He'd got quite used to the regular ebb and flow of the throng below as it jostled its way to the gate. Which is why the two figures first came to his attention. If he'd been stood down at the gate himself, he probably wouldn't have noticed them through the crowd around the entrance. It was only from above that they revealed themselves as something out of the ordinary.

The two figures wore heavy riding cloaks with their hoods up. As the day was warm, they must have been sweating, although they could have good reason for the hoods if they were lepers. The problem was they didn't flow with the rest of the pilgrims, but floated around the edges of the throng as though waiting.

Osbert studied them intently from his window but try as he might he couldn't see their faces. They obviously intended to enter the precinct but there didn't seem to be any logical reason for them not to follow the throng, unless they were nervous of something. He decided the safest thing was to make his way down to the gate.

He hurried down the narrow stone steps and emerged just under the gate. The two gatekeepers were on the opposite side of the entrance. He tried to attract their attention, but a mass of people were pushing through the gateway in both directions. He stepped out into the stream of people and pushed his way through.

"Thought you'd gone to sleep up there lad. What's up?"

"It might be nothing, but there are two figures hanging about on the fringes of the crowd. If they're real pilgrims, I can't see any reason they wouldn't come through the gate."

"You think it's your two sanctuary seekers then?"

"I can't be sure, they're just behaving oddly."

"We can't be stopping everyone who looks a bit odd from wanting to come in lad, it'd be chaos. We need to keep them moving through."

The other gatekeeper nodded his agreement. "I've seen just about everything doing this job. Nothing surprises me these days. Do you realise how much coin this lot contributes to the cathedral?"

"I understand. It's the same at Draychester, but will you humour me and stop these two if they try to enter?"

"We'll certainly ask them their business and you can take a closer look and see if you recognise them. The bishop's orders are to stop them entering if they're your boys."

"What they seeking sanctuary from then?" sniffed the other man.

"Murdered their own father."

"Gawd. Nasty one that, it's a hanging at the very least. Worse if the wrong people catch up with them," he said eyeing up Osbert speculatively.

"We want to see justice done that's all."

"Well then lad, I suggest you go and stand at the bottom of the stair doorway over there. Keep out of sight, you don't want to frighten them off."

Osbert squeezed his way across the narrow gateway between the hurrying pilgrims and positioned himself two steps up the stairway. Close enough to see but mostly hidden from all but the most curious passerby."

His legs got stiff stood on the stone stairway. Minutes passed without the two figures trying to enter. Osbert began to think they'd decided not to chance their luck even though they must be desperate. Perhaps they had anticipated that the bishop's men would surely be looking for them here.

But suddenly he saw the two dark cloaked figures

approach. His stomach lurched in anticipation. One of the gatekeepers looked across at him and he gave a nod. The larger of the two stepped out and blocked the cloaked figures's way

They tried to step around him but he moved into their path once again.

"Hang on there friend. You're a pilgrim?"

Osbert heard a familiar voice reply, "We are sir, let us pass I beg you, for we're lepers seeking Saint David's blessing, perhaps he'll heal us."

The gatekeeper stepped back a pace, as if ready to move out of the way. "Lepers is it?" he nodded amiably before his hand shot out and flicked the hood of the lead figure back.

Richard Phelpes blinked back at him. Osbert stumbled from the doorway and cried, "It's them!"

Richard's gaze flicked to Osbert and then back to the gatekeeper, who he then shoved hard. The gatekeeper fell backwards onto the cobbles, scattering pilgrims as he went down. There were angry shouts and a jumble of arms and legs as people struggled to get up. David Phelpes jumped over the struggling gatekeeper and both brothers ran onwards barging through the crowd. Osbert struggled out of the doorway and dodged around startled pilgrims. He ran towards the steps to the cathedral. Ahead of him the Phelpes brothers were hurtling downwards, three steps at a time. They exited the bottom of the steps and charged along the last stretch to the cathedral's east door scattering pilgrims and disappeared inside.

Osbert followed as fast as he could, knowing it was already too late. He entered the cathedral and looked towards the high altar just in time to see the two brothers collapse on the altar steps gasping for breath. A curious crowd soon gathered in front of them. A canon pushed past and demanded to know what the commotion was about.

David said, "We're claiming sanctuary, go tell who needs to know. We'll not be moving from here."

"And what crime do you flee from?" asked the canon sceptically. "You don't look like our normal cases. If you've short changed your customers, then you'd be better off taking your chances with the town council."

Richard glared at him and said, "Murder is our crime friend, not some petty theft."

The canon blanched.

## 22

## TRIAL AT THE CHAPTER HOUSE

Will, feeling guilty at leaving Osbert on his own at the gatehouse, had already started to make his way up from the bishop's palace when the commotion started. He saw the two figures shoot out of the gatehouse and come hurtling down the stairs towards the cathedral. He swore under his breath, he had no doubt it was the Phelpes brothers. He ran across the small bridge that separated the bishop's palace from the rest of the cathedral precinct. He was too late to intercept them before they entered the cathedral. In any case the path was thronged with pilgrims and he wasn't about to knock them aside in the brutal fashion the desperate brothers had. There was an angry buzz amongst the crowd as various figures got to their feet or were hauled up by concerned companions. Will, joining the mass, was almost swept off his feet as the angry crowd surged forward and pushed their way through the entrance into the cathedral.

He found Osbert inside.

"It's too late, I saw them but they managed to push past the gatekeepers. I'm sorry Will."

Will stood beside him and shrugged resignedly. "Don't be sorry Osbert, it's not your fault. Fate seems to be against us my friend."

Osbert gestured at the brothers sprawled against the altar. "And the brothers, they escape justice? It doesn't seem fair."

"Fair, no I suppose it's not. Still, I dare say we may be able to influence things a little."

"I don't understand."

"You explained the process to me Osbert. The coroner is still to be called. The fugitives need to admit their guilt and the port of departure to be decided."

"It could be days before all that happens. I hope we'll be on our way home long before then."

Will spied Thomas the bishop's clerk pushing his way through the crowd. He joined them staring at the spectacle of the two fugitives sat beneath the altar.

"I take it those two are the ones you sought."

"The very same."

He sighed wearily. "You do seem to have brought me a burden of problems. Now these two have claimed sanctuary you realise they have forty days to decide their fate."

"I understand but they don't have to wait the full forty days, they could be persuaded to decide at any time. If you were to summon the coroner then this mess could be over with today."

Thomas rubbed his chin in thought. "For the sake of the bishop's health, and regaining some peace about the place, I'm of a mind to be persuaded. I'll have to speak with the bishop of course, as it's not my decision to make."

"I'm sure your opinion will make all the difference. The coroner, where does he reside?"

"The coroner is the mayor of Saint Davids, he answers to Bishop Mone."

Will grinned. "How convenient."

∼

Will stood against the back wall of the chapter house as the mayor, acting as coroner gestured to his clerk. The clerk said to the Phelpes brothers, "Place your hand on the holy book." They shuffled forward on their knees and each placed a hand on a corner of the bible which sat on a golden cloth before them. The clerk continued. "You will swear to the following. You will leave the realm and never return without the express permission of our lord the king or his heirs. You will hasten by the direct road to the port allotted to you and not leave the King's Highway under pain of arrest or execution. You will not stay at one place more than one night and will seek diligently for a passage across the sea as soon as you arrive, delaying only one tide if possible. If you cannot secure such passage, you will walk into the sea up to your knees every day as a token of your desire to leave. Do you so swear?"

"I do so swear," both murmured.

The men made to get up. The coroner growled, "Stay down you churls, we haven't finished yet." They sank down again. The coroner glared at his clerk who started to speak again.

"You will cast off your own clothing, which will be confiscated and sold. You will be provided with sackcloth only and you will walk bareheaded, carrying a wooden cross before you, made with your own hands. You will tell any that question what you are and you must take care not to stray from the highway nor stay in any one place more than one night. If you ever set foot in this realm again you will be declared outlaw and your life forfeit. You will be given enough coins to buy passage. As for the port of departure that is at the coroner's discretion. Master?"

The coroner smiled cunningly. Will knew he'd had his instructions from Thomas the bishop's clerk. "Porthclais had crossed my mind, after all it's but a mile or so from here. The crossing to Ireland is short." The two men, both still on their knees, sighed with relief. Then the coroner spoke again. "However, I thought it more appropriate that it be Tenby."

There was a collective intake of breath around the room. The two men struggled to their feet visibly shaking. Richard Phelpes said, "Are you mad? We can't go back to Tenby that's where we have fled from. It's a virtual death sentence. We came here for sanctuary."

"Silence! You've heard my decision, you gave up any rights when you admitted your guilt. I suggest in the little time you have left you prepare for the journey ahead. I fear it may be challenging."

"You put him up to this," hissed David Phelpes pointing accusingly at Will.

Will, still leaning against the wall, simply shrugged. "It's the choices you made all by yourself that have led you here. Don't lay the blame at anyone else's feet. I'll be sure to pray for your father, he didn't deserve this."

"Bastard," said Richard. Will wasn't sure if it was directed at him or the coroner. He didn't suppose it made a great deal of difference.

## 23

## DEPARTURES

The struggling man lunged forward in an attempted head butt. The sergeant jerked out of the way at the last second. Two more members of the watch grabbed Sir Roger's arms and restrained him.

"Easy Sir Roger. It's nothing personal, it's the bishop's direct orders."

"Do you realise who I am? I've dispatched a thousand worms like you before breakfast."

The sergeant said, "That's as maybe but we're not letting you loose. Now if you'll be so kind as to refrain from attacking myself and my men, we'll get you safe away down to the harbour. There's a ship in from Pembroke. It returns there before nightfall and you're to be on it."

"Listen you cretin. I'm not going anywhere without my property. I've three trunks and my idiot servant, Travis."

"No need for that tone sir, we're only doing the bishop's bidding. Your trunks are already loaded up on the cart. Your servant is waiting outside."

"And I'm to be tied up like some common criminal?"

"I've had my instructions. The bishop says you're to be

restrained and placed down below with the ship's cargo and only released in Pembroke. The mess you caused fighting that big fella the other night I don't blame him."

"The bishop of Draychester's man, what's become of him?"

"Now don't get any ideas, the same applies to him. You'll both be released when the ship reaches Pembroke. After that, well if you want to try and kill each other again, that's up to you. Seems a damn foolish thing to me; lots of ways for a man to get hurt without bringing it on yourself."

"Why don't you mind your own damn business."

The sergeant growled at him and said, "With pleasure," and promptly shoved an old turnip sack over Sir Roger's head.

"Get him out of here lads."

∼

"What's that Mudstone? Better speak up, you're a bit muffled." The hooded figure let loose another muffled stream of oaths. He struggled against the ropes that bound him tightly, nearly falling out of the back of the cart carrying them. The absurd spectacle set Bernard roaring with laughter. The fact that his own arms were bound behind his back didn't bother him too badly. Two men of the town watch walked behind and periodically shouted at Sir Roger to hold his tongue, with little effect.

Bernard was content to let the watch carry out Bishop Mone's orders. In truth he felt a little sorry that the bishop's peace had been so sorely disturbed. In any case, he would be free soon enough and he intended to settle the score with Sir Roger once and for all. Behind them came another cart carrying Sir Roger's three trunks, on top of which sat a grim-faced Travis. Bernard grinned at him cheerfully and shouted, "Nice day for it, eh?"

Travis shook his head in despair and shouted back, "My master will be in such a rage as will know no bounds. I'll pray for our safety."

"Why do you stay with him Travis? He treats you worse than a dog."

"He's my master. Where else would I go, what would I do?"

"Come with us, get away from him. If ever there was an evil man, it's him."

"You don't know him like I do. He'd find me for sure. You don't know what he's capable of."

"He's capable of nothing if he's dangling at the end of the hangman's rope."

Travis shook his head sadly. "You don't understand. Sir Roger will never hang, the devil protects his own. He always finds a way."

"Well, don't say I didn't give you the chance." Bernard sat back in the cart and enjoyed the brightness of the day. The carts carrying them rocked their way slowly out of the west gate of the cathedral precinct and down the hill towards the harbour at Porthclais.

～

"The cart is leaving," hissed Osbert.

"I can see that," said Will watching Bernard and the hooded Sir Roger sitting in a cart leave the courtyard of the bishop's palace, followed by another cart carrying Travis and the cabbage and turnip filled trunks. Will smirked to himself.

"No, the other cart, " said Osbert tugging on his arm. He

turned around and saw that indeed the vegetable cart was getting ready to leave as well. The carter was preparing the two horses.

"You have the note and coins?"

"Here," said Osbert handing over a folded bit of parchment, which he had sealed shut with wax and imprinted with his seal. He also passed over a fistful of pennies. "Let's hope the good brother can read it."

"The seal should be enough for him to know the message delivered by the carter is from us. Anyway, I suspect Brother Howell at Tenby is more educated than you might believe. Frankly, I can't think of anyone else I trust. We're sorely short of friends here in Wales Osbert. "

"And the carter, he'll surely be tempted to open the sacks?"

"Don't worry. I'll put the fear of God into him and promise him more coin on arrival. You've said that on the note to Brother Howell?"

Osbert nodded. "I have and I hope you're right about this. I fear this is complete madness. You're letting a peasant ride off with a fortune."

∼

"So friend you're clear about what I've asked of you?"

"Yes sir. I'm to deliver these five bags of cabbages and turnips to Brother Howell at Tenby and give him your letter."

"As I said, the good brother did my master a great favour by assisting us. It's the least we can do. The friars can always do with more supplies and no harm in putting a bit of coin in your own pocket eh? We're all men of the world here friend, so no need to tell anyone of your extra journey."

"Leave it to me sir. Brother Howell will give me the same coin again on delivery?"

"As long as you give him that letter I've given you. You'll be sat with your feet up with a pitcher of ale tonight in Tenby with a good few coins to spare. And a good deed will have been done."

"Right you are sir."

As the cart trundled away from the yard, Osbert crossed himself and said, "God save us. I dread to think what our lord bishop will say about this when he hears."

"There are some things Osbert that perhaps you don't need to record for our bishop?"

Osbert looked puzzled. "Not record? But that's my task."

Will sighed and shook his head. "Never mind. Come on, we need to catch up with the others. I dare say the master of the ship will be anxious to depart before the tide turns."

Will took a last look around at the splendour that was the bishop's palace. Unsurprisingly, Thomas the clerk was nowhere to be seen. He would have done the same in his place. The man was no doubt glad to see the back of the troublesome Draychester men. They'd more than outstayed their welcome.

## 24

## THE BRETON

They'd left the harbour at Porthclais behind by no more than an hour when the ship's master suddenly gave a sharp intake of breath.

"What is it?" said Osbert curiously.

"There's a sail off to the West."

Will screwed his eyes up against the reflection of the sun on the waves. He followed the direction of the master's shaking finger and on the far horizon he could just make out the outline of a small ship.

"I see it, what of it? A merchant coming back from Ireland?"

"Maybe, maybe not."

The master began barking orders to the crew who scurried to adjust the sail. They began to pick up speed.

"Better safe than sorry," muttered the master looking at the ship on the horizon. There were more barked orders and over the course of the next fifteen minutes they drew closer to the shoreline as the other ship drew closer to them.

"Why are we so close to the shore?" said Osbert peering

at the waves breaking against the rocks not a quarter of a mile away.

"Just leave the sailing to me lad," snapped the master.

Will didn't understand the sudden change of atmosphere. The crew in between hauling ropes looked tense and gave several anxious looks at the approaching ship. One of them paused at the rail and stared intently at the other vessel.

He suddenly turned to the master, his face grey, and said, "Christ's bones, it's him, it's the Breton himself!"

The master, a quiver in his voice said, "You're sure?"

"Aye, it's him right enough. I'd recognise that ship anywhere. I was on the Saint Anne when he took her. I'm not mistaken master."

"The Breton?" asked Will.

The master, looking fearfully at the fast approaching ship said, "A murderous, thieving bastard. They say he's a Breton, but no one really knows for sure. Always comes out of the west. He'll try and board us if he can and take the ship and the cargo."

"And the crew?" croaked a frightened Osbert.

"If we're lucky, he'll throw us overboard."

Osbert licked his dry lips nervously. "And if we're not?"

"He'll kill us first, then throw us overboard. I doubt you two are worth ransoming. There's six ships been taken in as many months."

"I can't swim," wailed Osbert.

The master shrugged. "Neither can I."

"Can't we go any faster?" asked Will.

"We've got a full hold and we're not built for speed. I can tell he has no cargo aboard, he's high in the water and twice as fast as us. We need to lighten the load and hug the shoreline. He won't dare approach this close, we've got a much shallower draft than he does."

Osbert said, "What do you mean lighten the load?"

The master ignored him and shouted orders again, and the crew immediately started to throw the on deck cargo overboard.

"Is that going to help?" asked Will.

"Probably not but it makes me feel better. I wish I could chuck your bloody wine cask overboard but it's too heavy to move except in harbour. Anything else we can shift from below deck is going to go over the side."

Will said, "You need to release our friend from down there. We'll need every man to fend this Breton off, and I promise you our friend is a formidable fighter."

"Let Sir Roger up. He'll kill them all," said Travis.

"Aye and us in the process," said the master. "I've heard about him and I'm more inclined to throw his arse overboard."

"Please don't let Mudstone up on deck," pleaded Osbert. "He's insane."

"That's as maybe lad, but if the Breton looks like he's going to board us, I'll have no choice. As your friend says, we'll need every man. The big man can come up now. As for Sir Roger, let's hope we don't need his help." He nodded to one of the crew who lifted off the hold cover and climbed the ladder down into the darkness.

Bernard blinded by the bright light from the open hatch croaked, "We there already then?"

"You're needed on deck big man. I hope you can fight as well as your friends say you can. We've got a problem."

"What's going on you worm?" hissed Sir Roger, rattling his chains.

"Don't worry I'm sure you'll get your turn soon enough. The Breton doesn't take prisoners."

"Don't talk in riddles man, who the hell is the Breton?"

A shout from above had the man hurrying to unchain Bernard. The big man groaned as he got to his feet, his stiff limbs aching. He peered at Sir Roger through the gloom of the hold. "Don't go far Mudstone, we have unfinished business." Sir Roger just glared back. Bernard grinned maliciously and then quickly followed the crew man back up on deck.

Off to the seaward side a cog not unlike their own was closing fast at a forty-five degree angle.

"I thought you said he wouldn't dare come in this close, " shouted Will to the master.

The master cursed. "He must be mad, he's going to run us both aground at this rate."

The Breton's cog had her bows and stern built at a higher level than the rest of the ship in order to form a castle like structure. At the front stood a black-cloaked figure, both hands braced against the rail. With his cloak billowing out behind him he looked like a giant crow.

The crew of their own cog started to cross themselves. Osbert, his eyes fixed with horrified fascination on the figure, began reciting a prayer in a low mumble.

Two men joined the black-cloaked figure on the fighting platform. They each raised something up.

Bernard squinted against the glare of the sun then suddenly bellowed, "Christ's bones, they're archers, get down."

He crashed to the deck, drawing Will down with him. Osbert stood frozen, arms around the mast. A cross-bow bolt thudded into the wood just above his head and he slumped down in a faint. Another bolt took the master in the side just below his armpit. He fell to his knees blood gurgling in his throat as he fought for breath. He collapsed on the deck, a red pool of blood slowly spreading from his wound. The ship gave a great lurch to one side and slowed noticeably. Will looked back and saw nobody at the rudder.

"We need to get up there," said Bernard gesturing towards the bow castle of their own vessel. "Maybe we can hold them off. I need a weapon."

He crawled over to the master and relieved him of a short sword. Will drew out a small dagger from under his cloak. He looked at it sadly, it was ridiculous under the circumstances but the best he could do. Anything more deadly was with their packs down in the hold and this was no time to be rummaging around in the dark.

～

The two ships came together with a massive jolt. The bow of the Breton's ship was driven hard into the stern of the other vessel. The first man to cross was built like an ox. He made even Bernard look small. In one hand he bore an axe and in the other a small dagger. Despite his bulk he had clambered across skilfully enough and now stood on the stern castle. His face was round and bloated with two piggy eyes set deep into the flesh of his face. The nose was flat as though once crushed and he breathed heavily through a wide mouth of black tooth stumps.

One of the crew rushed at him, instead of retreating he lumbered forward swinging the murderous axe, catching the man a glancing blow to the shoulder that split bone and flesh. With a giant lurch he barged into the screaming man sending him flying over the side.

Then the Breton himself leapt over the short gap

between the two vessels, his cloak billowing in the wind. He landed directly in front of a quaking Osbert. He towered over the clerk and gave him a quizzical look.

Osbert, voice quavering, said, "I'm a bishop's clerk, you can't harm us."

The Breton held a wicked-looking dagger up to the very tip of Osbert's nose. The clerk stood trembling before him. The Breton laughed uproariously. In heavily accented English he said, "And who is this bishop that I should be afraid of him?"

The Breton tapped the clerk on his nose with the dagger to encourage him to speak. Osbert squeaked, "The Bishop of Draychester. He'll have you excommunicated. You'll burn in the fires of hell."

The Breton looked at Osbert incredulously as though he couldn't believe his ears, then roared with laughter again. "You joke, my little clerk, no? The devil, he will welcome me with open arms and I'll warm my feet by these fires you talk about."

He turned to Bernard. "You, big man. You are in charge, yes?"

Bernard smiled as if to answer then spat directly in the Breton's face. The Breton's immediate reaction was to smash his fist into Bernard's stomach, causing the big man to double up and retch onto the deck.

He turned to Will. "And you, will you also spit in my face?"

"That depends on what you're asking me," said Will for want of a better response.

The Breton laughed and said, "You are a funny man, yes?" before back-handing Will in the face, causing the blood to run freely from his nose. The Breton grabbed Will's chin and wrenched his head up.

"There is a man on board, his name is Mudstone, an English knight?"

Will struggled to nod his head in the other man's vice like grip. The Breton tightened his grasp on Will's chin. "Answer me."

Through the blood and snot from his nose he managed to blurt out, "He's chained up down below."

The Breton grinned. "This is good."

He gestured to the giant man who had jumped across first. "Jupp, find him, bring him up on deck. Hugo, Thomas, John, bring up anything of value from below and get it back across. Better hurry."

Sir Roger was literally dragged on deck gripped around the neck by one of Jupp's huge arms. He dragged him without releasing his grip across to where the Breton stood with the bishop's men.

"Pretty. Jupp likes, Jupp wants," rasped the giant of a man in a strangely childlike manner. He stroked Sir Roger's head with one paw like hand then traced the burnt letter M on Sir Roger's cheek with a fat finger. Sir Roger flinched in alarm and Jupp tighten his grip around his neck.

The Breton looked at Sir Roger curiously. "So you are Mudstone, yes? Jupp here, he likes you. Play later Jupp, I promise. You're not to damage him, understand?"

He punched the giant on the arm in a friendly gesture. Jupp grunted. "Understand, play later, no damage."

"Release him please my friend," said the Breton.

Jupp released his grip and Sir Roger fell gasping for breath onto the deck besides Bernard.

"Christ's bones," gasped Sir Roger looking up at Jupp. "A formidable man to have at your back. Pity he's a half-wit. I wager easier to control that way though?"

The Breton looked down at him with contempt. "See

how much pity you have when you're wrapped in his bedroll tonight."

The Breton's crew laughed uproariously. The Breton himself grinned and said, "Perhaps you'll still be able to walk tomorrow or perhaps not."

~

"Is there anything else?" asked the Breton.

"Nothing that we can move easily. Some wine casks."

"I was told gold and silver."

"No gold and the only silver is the coin they had on them, and little enough of that."

The Breton grunted his acknowledgement. "Take a hatchet and put a hole in the hull."

"No, you can't," cried Bernard with desperation in his voice. "Some of that wine is our bishop's, we've followed it across half of Wales. I won't let it all be for nothing."

The Breton slapped him hard across the side of the head, then punched him in the cheek on the other side. He collapsed onto the deck.

"I can do anything I want. What do I care for your bishop? You can tell him that when you meet in hell."

Bernard spat out a broken tooth and glared up at the Breton and hissed. "Never fear, I'll pass on the message personally."

Sir Roger, still on his hands and knees said, "Your men haven't searched thoroughly enough, there's three trunks below full of silver and gold I took from the Welsh. Sink the ship and you send them to the bottom."

The Breton drove a foot hard into Sir Roger's stomach, "You think my men are fools? Perhaps you think I'm a fool, is that it Sir Knight? You think me foolish?"

Sir Roger, wiping a hand across his vomit stained mouth looked up and said, "I saw them loaded up myself, I was chained up next to them in the hold."

The Breton turned to one of his crew. "John?"

"It's true, three chests in the hold. Full of cabbages and turnips. I opened them myself."

Sir Roger, with a face like thunder, looked at Bernard and hissed. "What have you done bishop's man? Do you know how I worked for that coin? You've taken from me again I know it. What have you done with it?" He lunged at Bernard but was roughly pushed back by the Breton who laughed uproariously.

"It seems you are not a careful man Sir Knight, to lose such treasure is, how do you say? Unfortunate."

"You stinking turd faced frog," roared a red-faced Sir Roger lunging this time at the Breton who sent him back to the deck with an elbow to the face.

The Breton still laughing said, "Enough. John put a hole in the bottom. Jupp, this one," he said pointing at Sir Roger, "comes with us; the others, toss them over the side."

Jupp grabbed hold of a wailing Osbert, lifted him bodily over his head and threw him into the sea. Bernard managed to scramble along the deck a few feet but Jupp caught him and sent him hurling into the sea with a shove from one of his giant feet. Will stood frozen to the spot near the edge of the deck, his face a mask of horror. Jupp grinned and shot out a hand that toppled Will gently over the side.

A minute later and the sound of splintering wood came from below. The Breton's crew man emerged from the hatch and said, "It's done."

The ship lurched under their feet as it began to take on water. The Breton roared at his crew, "My friends, we have finished here. Return to our ship."

## 25

## ON THE BEACH

Osbert entered the water head first, like one of the local seabirds diving for fish. He shot downwards, his descent slowing with every foot. His slim frame helped, and he soon rocketed upwards where he briefly broke surface and the waves rolled him towards the shore away from the sinking ship. Occasionally his head popped up above the surface, allowing him to gasp for air as he was swept along with increasing speed and tumbling limbs. He had no thoughts of survival, a sudden calm came over him. He stopped struggling and he let the waves take him where they wished.

Will had toppled backwards over the side and entered the water on his back. He only went below the surface for a few seconds before emerging once again on his back. He was still near enough to the ship to reach out and cling onto the side. By this time she'd come to a complete stop in the water. There was no way he could climb up from where he was and he slowly, hand over hand, moved himself to the stern. Will thought perhaps he could somehow use the rudder to haul himself back onboard. There was an

## Death Of The Vintner

ominous splintering sound and muffled shouts coming from above him. Will realised someone was likely putting a hole in the hull. He continued around the ship and discovered the Breton's vessel was still hard against the side of the sinking ship. It couldn't be long before they'd cut the ropes holding them fast. The ship above him seemed to lurch and settle into the water. She was sinking fast. Suddenly the side leaned in towards him and debris starting raining down from the deck. A large wicker basket fell directly in front of him. Will grabbed hold of it and half climbed out of the water. Kicking with his feet he backed away from the sinking ship and forced his way back around the other side. The ship was keeling over, half the hull was now exposed. How far she'd actually sink he didn't know, they'd come close to shore, and the sea was shallow. Perhaps she'd lie here like a beached whale until the tides and the storms broke her up. The waves started to push him towards the shore.

Bernard had gone over the side and sunk like a stone. Before Jupp had kicked him into the water he'd already been barely able to move from the pain of the beating the Breton had dished out. The shock of the cold water served to revive him, but he knew it was just as likely to kill. It wasn't winter, but the sea was still deadly cold. By instinct he had the sense to free himself of the heavy boots he wore and then kick for the surface. He was a poor swimmer and never before in the sea. Bernard had sometimes swam in the shallow river during the summer in Draychester, but this was something entirely different. He struggled to the surface and with his head above the water he struggled even more to stay afloat. He bobbed with the waves for what seemed an age. Occasionally he caught sight of the ship, which was listing over at a crazy angle. A length of wood trailing a tangled mass of rope came towards him. He clutched at it desperately. It wasn't much, but it gave him the extra buoyancy to keep his head above water. He looked around, hoping the others were still alive but saw no one. The waves soon started to push him towards the rocky shore. Bernard thought it unlikely he'd survive the pounding surf and his arms clutching the wood were growing numb with the cold. If he let go now, he was sure to die. There was a shout above the crashing of the waves. Bernard looked but saw no one in his limited vision. His grip on the wood started to weaken. He heard a shout again. A figure was moving towards him through the heavy swell.

"Travis!" he gasped.

Sir Roger's grey faced servant drew close to him. He was pushing what looked to be the hatch cover in front of him. Bernard struggled towards him, eventually getting an arm over the square wooden cover.

Travis said, "I'm sorry I can't do any more. I need to find my master."

"I'm glad for the help Travis but your master is gone with those who took the ship."

"If I swim hard I may catch them."

"Don't be a fool, you owe him nothing and you'll drown for sure."

Travis said, "Before the ship went down, I saw your companions being swept toward the shore." With that he turned his back on Bernard and swam off in the opposite direction.

"Travis come back, you idiot," shouted Bernard, but it was no use and the figure soon disappeared amongst the waves.

Bernard briefly hauled himself higher on the hatch and he could just make out the shoreline. It looked impossibly far, but he knew in reality it had to be close. He clutched tight to the hatch cover and prepared for the worst.

∽

Will was swept around the rocks of a headland and pushed towards the beach. Finding himself in the shallows he managed to touch the bottom with his feet. He struggled ashore, bedraggled and exhausted and dragged himself up the beach until he reached the dry sand. He sank down on his backside, head on chest too tired to move further. Eventually he lifted his head and scanned the beach for any sign of the others, but it was completely deserted. There was no sign anyone else had come out of the water. Perhaps they had been swept onto another beach, the coast here was one headland and beach after another. He could only hope.

Will got to his feet and slowly made his way to the top of the beach. Finding a path he climbed up from the sand and onto the headland itself. The way was steep, and he was already exhausted, but he needed to find the others if they were still alive. From the headland Will could see out to sea and down into the next bay. On the horizon he could see a sail. It was too far away for him to make out but Will guessed it was the Breton's ship. Just off shore the surf was breaking over what looked to be the remains of their own vessel. Will couldn't see any movement in the surrounding water. He turned his attention to the beach beyond the headland he stood on. There was something right at the water's edge, riding up with the waves then being dragged back into the water as they receded. It looked like a figure lying face down, around it were bits of wooden debris. Will ran down a steep path that led to the beach below. He lost his footing several times and ended up sliding on his backside. Back on the sand he stumbled down the beach to the water. Bernard lay face down at the water's edge. He managed to tumble the big man over. His face was grey, eyes shut tight, he didn't appear to be breathing. Will grabbed him under the armpits and attempted to get him clear of the water. The big man was heavy and Will struggled, his feet sinking into the sand as he dragged him up the beach. When he was out of the water he turned him onto his side. He forced Bernard's mouth open and was horrified at the water that ran out of both his mouth and nose. He thumped hard on his friend's back in an attempt to clear the water and force him to breathe. Bernard lay motionless, with no signs of life. In desperation Will rolled him on his opposite side and thumped him again on the back. His friend suddenly twitched, and the retched up what seemed to be a gallon of water onto the sand. He began coughing and spluttering and gasping for air.

Will slapped him on the back again. Bernard opened his eyes, managed to focus on Will and wheezed, "That'll do! I'm not bloody dead yet."

"God's teeth. I thought you were drowned for sure."

"Get me up lad."

Will helped the big man to his feet. With one huge arm around Will's shoulders, they struggled up the beach.

"Where's Osbert?" wheezed Bernard.

Will said, "I fear he must have drowned. I've not seen him anywhere. I came ashore around the headland over there and he was nowhere to be seen."

Bernard shook his head sadly. "He was terrified of the sea. Always saying he couldn't swim. I'm ashamed we made fun of him. We need to search. I'll not leave the lad washed up on a beach somewhere, drowned or not."

"You need to rest, sit down just for a while, you're in no

condition to do anything. Let me go and look. Whatever has happened he will have come ashore close by."

Bernard sank down onto the soft sand at the top of the beach. He was exhausted. He just said, "You'd better find him before nightfall then. It's bloody cold in that water." He closed his eyes and was asleep before Will could respond.

Will went down to the waterline again and walked along it, as far as the beach ran. There was a fair amount of debris that seemed to have come from the ship, but he saw no one in the water. The beach came to an end at another headland of tall rocky cliffs. He made his way back up the sand along the side of the headland until he found a way up among the rocks. It was steep, but with legs aching from the climb, he soon emerged on top. The headland was a windswept open grassland, and he quickly made his way to the cliff edge. Will thought he heard a faint cry on the wind. He inched forward and looked down. It wasn't a sheer drop. The cliff tumbled away down to the sea in a series of ledges and slopes. It looked like there had been a landslip at some time in the past. Will listened intently and mixed in with the wind and cries of the whirling sea gulls he definitely heard a human voice.

He cupped his hands to his mouth and shouted down, "Hello?"

There, he heard the cry again. It was coming from below he was certain now.

"Osbert is that you?" he bellowed.

He was rewarded with a faint, "Help."

Gingerly Will lowered himself down onto the first grassy ledge below. It sloped downwards, and he followed if for perhaps fifty feet. He shouted out again and this time much clearer he heard a voice call back.

"Thank God. I don't think I can hold on much longer."

Will continued down the narrow ledge until it came to an abrupt finish. Looking over the edge he saw a small figure clinging to the rocks about ten feet below him and far below that the sea crashed against the bottom of the cliffs.

"Osbert are you all right?" asked Will.

"That's the most stupid question you have ever asked me," replied a white-faced Osbert looking up at him.

For the first time since they'd been shipwrecked Will smiled. "I thought you were drowned for sure my friend."

~

The three of them reunited on the beach where Bernard lay resting. The big man's face split into a broad grin when he saw Osbert. "As annoying as you can be, I'm truly glad to see you lad."

Osbert sank onto the sand beside him and solemnly said, "It's a miracle all three of us are still alive. God must have some further purpose for us, probably unpleasant."

Bernard grinned again and said, "If it's to hang that sod Mudstone and the Breton at the nearest gallows I'm all for it. As for Mudstone's loot I presume that it wasn't a miracle that filled those chests full of turnips and cabbages rather than coin?"

"That was us last night. Mudstone can hardly have left a Welsh coin untouched, nor a Welsh church with its plate intact. There's a fortune concealed on a vegetable cart on its way to Brother Howard at Tenby. It's the best plan we could come up with. I pray to God it's still undiscovered. It'd be a fearful temptation for any man."

Bernard's eyes widened in surprise then he nodded. "You did well, but perhaps we'd better intercept this cart. If Mudstone ever escapes the Breton, he won't rest until he recovers the loot. The sooner we get it to our own bishop the better."

Will said, "I'm not sure where we are but surely we can't be that far from Pembroke?"

"So what have we between us?" asked Bernard struggling to his feet. Will marvelled at the big man's stamina. An hour's sleep on the beach seemed to be all he had need of to revive him.

Osbert, knees drawn up to his chest and shivering in his damp clothes said, "I've still got my seal around my neck but the bag of coins is gone, probably at the bottom of the sea. I don't know what my lord bishop will say about it."

"Don't worry lad. He'll say he's glad we're alive," said Bernard, clapping one giant hand on Osbert's shoulder.

"And my pen, ink and parchment is lost," added Osbert sadly.

"Will, what about you?"

"Still got my seal, much good it'll do us. I'd rather have some bread and cheese. I've not so much as a penny. Everything is lost on the ship. At least I still have my boots."

Bernard looked down at his bare feet. "Bloody good pair of boots I've lost. Still if I hadn't taken them off I would have drowned." He rummaged under his sodden tunic and produced a little leather bag. He opened it and emptied a few silver pennies onto the palm of his hand. "Enough so we won't have to walk all the way to wherever we're going. Any suggestions?"

Will shrugged and got up wincing at the pain in his battered limbs. He said, "Well we can't go back to Saint Davids so to Pembroke? The vegetable cart with Mudstone's loot goes by way of a place called Carew first. That's where the carter said he was from. He's supposed to carry on to Tenby and deliver our sacks."

"Back to Pembroke then," said a damp Osbert with a sniff.

Bernard nodded and offered him a hand. Osbert reluctantly used it to haul himself off the sand.

"Let's go," said Will.

∽

"How far is it to Pembroke?" asked Will.

They'd stopped to talk to a group of men working in a field by the side of the road. They were digging some sort of ditch, for what purpose they didn't say and the bishop's men didn't ask.

One of the serfs gave them a good long hard look before a rattling cough took over him. He wheezed away until he eventually brought up a mouthful of phlegm and spat it out. A disgusting green mass landed next to Bernard's bare feet. Bernard stepped forward angrily but Will placed a calming hand on his friend's arm.

The man wiped his mouth with the back of a grubby hand and said, "Suppose it's fifteen miles on a good day, course I never been there myself, why would I?"

Another one scratching his arse absentmindedly looked at Bernard's bare feet and said, "Be slow walking without boots. You'd be faster by water, coast isn't far."

"I'm never taking another passage by ship as long as I live," muttered Osbert, shivering in his damp clothes.

"What about you? Have you been there?" demanded Bernard.

The other man momentarily stopped scratching and gave an indifferent shrug. "Once when I were a boy. I didn't care for it much. If you're looking for a ride, you'd be better asking old Godwin, he goes there all the time."

"And who's he?" asked Will patiently.

"He's the carter of course. You'll find him at the alehouse in the village. Keep following the road. He's probably pissed by now though, it's gone noon. As for us, well this ditch won't finish digging itself."

"God's teeth," sighed Bernard.

"Come on," said Will pulling on Bernard's arm with one hand and pushing Osbert forward with the other. "Sooner we get there, the faster we can be somewhere else."

## 26

## IN PURSUIT

The village alehouse was a turf roofed cottage that sat slumped by the side of the road. A feeble waft of smoke drifted up from a crude hole cut in the centre of the roof. A cart stood outside with a dejected looking horse tied to a wooden post.

They had to crouch to enter via the doorway which was covered in a scruffy leather hide. The interior was almost dark. A weak fire spluttered in the hearth making the air thick with smoke.

They found Godwin the carter with difficulty, only locating him by his snores which were loud enough to wake the dead. He lay in a drunken stupor under a long bench, only his boot clad foot visible at first.

"Christ's bones, look at the state of him," said Will.

Bernard reached down and grabbed hold of the drunken man's legs and pulled him none too gently from under the bench. The man's snores stopped briefly, and he murmured something unintelligible, before resuming again.

Bernard said, "We need to sober him up, but let's get out of this bloody smoke first." Bernard grabbed one of

## Death Of The Vintner

Godwin's feet and dragged him across the room and out through the door. He dumped him besides what was presumably his cart.

"Find me some water if you can," said Bernard, slapping Godwin's cheeks. "Wake up, damn you. We have need of your services."

Will looked down at the drunken man thoughtfully and said, "Why not just take the cart, we don't actually need him do we?"

"We can't take the cart. We're not common thieves," said Osbert.

Will shrugged, "We'd only be borrowing it. I believe our need is greater than his at the moment. Bernard you still have your coins?"

The big man said, "What are you thinking?"

"Leave half in Godwin's grubby hand. We can send the cart back when we get to wherever it is that we're going."

Bernard nodded, took out his bag of coins and stuffed three sliver pennies into the unconscious Godwin's hand and said, "Come on get in the cart. I've walked far enough today, and this fool is in no fit state to take us anyway. We'll just have to ask directions."

~

"God's teeth, I can feel every rock in the road," wailed Osbert. Bernard was urging the horse on and the cart was bouncing around behind, crashing over every rock and into every rut in the road. Will felt that every one of his internal organs had taken a beating.

Bernard looked over his shoulder at Osbert who lay in the back of the cart. "At least you're not walking lad. If you hadn't noticed, I don't have any boots."

Osbert glowered back at him. Will, sat next to Bernard at the front, grinned to himself, Osbert must be feeling better. They came to a crossroads, but there was no indication which way Pembroke lay. There was, however, an old woman sat on the grass verge eating bread and cheese. Will could hear Bernard's stomach groan as he caught sight of the food. They hadn't eaten for what seemed like hours. Bernard brought the cart to a halt.

He grinned at the woman and shouted down, "Perhaps you have some bread to share mother? A penny for your trouble?"

The woman looked up at them with her mouth open, chucks of bread falling out. From the glimpse Will got, she had only one tooth left in her head. She cupped a hand around an ear and shouted, "I'm deaf dear. Can't hear a word you're saying. What you want?"

Bernard mimed shoving food into his mouth then offered one of their last silver pennies to the woman.

"Bread is what you're wanting is it? Well why didn't you say so?" she fumbled in a rough leather bag at her side and brought forth a rough loaf of bread and some grey looking cheese.

"Penny for the bread and another for the cheese."

Osbert mumbled, "That's ridiculous."

Will said, "I'm hungry. Give her what she asks Bernard."

He grinned down at the woman and handed her two coins. She passed up the loaf and cheese. Osbert waved a hand to draw the woman's gaze. He shouted at the top of his voice, "Which is the road to Pembroke?"

She chuckled, revealing a single blackened tooth. "No need to shout like that son, I'm only deaf not dead. Take the road to the right." As they set off again, she raised an arm in farewell.

The cheese turned out to be as tough of old leather and the bread full of grit. As he chewed on his share, Will said, "If she eats this every day, it's no wonder the old crone only had one tooth in her head."

Osbert shrugged. "I'm so hungry I'm not sure I care."

Bernard spat out an inedible lump and said, "When you've got as few teeth left as I have, you'll regret saying that."

The road was badly rutted and barely wide enough in places for the cart to pass. They bumped along at little more than walking pace. If it wasn't for Bernard's bare feet, Will would have suggested they abandoned the cart altogether. Finally they emerged onto a much wider track. It looked well travelled.

"So which way now?"

"Right," said Will.

"Go left," said Osbert.

Bernard sat for a minute looking left then right. The road was empty in either direction. He looked at Will, who raised his eyebrows. Bernard nodded and turned right.

"You never follow my advice," said Osbert sulkily.

Will shrugged. "It's not your advice we're worried about, just your sense of direction."

Under his breath Bernard said, "Let's hope he's wrong else we'll never hear the last of it."

Bernard picked up the pace again, the ruts in the road inducing bone jarring bounces. Will started to lose track of how far they'd travelled. The road seemed to go on forever. He was so tired he momentarily fell asleep at times and had to pinch himself to stay awake. If he didn't stay alert, he'd probably end up under the wheels of the cart.

Bernard suddenly said, "Looks like some monks or maybe a couple of friars up ahead. What do you think?"

Will shielded his eyes against the sun and grunted. "Looks like it. Finally, someone we can get some sensible answers out of. Osbert, are you still awake back there?"

"How can I sleep? Every bone in my body aches from the ride."

∽

Bernard brought the cart to a halt beside the two black cloaked figures who had stepped onto the verge in anticipation of them passing. Will looked at them curiously, he took them for Benedictines from their black cloaks. He let Bernard do the talking.

"Greetings brothers. Can we offer you a lift? You look a little weary and we have need of directions."

The two monks looked up at them suspiciously. One was just a boy, the other was much older. He said, "Depends on where you journey my friend. We travel to the priory at Pembroke."

Osbert said from the back of the cart, "Finally, fortune favours us."

The boy darted a glance at him. The older man looked them over once more. He didn't seem inclined to accept the offer. Will couldn't help but laugh. "Don't worry brother, I can see your doubts, we're not as rough as we appear. What you see is the result of recent misfortune. We mean you no harm, and we'd be grateful for your help. Believe it or not we're the bishop of Draychester's men."

Will offered the man his seal. He took it and peered at it curiously before handing it back. He grunted and said, "You're a long way from home. I've been to Draychester once, the cathedral is a wonder. The lad is Brother Willard, I'm Brother Matthew."

Bernard said, "Climb aboard brothers and we'll tell you our sorry tale as you guide us."

∼

Monkton Priory was set on a hillside overlooking Pembroke. The welcome from the prior, Gervase le Brek, was somewhat chilly. He said in a heavy French accent. "Brother Mathew and Brother Willard seem convinced of your tale. I suppose I'll have to take your word for it." He held Will's seal matrix in his hands disinterestedly.

Bernard bristled at the implied insult. "If the constable is back at the castle, he'll vouch for us. The bishop of Saint Davids knows us as well."

Le Brek shrugged. "I've been here but a short time. I've yet to meet either the bishop or the constable. My first allegiance is to our mother abbey of Séez and to its abbot. The priory has been badly run, things are slack, discipline is lax. There are but six of us here and I have much to do. These petty local squabbles you have been involved in are of little concern to me."

Will said, "We simply seek assistance as would any other traveller. As you have heard we have been attacked, robbed and ship wrecked. We have lost all our belongings. We seek assistance from you as officials of the bishop of Draychester. We need to send dispatches to our lord bishop and we would also appreciate some simple clothing and provisions."

Le Brek looked at them with distaste. "My understanding is the constable is away in the north, some trouble with these savages the Welsh. I suggest you report your misfortune to him. Why is it you come here and not the castle if you are known there already? We have little here as it is."

Osbert snapped, "Are you refusing us assistance? Surely hospitality is part of the rule you live by? It is your duty is it not?"

Le Brek turned to him and laughed without humour. "Duty? And what do you know of duty boy? By the look of it you've hardly lived."

Osbert glowered at him whilst Bernard was turning a beetroot red from the neck upwards. Will, trying to keep the conversation civil, said, "We can certainly carry onto the castle. As you say, we need to report these crimes against us. You were the first place we came to before the town itself. I've never known the Benedictines to be anything less than hospitable. I'll be sure to let our lord bishop know of our welcome here."

Le Brek sighed. "I never said I wouldn't help you. Just that you are yet another drain on our resources. These are difficult times. Do you know how many pilgrims seek shelter every night on their way to Saint Davids?"

Bernard growled, "Our lord bishop will recompense you twice over for anything you may supply. I give you my word."

Le Brek sank back in his seat and regarded them silently. Finally he waved a dismissive hand at them and said, "Go, find Brother Mathew. Tell him he has my permission to clothe you and give you any provisions as we can spare. Now if you'll excuse me I have God's work to do."

As they left the prior's chamber, Bernard said loud enough to be heard, "Sanctimonious turd."

∽

For all Le Brek's coldness the welcome from his fellow monks was genuine enough. The three bishop's men were soon sat at a bench warming before the fire in the priory guesthouse. One of the brothers brought them some ale and bread and cheese which they devoured ravenously.

"Don't mind the prior. I suspect he feels he's been sent here as a punishment. It certainly wasn't by choice, of that I'm sure," said Brother Matthew.

"The priory's mother house, it's in France?" asked Osbert curiously.

Brother Mathew nodded. "It is, at Séez. Most of the Benedictine priories in this part of Wales owe their allegiance to Séez. The prior is recently arrived from there."

Another brother laughed and said, "The prior, bless his soul, is a long way from where he feels comfortable. He's only been here a month, give him time and he'll come to appreciate Pembroke."

The brothers supplied them with some rough work robes, a thin cloak each and some ill-fitting boots for Bernard. Osbert persuaded them to find him some writing materials and was soon lost in scribbling their latest adventures. Finally a battered bag containing a day's worth of provisions was handed to them. As they made ready to leave Brother Mathew said, "Now if it's horses you need you'll have to ask at the castle."

Will grasped his hand in thanks. "You've done more than enough for us brother, probably more than your prior intended."

"Aye well, never mind about him, we haven't trained him to our ways yet."

Bernard laughed and said, "Even if he is a sanctimonious sod, we're in your debt. Our own lord bishop will hear of your help."

"Go with God," replied Brother Matthew.

～

As they trudged down the hill towards the castle, Will asked Bernard, "How far do you think the vegetable cart has got?"

Bernard shrugged. "He's had all day while we've been otherwise occupied."

Osbert looked up at the sun and said, "Even if he took his time unloading at Carew he can't be far from the gates of Tenby by now. You think there's any chance they'll lend us horses at the castle?"

Will looked him straight in the eye and said, "We're the bishop of Draychester's men aren't we? So of course they'll lend us some beasts."

Osbert gave him a sceptical look as did Bernard. Osbert said, "At least I can send despatches back to Draychester. There must be messengers going to and from the castle all the time."

"I'm sure the bishop and your uncle are going to be interested in what you have to tell them," said Will dryly. He rubbed his neck guiltily, he could still just about feel the scars the hangman's rope had once made about his neck. He didn't want to repeat the experience.

～

They found the sergeant sat in the guardroom at a table drinking wine with three of the castle guards. The room was small and stifling from a fire blazing in the small hearth behind them. By the state of them, Will concluded the session had lasted some hours. On the table sat a jug of wine, a collection of wooden cups, a leather gaming board with counters and a scattering of silver pennies.

The sergeant looked at them through bleary eyes. "Don't I recognise you?" he slurred.

When they'd told him a brief version of the day's events, the sergeant wiped the back of a dirty hand over his mouth and roared with drunken laughter. With tears in his eyes he said, "So the Breton has struck again has he? Personally I avoid sea travel, bloody dangerous at the best of times. He's left you looking like three beggars. What do you think lads?" The three guards joined in the drunken laughter.

Bernard walked over. Fists clenched, he brought them crashing down onto the table and sent the contents flying. He leant over and pushed his face into the sergeant's. "It wasn't bloody funny when he was throwing us overboard. If you knew about this Breton, why aren't you trying to stop him?"

The sergeant hastily pushed his stool backwards. He spluttered, "You think the constable has the funds to pursue every report we get? We're under manned here as it is."

One of the guards struggled to his feet and said, "Don't have a go at the sarge. We haven't even been paid properly for two months."

Bernard pushed him roughly back down into his seat. "I wasn't asking you."

Will said, "The ship was returning from delivering supplies, so technically it was on the king's business, does that not concern you?"

The sergeant shrugged. "There's always been pirates off this coast. You've got to expect a certain amount of losses whether it's pirates or storms."

"I wonder what your master the constable will have to say about it? A ship on the king's commission attacked, crew killed, stores stolen, a prisoner onboard released. Three bishop's men thrown overboard and left for dead. Shouldn't you be raising the alarm?"

The sergeant smiled and said with some satisfaction, "I leave those sorts of decisions to my lord. He's taken most of the men north, there's trouble with the Welsh. I don't expect him back for days if not weeks. I can't act without his orders."

"Then you're in charge until his return?" said Bernard not hiding the contempt in his voice.

"I am."

Bernard just shook his head in disgust. Will grabbed the big man's arm before he could say anything further.

Will said, "At the very least sergeant you'll do us the courtesy of lending us some horses. We need to get to Tenby."

The sergeant looked at them coldly. Finally he said, "If you insist, I warn you though, there's not much left in the stables. You'll have to ask one of the lads down in the yard, you can see we're busy."

Before a red-faced Bernard could react, Will started to push him through the door. The big man let loose with a string of curses. The sergeant simply raised his cup of wine in mock salute at them and his companions roared with laughter.

As they made their way to the stables, Bernard still fuming said, "That bastard is so lax his own mother could take the castle single-handed. I hope for his sake the Welsh never turn up at the gates."

"Let's not argue with anyone else," said Will running a hand over his stubbly chin. "At this point I just want to catch up with that vegetable cart. I'm coming to regret hiding

Mudstone's loot with the cabbages. I must have been out of my mind."

Osbert nodded and said smugly, "Did I not say as much at the time."

Bernard and Will both turned to him and simultaneously shouted, "Shut up!"

∽

A stable lad hobbled into the castle yard leading a shabby-looking beast. It regarded them with a critical eye.

"God's teeth, is this the best there is?" asked Bernard exasperated.

The stable lad shrugged. "The constable and his men have taken most of them, Molly here is all right, she's getting on a bit I suppose, but she's sound."

Will said, "We'll not be galloping that I can see, the beast looks like it'll drop dead if we go faster than a walk. Also, if you hadn't noticed, there's three of us."

The stable lad looked at them for a moment in thought and then said, "Well there's only Shaker left, he's as mean spirited as they come. No one wants to ride him. Kicked me in the shin only this morning, hurt like hell it did. The sergeant says he's only fit to be made into pies."

Bernard sighed, looked up to the heavens and said, "I'd expect nothing less." He stabbed a finger at the stable lad. "Bring him out boy, we've no choice and we're in a hurry."

## 27

## THE BELL TAVERN

As at any city gate, there was the usual cluster of beggars and others hoping to earn a penny or two from the passing trade. The west gate of Tenby was no exception. Will approached a young lad with ragged clothes. He was thin-faced, with a runny nose and beady eyes that seemed to miss nothing.

"Seen a cart today lad?"

The lad gave him an appraising look. He didn't seem that impressed. Finally, and somewhat reluctantly he said, "Seen a few, what sort of cart you looking for?"

"One filled with sacks of vegetables."

The lad licked his rough dry lips and said, "What's it worth to you?"

"How about a clip around the earhole?" said Will. He tweaked the lad's ear.

"Ouch!"

"Have you seen a cart today like that or not?"

The lad rubbed his ear then shrugged. "Saw one earlier at the gate. Think it's one from Carew. Comes here quite often."

"What do you mean earlier?" demanded Will.

"I don't know, maybe an hour since. I've got better things to do all day than watch for sodding vegetable carts. How about a penny for my trouble?"

Will already moving away looked back over his shoulder and said, "If we meet again I'll be sure you get one, a bit short of funds lad."

The lad shook his head and muttered, "Should have known. Bloody skinflint." He peered after Will and calculated there was still a penny to be made. He'd survived this long on his wits and they hadn't let him down yet. It might be something or nothing but he'd drop his scrap of information into the gatekeeper's ears.

∽

Will walked back down the road away from the gate and the town walls. Bernard and Osbert were stood with the horses just out of sight.

As Will approached them he shook his head and said, "We're too late, the cart passed through the gate an hour ago."

"God's teeth," said Bernard. "It's like we're cursed. "

"What did I tell you," said Osbert, which drew withering looks from the other two.

Bernard ran a hand over his tired eyes and said, "So to the friars again. Let's hope your faith in Brother Howell isn't misplaced Will."

"He's a man of God," said Osbert simply.

"And I pray that you're not really that naïve boy," snapped Bernard.

Will sighed, grabbed hold of the horse's reins and started for the gates. "Put your hoods up and keep your head down. No point in letting the whole town know we're back."

The gatekeeper didn't give them a second glance, but Will was sure they wouldn't go unnoticed for long. They quickly made their way through the streets to the whitewashed walls of the friar's little chapel.

Will gave the reins of the horses to Osbert and said, "See if there's somewhere around the back you can tie them up out of sight."

Bernard tapped lightly on the door to the chapel. They could hear footsteps from the other side of the door. Then a voice said, "Who is it?"

"Doesn't sound like Brother Howell," whispered Will.

Bernard shrugged and said, "Officials of the Bishop of Draychester. We were here with Howell a few days ago."

The door opened and a little cowl clad figure stood at the door. He smiled weakly at them. "Howell mentioned you. I'm Stephen. If it's him you seek he's gone to the hospital outside the west gate. He'll be back soon. You return our spare cloaks perhaps?"

"May we come in brother?" asked Will.

Brother Stephen opened the door wide and beckoned them in. Will said, "Tell me brother, did a carter from Carew call earlier and drop off some sacks of vegetables? He also had a letter for Brother Howell."

The friar shook his head. "I have no reading I'm afraid. Howell, on the other hand, reads well."

Bernard stepped forward impatiently and said, "You haven't answered the question Brother. Has a cart been here or not?"

The little friar looked at him in bewilderment. "No one has been at the door since Howell left earlier. I'm not expecting anyone let alone a carter."

Bernard reached out as though to grab him and the little friar shrunk back in alarm. Will grabbed Bernard's arm. He said sharply, "Bernard leave him be. I believe what he says, he knows nothing of this."

"Then where the hell has the carter gone?"

"He'll be away to the tavern. I gave him enough to spend the night pleasantly with his belly full and his feet up in front of the fire. Perhaps he plans on unloading the sacks when he leaves tomorrow."

Bernard said, "Osbert stay here with the brother. If the carter shows up get the sacks inside out of sight."

"Where are you going?" asked Osbert.

Will, ignoring him, turned to the still bewildered Brother Stephen. "Brother, which tavern in town would you go to for the night if you were a carter?"

With some scratching of his head, the friar said, "Well I suppose the Bell; you can put the cart around the back and there's some stabling."

"And where exactly is this tavern?" demanded Bernard.

"You can't miss it, go back onto the main street, past the church towards the north end of town. It's near the end of the street, the yard and stable backs up against the town wall."

Bernard was already turning towards the door before the little man finished speaking.

Will clapped the friar on the shoulder. "Thank you brother. We'll find it and with luck we'll be back soon."

"I really don't understand what all this is about."

Will said, "Osbert here will explain, well at least some of it anyway." Osbert raised his eyebrows as Will disappeared through the door.

Mayor Watts screwed his face up in frustration.

"You sure it's them?"

The gatekeeper nodded. "Plain as day, I was down on the quay the day Phelpes was tipped out of the barrel in front of them. All three came in the west gate."

Watts banged a fist down on the tabletop. "Why in God's teeth are they back here again? As if we don't have enough to deal with."

One of his men said, "Let me go and find them John. Me and the lads can get them to tell us whatever you want to know. We won't hold back this time."

Watts pointed his finger at the man and said, "Go and bring them back here, I don't care if they aren't willing, make them, you understand me? And watch out for the big man, he's dangerous."

∼

It was twilight as they left the chapel of the friars. Will wasn't sure how soon the curfew bell would be sounded. There were still a few people on the streets and they didn't seem to be in a particular hurry.

The Bell tavern was just where Brother Stephen had described. They could just about see the sign hung over the door in the deepening gloom. From the outside, the place looked respectable enough. Bernard opened the door and took a step down onto a well-flagged floor scattered with rushes. A cheerful fire burned low in a hearth in the centre and there were low trestle tables, benches and stools set around it. A scattering of candles cast a golden glow over the scene. Will thought he hadn't seen a pleasanter place since they'd stepped off the boat in Tenby.

Will looked around. Only a few of the tables were occupied, a few blearily eyes drinkers looked up at them but he recognised no one.

"You see the man?" asked Bernard.

Will shook his head. "I don't see him. Maybe he's been and gone. He must be bedded down somewhere."

A man got up from one of the tables and ambled over, presumably the landlord. He looked them over curiously.

"A drink sirs? It's getting late but we don't hold too closely to the curfew." As if to clarify he added, "Half the watch drink in here."

Will was about to reply when from a doorway at the back of the room the carter stumbled in and sat down. He put his head face down onto his folder arms on the table and appeared to instantly fall asleep.

The landlord said, "Doesn't seem to be able to hold his ale that one. Spent more time stumbling about and pissing out the back than he has drinking. Friend of yours is he?"

"We're acquainted," said Will vaguely before heading over to the carter.

"Bring us a pot of ale landlord," said Bernard before following his companion.

∼

The carter was snoring heavily as Bernard sat down next to him and lifted his head up from his arms by grabbing a handful of thinning hair. He blinked sleepily at Will sat across the table from him.

"You remember me don't you," said Will.

The carter tried hard to focus his bloodshot eyes and then suddenly slurred, "From Saint Davids, asked me to deliver the sacks? Bloody long day it's been, thought I'd have a couple of drinks in here first."

"That's right my friend. I can see you've had a few. So the sacks for the friars are still on your cart are they?"

The man hiccuped and belched a sour ale laced waft of air directly at Will. "That's right."

As though addressing a child, Will said gently, "What have you done with the cart?"

"Why?" said the carter as suspiciously as a drunk man can.

Bernard still holding the man's head up by the hair shook it about a bit. Will winced as did the carter.

"Ouch, hurts," he slurred. "It's in the yard."

Bernard said, "Thank Christ for that." He let go of the carter's hair, the man slumped back down and was almost instantly asleep.

Just as they were about to get up, the landlord came over and slapped down a pot of ale and two wooden cups beside them.

"Penny," he said.

Bernard handed over one of their remaining pennies, poured a cup of ale for himself and Will and toasted the Landlord. "Your good health."

The landlord looked at them suspiciously, grunted, and finally walked away from the table.

"Going to look bloody funny if we both disappear out the back almost as soon as we've walked in," whispered Will.

"I'll keep our sleeping friend here company. You nip out back as though you're desperate for a piss. If the cart is still in the yard check for the sacks. Then come back in, we'll have another cup of ale and leave through the front."

"Then what? There are too many sacks to carry at once."

"We take the cart out of the backyard, the friar's chapel is only a few streets away."

"What about the curfew, we'll make enough noise to wake the dead."

"Have you got a better plan? There's a fortune sat out the back on that cart. I'm not leaving it there."

Will shrugged, got up and said loudly, "That ales gone straight through me." He disappeared through the dark doorway behind the table.

The yard behind the tavern was dark and muddy underfoot. At least Will hoped it was mostly mud but the foul smell suggested otherwise. The town wall formed the back to the yard and he could just make out the shape of a cart drawn up against it. On the left-hand side was what he took to be a stable. A dark alleyway led out of the yard on the right back to the main street. He squelched his way across to the cart. A pile of sacks still sat in the back. With pounding heart he climbed up onto the cart. He quickly pushed away the topmost sacks that he knew were filled with cabbages and turnips. The sacks at the bottom were lumpy and misshapen. He pulled one out and opened it and with shaking hands drew out a silver plater. He quickly thrust it back into the sack and pulled the vegetable filled sacks back on top. Will, still shaking, quickly strode back into the tavern. He sat down opposite Bernard and the snoring carter. "It's still there, under the real vegetable sacks on the back of the cart. Didn't see the horse but it must be in the stable. He'd no intention of delivering the sacks tonight that's for sure."

Bernard let out a deep breath, grinned and poured them both another cup of ale.

"Drink up lad, then we've got work to do."

They left the tavern and turned left heading for the entrance to the alleyway that led to the tavern's yard.

"We're being followed," said Bernard matter-of-factly.

Will gave a quick glance over his should and replied, "I know. I saw them as soon as we came out of the door. They were lurking across the street in the shadows."

Bernard grunted and said, "You didn't say anything."

"I didn't want to worry you."

"I'm not worried lad. Fact is, the more we take down now, the less we have to worry about later. "

"I admire your confidence but we're outnumbered."

The men were rapidly gaining on them. There were four of them. The leader of the bunch had a thick wooden staff, the man immediately behind carried a short blade in his left hand. The other two had wooden cudgels. Bernard and Will picked up their pace.

"Quick, down there," said Bernard, pushing Will into a narrow passageway. If the street had been gloomy, this was even darker. "They'll have to come at us one at a time now."

Bernard virtually blocked the passageway with his bulk. Will backed up behind him. The passageway came to a dead end twenty feet behind them with the outer wall of the town defences. Either side were the walls of the houses that had shop fronts and entrances on the main street. The upper floors stuck out over the passageway almost touching.

Will whispered, "I hope you're sure about this because there's no way out back here unless you fancy climbing the town wall."

"Just back up a bit, it's not the first time I've broken heads in some back alley. I'll reduce the odds a bit in our favour."

Will moved further down the passageway, while the big

man pressed himself against the wall as much as possible in the confined space.

The first man barged around the corner. Wooden staff held out before him. He squinted and then carefully started to move forward. Bernard pumped a huge fist into the side of the man's head with enough force to throw him into the opposite wall. He slid down onto his knees, face against the wall. Bernard hauled the man up by the scruff of the neck, twisted him around and then viciously elbowed him in the face. There was a sickening crunching sound. Bernard released his grip, and the man dropped unconscious onto the ground. Bernard ground his heel into what probably remained of the man's face.

"I think you might have killed the poor sod," whispered a shocked Will from behind. He was thankful it was so dark that he couldn't see the damage.

Bernard said softly, "This isn't a game lad, you'd better understand that. It's us or them."

Bernard grabbed the man again by his leather jerkin. He hauled him up and out of the muddy alley and onto the main street directly in the path of his following companions. Will, still in the dark passageway, bent down and quickly scrabbled around on the muddy ground near to where the man had first come in contact with the wall. His hands soon found the wooden staff. Armed with his newfound weapon Will crept forward and gazed out onto the main street from the shadows. Bernard stood directly in the middle of the street, the fallen man face down in the filth in front of him. The remaining attackers, gazing in horrified fascination at their fallen comrade, slowly backed away. Bernard stretched his arms wide is if to embrace them and grinned. "Come on lads, let's settle this like men, or have you gone all faint-hearted on us now?"

The biggest of the bunch took the bait and growled, "You shite sucker. I'm going carve that grin off your ugly face." He lunged at Bernard with a short blade. Bernard had been in more back street brawls than he could remember and easily dodged the weapon. He grabbed the arm that bore it and dragged the man forward, jamming a finger into one of his eyes. His attacker howled in agony and dropped the blade. With the man now disarmed and disorientated Bernard stomach punched his attacker with such force he crumpled in two and sank to the ground. Bernard gently pushed him over with a booted foot and he came to rest face to face with the first attacker in the mud. The two other would-be attackers slowly backed away until they reached the entrance to an alleyway and turned and fled.

Will bent down and checked on the second fallen man, he didn't seem to be breathing. "God's teeth, couldn't you just have knocked him out or something?" he hissed.

Bernard shrugged. "He'd have killed us both without a thought. Better be prepared, this is just the warm up lad, things might get brutal."

Will shook his head and sighed. "The mood you're in, we'll end up leaving a trail of bodies for someone to follow. Let's at least drag them into the alleyway and out of sight."

～

There were two horses in the tavern's stable. They both looked capable of pulling the cart. Will didn't know which was actually the carter's. He grabbed the one from the nearest stall and it came out willingly into the yard without much fuss or noise.

"That's his horse is it?" whispered Bernard dubiously.

"How should I know, can't say I paid much attention to the bloody horse in Saint Davids," hissed back Will.

"Christ's bones, keep your voice down. Here, let me back it up to the cart shafts."

Bernard stroked the horse's head and whispered softly in its ear and gave it a gentle nudge. Miraculously it backed up between the cart shafts. Bernard went back into the stable and after a bit of stumbling about in the dark brought out a leather harness. The horse seemed comfortable if a little bemused at getting ready to go out to work at this hour of the day.

"Give me a hand," Bernard whispered. Together they got the harness over the broad shoulders of the horse and attached the cart shafts to the leather straps the best they could in the gloom. Bernard said, "It'll have to do. I'll lead the horse you get up on the cart."

"I hope to God we aren't going to leave the cart sitting in the middle of the street," said Will before climbing up onto the front and taking hold of the long reins. He lightly tapped them and Bernard gently tugged on the horse's head. With one squeaky wheel they creaked into motion, Bernard leading them out of the yard and onto the main street. There was nobody about although Will hadn't heard the curfew bell sound yet. By now the daylight had gone and the stars could be seen overhead in the thin slit of sky visible between the dark sides of the tall buildings. The street was cobbled, and the cart rumbled along squeaking madly from one wheel. Perhaps the carter was deaf, Will was certain a few miles of that noise would be enough to drive anyone mad.

Will grimaced. "God's teeth, this is noisy."

"What you say?" hissed Bernard.

"I said it's noisy and we need to hurry!"

As they turned off the main street, the cobbles gave way to a hard rutted mud surface. The cart rolled over each rut with a loud crash and a shudder.

"Not far now lad," hissed Bernard.

Will looked behind them, but apart from the odd barking dog in the distance, he couldn't hear or see anything. Eventually Bernard led the horse and cart hard against the side wall of the friar's little chapel.

Will jumped down from the cart and said, "No time to lose, let's get this stuff unloaded."

Bernard knocked gently on the door to the friars.

A voice said softly, "Who is it?"

"It's us brother, let us in."

"You're alone?"

"Just the two of us, now for God's sake open up."

"The door open slowly and an anxious Osbert slipped out from behind Brother Stephen.

"You have it?" gasped Osbert.

Will said, "Of course we do, now help us carry it in. You too brother, we need to hurry."

"What is it you have there?" asked a worried Brother Stephen. "It's not a body is it?"

Bernard forced a chuckle. "What do you take us for brother? We'll tell you the tale all in good time brother, all in good time. Give us a hand or stand out of the way, one or the other."

Between them, they half carried half dragged the sacks in through the door of the chapel.

When they were done Will said, "We can't leave the cart outside the door. Perhaps we should take it back to the tavern?"

"No time for that. If those were Watts's men we ran into, then he will be back to search for us."

"Then we need to leave it somewhere else."

"You say you've had trouble with Watts's men. Are they coming here?" asked Brother Stephen anxiously.

"I bloody hope not," Bernard said. "Now, tell me brother, where would we leave this cart to draw the least attention?"

Brother Stephen pointed a shaky finger down the muddy street. "There's an ally just down there on the left, it's a dead end, you could leave it there, but someone will see it in the morning for certain."

Bernard shrugged. "I don't care about that as long as it's not sat outside the front of your little chapel brother."

Will said, "Get inside. I'll move it. I won't be long." With that he grabbed the reins and urged the carter's horse forward.

~

Watts studied the letter that they'd taken from the drunken carter when they'd searched him. It had been tucked into his waistband. Watts wasn't good with his letters but he could decipher enough to know it was addressed to Brother Howell. He looked across the table. A quickly sobering carter looked back at him, his arms pinned behind his back by two of Watts's men.

"I won't ask you again. What else was on your cart?" The two men holding the carter forced his arms back even further. He winced in pain.

"I swear master he gave me that note for the friars and asked me to leave them some sacks of turnips. Paid me well to do it as well. There was nothing else I swear, the cart's still out the back."

Watts glanced up at another of his men and said, "Check it now." The man hurried out the back door of the tavern.

Watts tried again. "Why are the bishop's men back in Tenby? There must be some purpose?"

"I know not master, I left them at Saint Davids this morning. You know me master, I'm just a simple carter nothing more."

Watts's man emerged through the door that led to the yard. He shook his head. "There's no cart in the yard John, nor cart horse in the stable."

The carter wide eyed said, "They must have taken it master, who else would have cause?"

Watts sat brooding for a moment. He fixed the carter with an intense stare and said slowly, "At least one of my men is dead outside and you know nothing about anything. You make a mockery of me in my own town." He took out a small knife and with lightning speed slashed the carter brutally across the face. Across the room, the landlord gasped.

The man holding the carters arms swiftly released him as hot gore splattered his bare arms. "Christ's bones John. What you do that for? I don't think he knew anything."

The carter clutched at his face, trying to hold the deep cut together. He moaned as blood trickled through his fingers and pooled on the table before him.

Watts brandished the knife at his man and snapped, "When I want your opinion, I'll ask for it. I'd hold your tongue if you don't want to lose it. Now get the others together. We're going to pay a visit to the friars."

∽

Will hurried down the street with the cart. There was nobody anywhere in sight. The noise from the cart seemed deafening. He quickly led the horse towards the alleyway

Brother Stephen had pointed to. It was dark, and the horse wasn't keen on advancing into the unknown. He pulled on the reins and coaxed the beast forward with a gentle pat and a whispered word in its ear. The cart was now off the main street. He gave the horse a final pat and quickly made his way back towards the friar's chapel. A light tap on the door and he was inside breathing a sigh of relief.

Will said, "Now what? It'll not take Watts long to find us. One of his men is dead. I know his sort, self defence or not, he'll not rest until we're strung up or worse."

Brother Stephen crossed himself and murmured, "Dead you say. Christ save us. Where is Brother Howell? He'll know what to do?"

Ignoring the question Bernard grabbed the little man by the shoulders and said, "Is there any other way out of the chapel?"

"No, well, yes."

"Think man, which is it?"

"There is no other door but there is another way out."

"Where?"

"Well there's the tunnels. Brother Howell could tell you more. I've been here but a year."

"When was he due back?"

"He's normally here by now. He goes down to the hospital outside the west gate every afternoon."

The door opened with a creak making them all jump back in alarm.

∽

"Thank God you've returned Howell," said Brother Stephen, clutching the sleeve of the other monk's cowl in a vice like grip.

"Calm yourself brother, I stopped off to see an old friend just inside the walls. Now what ails you? I see we have visitors as well. I didn't think we'd be seeing you again my friends."

"We bring trouble I'm afraid brother," said Will apologetically, before pushing past him to shut and bar the door.

"And that trouble would involve Watts and his men would it? Only there seems to be a great many of them in the streets tonight."

"It was quiet but a few minutes ago. You think they head this way brother?" asked Bernard worriedly.

Howell shrugged, "That was my impression as I made my way home. Although I didn't think our little chapel was their destination then. You better tell me quickly what this is all about. I'll help if I can."

Osbert crossed himself and said, "They'll murder us all. We're trapped."

A moment later and there was a hammering on the door that had the wood vibrating in its frame.

A gruff voice called, "Open up or I swear we'll break this door down"

Bernard said, "Brothers I don't agree with Osbert's dire warnings often but open that door and I don't believe any of us will leave this place alive. Howell, there's a tunnel that leads out?"

There was a massive crash and the door groaned and shuddered. They were using something seriously heavy to batter it. Howell nodded to the far end of the chapel.

"There are tunnels under most of the town. You'll find the entrance to one under the rushes. It's right up against the wall. There's a trap door."

They followed him to the back and quickly brushed the old rushes away from the wall with their feet. There was a trapdoor set flush to the floor. A small iron ring allowed Howell, with some effort, to pull it open. They stood around the small square hole looking down into the dark.

William said, "Where does this lead brother?"

"A hundred yards and the tunnel splits, to the left I believe it eventually comes out under the parish church, although its many years since I went that way. It could be blocked now I can't say for sure."

"And the other way?"

"The passage slopes down towards the beach between the harbour and the next headland. It comes out in a cave in the cliffs."

"This cave, it's always free of the sea?"

There was another tremendous crash from the far door which they tried to ignore.

"I think so, at least it has never been with water when I've been there. Perhaps on a spring tide but we should be safe tonight. The passage was still clear and free this time two years ago."

Brother Stephen looked at his fellow brother curiously.

Brother Howell smiled faintly. "Never mind why brother, it's all in God's plan."

"I don't doubt you brother," Stephen replied meekly.

Bernard said, "I think perhaps you should both come with us. It's not safe for you here. I swear that the bishop of Draychester will look more than favourably on you and your chapel in this town. There is yet to be a reckoning here and I fear for your lives as well as ours."

Will said, "What about the sacks?"

"I'm not leaving them for the mayor. Let's drop the lot down into the tunnel, carry what we can and hide the rest."

The chapel door groaned as if under tremendous pressure.

Will nodded. "We'd better be quick about it then, that door won't hold much longer."

Howell picked up a burning tallow candle from a niche in the wall and used it to light others for each of them. "Try not to let them go out. There's no light at all until we get close to the sea cave and it would be a long walk in the dark."

## 28

## SECRETS OF THE PRECINCT

Bishop Gifford and his clerk, Scrivener, sat at the end of one of the long tables in the great hall of Draychester's bishop's palace. It was late, there were only a few others in the hall but none close enough to overhear their conversation. On the table between them was a jug of wine and two cups.

"I've been making some investigations my lord."

The bishop studied his friend's face. He thought he looked tired. "About what exactly Scrivener? You look very serious, should I be worried?"

"You mentioned you had a feeling about a possible spy? Someone lurking in the background."

The bishop smiled. "Perhaps I'm just getting old my friend. Maybe there was nothing more to it than that."

Scrivener pointed a finger at his master. "Come now. I know you too well my lord. You don't bring these things up on a whim. I trust your instincts, so I looked hard and there may be something."

"So, what is it you've found Scrivener?"

Scrivener hesitated a moment then said, "In Bishop Thorndyke's time there seems to have been someone here within the precincts who manipulated things."

"Surely Thorndyke himself?" replied the bishop.

"Thorndyke was far from a stupid man my lord," acknowledged Scrivener. "However, it seems there was some other devious presence here within the walls. Someone of a much darker nature."

"And this man is still here and still active?"

Scrivener nodded. "I believe he is."

The bishop leant forward. "A member of the chapter?"

"I don't know as yet my lord, that remains to be discovered."

The bishop leant back again, a puzzled look on his face. "Of those members I've come to know, it would seem barely credible that any would scheme against us and if so to what end?"

"I agree, nevertheless I suggest we rule no one out."

The bishop picked up the jug and poured himself some wine. He took a sip and said, "Perhaps we should set a trap Scrivener?"

"That idea had also occurred to me my lord. It won't be easy I fear. We should exercise caution, for it needs some planning"

The bishop looked at his friend and nodded. "You do that my friend, but don't tarry too long. I don't take kindly when someone interferes with our plans."

They sat in silence for a moment before the bishop said, "So, lighten my spirits old friend, what news comes from your nephew?"

Scrivener smiled. "Nothing directly for a day or two. Via other channels, I hear tell of a disturbance at Saint Davids that has upset the bishop there. I fear it bears all the hallmarks of our three officials."

"Excellent, tell me more."

## 29

## THE TUNNELS

There was smoke in the tunnel which came billowing down the passageway towards them. They picked up the pace as best they could in the narrow space, just managing to outpace the smoke. They could hear muffled shouts and curses behind them and then the sounds of someone coughing their guts up. Evidently whoever had the plan of smoking them out had seriously misjudged the effects.

Will said angrily, "What fool would start a fire to smoke us out and then come in after? I hope they choke."

Bernard put his hand on Will's back. "Just keep moving, well be in trouble if the smoke reaches us."

Ahead of Will in the passageway a panicked Osbert gasped, "I'm not sure I can go any faster. I can hardly breathe as it is."

Will pushed him forward. "Then save your breath complaining, and if I have to drag you out by the ears, I swear I'll do it Osbert. Now keep going."

The two friars were in the lead. They soon came to a

fork in the tunnel just as Brother Howell had said earlier. Taking the way to the right they led onwards, the passageway noticeably starting to head downwards. For the moment the smoke was left behind.

Bernard called ahead, "Stop a moment brothers." They came to a halt forcing all those behind to stop.

Bernard rested his bulk against the side of the passageway and tried to catch his breath. "We must be heading down towards the cave and the shore now. If they still follow, they may well head to the left and away from us."

Brother Howell nodded. "They may, if it's God's will. The distance to the cave is not too long now."

Will said, "Whichever turn they make, it won't be long before they follow us back down here."

Bernard wiped the sweat from his brow. "Then perhaps we should give them pause for thought."

"What do you have in mind?"

"Let the others carry on to the cave. You and I wait for our pursuers and ambush them."

"They'll kill you for sure, then I'll be on my own," wailed Osbert.

Will ignoring him said, "We need to stop them following or at least stop them knowing where we've gone."

Burned nodded. "I agree, if we carry on and reach the cave, what then? They'll be close behind. We need time to plan an escape, we can't do that with them breathing down our necks."

Will nodded. "Then it's agreed, Osbert and the good brothers carry on to the cave. You and I give our pursuers a surprise."

As the others carried on down the passageway, Bernard and Will made their way back to the fork in the tunnel.

Bernard whispered, "It'd be better if we were in the shadows. We'll see them first."

Will said, "Give me your candle. I'll walk back down the passageway and leave them as far back as I dare."

He walked back down the way they had just come. When Bernard had disappeared in the gloom, he placed both candles on the rocky floor. With one reluctant backwards glance, he walked away from the light back to Bernard. He advanced with one hand out before him and one hand against the wall. He soon bumped into the big man.

"Christ's bones, its dark," whispered Will.

Bernard grunted his agreement. "As soon as we see the light ahead of us, we rush out as fast as possible towards them. They won't be expecting it. Let me go first. I'll flatten the bastards."

Will nodded, unseen in the darkness. "At least in this passageway they can only advance one at a time."

Bernard hissed, "Sshhh, someone comes."

Will braced himself for the violence to follow. There was a glimmer of light ahead. The big man suddenly lurched forward and then with a yell that deafened Will, surged up the passageway. Will stumbled after his friend. Bernard piled directly into a figure clutching a candle to its chest. He sent it flying back onto the dusty stone floor and ran over it stamping as he went and Will coming up behind did the same. There were screams as bones broke below them and then they were clear and running into the next body. Bernard barged into the startled man and flung him into the side wall with a sickening crunch. He slumped down against the wall and Will grabbed a dagger away from a now limp hand.

"Bernard, dagger," he hissed.

The big man slowed just enough to take the weapon from him. There were two more men in the tunnel ahead. Both armed, one with a dagger and the other with a short sword. They each carried a flickering candle. Bernard yelled at them at the top of his voice. It was deafening. They stood, weapons thrust forward but shocked into momentarily inaction by the creature charging them out of the darkness. Bernard didn't hesitate, he brutally thrust the dagger up into the belly of the first man and literally shoved the poor fellow onto the sword of the man behind. He gave a great heave and pushed them both down onto the floor in a tangle of limbs and hot blood. He stamped down hard and the struggle slowly subsided beneath his feet. A single spluttering candle lay on the floor and cast a flickering light over the gruesome scene.

Bernard drew in great gasps of air, bracing himself against the wall with one bloody hand.

Will said, "Are you all right? Are you injured?"

The big man looked down at his blooded tunic and shook his head. "No, it's their blood not mine. Best find yourself that sword down there lad, could be more of the bastards up ahead."

Will gingerly pulled the short sword from under the two bodies. The hilt was slippery with blood. With the other hand, he rescued the candle from the floor.

They started to move forward up the passageway but soon ran into thick smoke and were forced to turn around. Bernard, eyes streaming and wheezing from the smoke spluttered, "This is going to take hours to clear. We're safe for now, no one's coming after us though that."

Will wiped his eyes, grabbed his friend's arm and said, "Come on, you've done enough. Let's find the others."

## 30

## NOXIOUS FUMES

Ralph of Shrewsbury let rip with a long fart. In the still air of the cathedral the noise echoed around the space. There were none but him and the young lad to appreciate it. As the noxious vapours slowly dispersed, Ralph, who'd been holding his breath, sniffed the air and chuckled to himself. After a long life he found the simple pleasures the only ones that gave him much joy these days. He looked down at Cedric who knelt on the stone floor before him massaging his bare feet.

"The little toe, rub it harder Cedric," he murmured.

The rheumatism didn't bother him much except in his feet, the lad proved himself useful in that respect.

"Is everything all right? Do things proceed to your plans master?" whispered Cedric.

Ralph contemplated the question and finally said, "Not entirely Cedric. Once you set things in motion, it's hard to predict the outcome. You'll learn these things yourself boy, that's if you live long enough."

Cedric looked up momentarily from his task and said, "You're displeased then master?"

Ralph shrugged, "Not at all. Things must be allowed to play out to their conclusions. Only then can we assess the success or otherwise of our schemes. Now the joint of the big toe please."

"You never interfere?"

"Of course. You can nudge, threaten, bribe, murder even, all of those things, but we must remain in the shadows Cedric."

"I'm not sure I understand master."

"Of course you don't boy, you have much to learn. Now start on the other foot."

The boy started to rub the pain away from the toes on the old man's left foot. Ralph sighed heavily. Lately he'd begun to think perhaps he was getting too old for the game. This new bishop and his clerk were more dangerous than he'd thought. He reflected that he may have underestimated them. He didn't feel in any danger of course, no, he thought himself much too intelligent for them to get close. He did however, feel slightly threatened. It'd been decades since he'd had the feeling. It gave him quite a thrill, and he nosily broke wind again in response to the thought. Cedric took the full impact and struggled to stop himself gagging. Ralph stifled a laugh and then contemplated the splendid vaulted ceiling above and realised he was mildly offended that the oaf Bernard and the two younger officials were still alive. The Breton was normally quite ruthless, perhaps it really was God's will that they yet lived. However their miraculous survival had been achieved, it had been careless on the Breton's part. He'd need to teach the man a lesson.

The boy lifted his hands from his master's feet and said, "Do you think the bishop's men still have Mudstone's plunder master? Will they bring it to the bishop or will they take it for themselves?"

Ralph smiled. He'd almost forgot how appealing greed was to the young. "It'd tempt many, but I'm a good judge of character boy, somehow I don't think they'll stray."

"Will you try to retrieve it from them master?"

He pondered on the question a moment then said, "Far too dangerous to have in our possession. A pity of course, it could have been put to such devious uses. Men like the bishop have such a limited imagination Cedric."

"Will Sir Roger not be angry?"

Ralph smiled wickedly as he imagined the rage Sir Roger would be feeling. "Angry? It will be a rage such as you've never seen boy. I can guarantee that."

A shudder ran down the boy's back at the words. Roger Mudstone's reputation was well known even here amongst the quiet life of the cloisters.

Ralph shook his head in wonder. The boy was still so naïve at the ways of the game, it was almost pitiful. "We can use that rage Cedric. We'll help Mudstone come looking for revenge. The man has a genius for causing mayhem wherever he goes."

"And that helps us master? How can we control such a man? I still don't understand."

Ralph looked down at the boy and chuckled. "Just rub my feet boy, your questions weary me."

## 31

## THE CAVE AND ESCAPE

"Another day, another cave. I hope this doesn't get as watery as the last one," said Will.

In the dim light from the cave's entrance, they could just make out Brother Howell's smile. "Don't worry my friend, the tide doesn't come this far up."

"I'm just happy to breathe some fresh air at last," said Bernard.

Osbert crossed himself and said, "It's a miracle we're still alive."

An anxious Brother Stephen said, "Will they come after us?"

Will glanced back at the dark opening to the tunnel. "Not that way at least. I dare say it's completely filled with smoke at their end. Do you think they know where the tunnel emerges Howell?"

"Perhaps, but these cliffs are full of caves and the town is riddled with tunnels. We have some time still."

Bernard said, "The sooner we leave this place the better, and I'd like to think we don't return empty-handed after all we've endured."

Osbert looked at the pile of sacks in the sand before him. "We brought what we could carry, the rest we hid in a side passage."

Will counted the sacks. "Well it's something. I'm sure the bishop can arrange for the rest to be retrieved. I'm not keen on going back in there."

Osbert shuddered at the thought. "It would be madness."

Bernard said, "Don't you worry about that boy, we've done enough. Watt's day will come, the bishop has a long reach and he looks after his own. The best thing we can do now is get ourselves away. You too brothers."

Howell shook his head. "We've still God's work to do here. Things will die down and we can stay outside of the town for a while, there are many who will give us shelter."

Will said, "Can we get around into the next bay and away?"

"It's possible. Let's wait until it grows fully dark outside. We can make our way along the base of the cliff and round the headland, it won't be the first time I've been that way. You might get your feet wet I'm afraid but if we stick close to the rocks we'll be fine, the waters shallow."

∽

As the last daylight faded, the cave became pitch black, and they edged their way slowly forward to its mouth. Under the starlight the beach appeared to be empty. They could hear the gentle lapping of the waves and see the white foam breaking upon the sand. The tunnel had run downwards towards the sea and the cave entrance was set far along the beach just to the north of the town. Looking back across the wet sand towards the distant harbour they could see no one in the gloom. The main part of the town itself was hidden out of sight on the cliffs above.

Brother Howell said, "I'd better lead, I know the beach better than any of you. Let's keep to the bottom of the cliff and work our way out to the headland."

Will handed out the heavy sacks to each of them, Bernard taking two, one under each arm. They set off following Brother Howell in single-file.

Bernard whispered, "Keep off the sand, stay in the water, don't leave footprints."

Osbert said, "It's wet sand, how can we not leave footprints?"

They hurried on along the edge of the beach scrambling over rocky outcrops and as they headed out towards the headland ankle deep water.

Looking back towards the harbour, Will saw a flare of light on the quay side then another and another. He said, "My God, look at that. They've seen us for sure."

Bernard peered back. "Perhaps not, but those are men with torches for certain. Watts is no fool, he must know where most of these tunnels lead out to. He'll have sent them to search the beach. All the more reason to get a move on!"

They struggled on, now more in the water than out of it. As Will, the last in line, rounded the headland, he paused and glanced back. The lights had made their way down from the quay and were at the very end of the beach. He quickly scrambled around the rocks, and they disappeared from sight.

"Where now Howell?" asked Bernard.

Howell, sack in hand, gestured at the next headland.

"Around the next one and then up onto the tops."

Without another word he set off through the surf and they reluctantly paddled after him.

Once around the next headland they headed towards the cliffs at the rear of the small bay. A small path, hardly more than a sheep track, led up away from the beach. Brother Howell silently led them up the winding way. At the beginning of the track it was dark and treacherous between the rocks. As they gained height, the seascape opened out below them, the water twinkling in the faint starlight. The path eventually emerged on the cliff top and Brother Howell came to a stop. He seemed hardly out of breath. The others sank down onto the grass, exhausted by the climb.

"Don't get too comfortable my friends. I suggest we keep moving. There's a place further along the coast from here, called Laugharne."

"How far is this place brother?" asked a weary Osbert, "I know not whether I have the strength to walk much further."

"It's a day's walk. My sister lives there and I am well known at the castle. We'll be amongst friends. You can take your leave by ship to Bristol from there."

"God's teeth, a day? It's the middle of the night as it is, how are we to find our way?" moaned Osbert.

"I know the way well my young friend, day or night. I grew up on this coast and I wasn't always a friar."

Bernard said, "Ignore him brother. I for one don't know how we will ever repay you. We'll be in your debt forever."

Will got slowly to his feet and held his hand out to Osbert. "Come on get up Osbert, we're not done yet."

## 32

## HOMECOMING

It had taken a good hour for Scrivener to read his nephew's account of events in Pembrokeshire. The letters had been carried from Bristol in only two days by a king's messenger no less, arriving along with the royal dispatches. It was late, and the bishop had already retired, but Scrivener, as usual, was still working at his desk in his day chamber. The messenger had been brought straight to his chamber and handed over a bundle of dispatches from the court. Then from under his leather tunic he had drawn out a smaller bundle and placed it on the desk.

Scrivener looked at him curiously. "And this?"

The messenger smiled. "From a friend my lord. He said it was most urgent and that you'd understand."

It was then that Scrivener recognised the hand that had written his name on the bundle. At first he'd been appalled at the audacity of his nephew bribing a royal official to carry personal dispatches. When he started reading he realised the bribing had probably been done by Bernard rather than the boy and with good reason. He also felt it merited disturbing the bishop's slumbers. He knew how much he liked a good story, and this was one of the best he'd hear in a long time.

"What is it Scrivener? It must be serious for you disturb me at his hour?"

"Letters from my nephew my lord, I think you need to hear this."

Scrivener plonked himself down on a stool at the end of the bishop's substantial bed and began to read aloud. The bishop sat up in his bed listening, eyes gleaming as the story unfolded.

"God's teeth Scrivener. Your nephew writes well when he isn't prophesying doom and gloom and boring us with the price of Welsh cheese. They've done well, particularly the lad, Will. Did I not tell you he'd turn out useful?"

"You did my lord and events seem to have proved you correct once again."

The bishop inclined his head. "Just so Scrivener, just so. And let's not forget Bernard of course, dependable as ever. We also seem to owe a great debt to some friars."

"Indeed my lord we do. I have to say our men seem to have left a trail of chaos behind them."

"That's the nature of a great adventure Scrivener. Tell me you don't wish you were twenty years younger and out there with them? I know I do. That turd Mudstone will answer for most of it. I'll see him hang or worse Scrivener. I swear it."

"With luck my lord, the Breton will throw him over the side. I can't think what he could possibly want with him. As Osbert writes it, Mudstone was singled out for capture whilst the rest were to be discarded. There's another hand at work here my lord."

"I grant you its strange. At least he was deprived of his loot. I think our men deserve an escort back from Bristol and I take it you'll try to retrieve the rest from below the streets of Tenby?"

"If it's feasible it will be done my lord. Then there's the question of the mayor?"

"Make sure a broken limb is the least of his worries Scrivener. If he's still breathing this time next week, I'll be most upset."

"Of course my lord, I'll see it's done."

# AFTERWORD
## FROM THE AUTHOR

Dear Reader,

Thank you for reading one of my books. I've always been an avid reader of historical fiction but also harboured the thought, like so many of us do, that I'd try and write something myself. What you have been reading was the second book I published. It took me a long time to finish the first one and have the confidence to put it out into the world. I worked in the IT and Telecoms industry here in the UK for many years, ended up running my own company, and inevitably life and job got in the way. I'd do some research, make some progress on the book, then leave it again.

In early 2018 a close family member became seriously ill. Writing offered me an escape from some of the stress and worry involved and gave me the motivation to get the first book over the finishing line.

After I'd completed that first book, I wrote the next two in the series in a just over a year. I learned a lot writing them. What I got over that period was validation from readers they enjoyed my work, which in turn encouraged me to keep on writing and improving.

The writing process can be both uplifting and disheartening in equal measure. I really appreciate every review you guys give my books. Every time you leave some feedback, good or bad, it helps validate that at least someone is out there reading them. I look at each review posted and take your comments to heart and hope to become a better writer because of them.

On Amazon, I've found it makes a huge difference for independent authors like me when prospective readers can learn more about a book from others who post a review. So, if you can spare a minute and share your impressions of the book that would be amazing.

Did you enjoy the book? What did you like about it? Who were your favourite characters? Should the series continue? Give me your thoughts via a review or rating on Amazon.

∼

*Be the first to receive the news of upcoming books in the series, exclusive offers and free downloads. Join my newsletter and...*

Get your free copy of
Death Of The Messenger
The Prequel to the
Draychester Chronicles

*You can sign up at this link:-*
*www.westerbone.com/newsletter*

*For lots more information visit my author website,*

*www.westerbone.com*

*You can also connect with me on Facebook,*

www.facebook.com/mjwesterbone

*and on twitter,*

www.twitter.com/westerbone

@westerbone

## Available Now
### Book 1 of the Draychester Chronicles
## Death Of The Official

## Available Now
### Book 3 of the Draychester Chronicles
## Death Of The Anchorite

Hope to see you soon,
M J Westerbone,
Hindley Green, England, U.K

# COPYRIGHT

**Copyright © 2021 by M J Westerbone.**
All rights reserved. Published by Irene Storvik Ltd, Hindley Green, Lancashire, UK. This is a work of fiction. Any resemblance to actual persons living or dead is purely coincidental. Reproduction in whole or part of this publication without express written consent is strictly prohibited.

Printed in Great Britain
by Amazon